Large Print Western KEENE James

Keene, James.

Seven for vengeance

[text (large print)]

Great Book

SEVEN FOR VENGEANCE

Center Point
Large Print

Also by James Keene and available from
Center Point Large Print:

Justice, My Brother

**This Large Print Book carries the
Seal of Approval of N.A.V.H.**

SEVEN FOR VENGEANCE

James Keene

CENTER POINT LARGE PRINT
THORNDIKE, MAINE

This Center Point Large Print edition
is published in the year 2018 by arrangement with
Golden West Literary Agency.

First US edition: Random House
First UK edition: Long

The text of this Large Print edition is unabridged.
In other aspects, this book may vary
from the original edition.
Printed in the United States of America
on permanent paper.
Set in 16-point Times New Roman type.

ISBN: 978-1-68324-795-1 (hardcover)
ISBN: 978-1-68324-799-9 (paperback)

Library of Congress Cataloging-in-Publication Data

Names: Keene, James, author.
Title: Seven for vengeance / James Keene.
Description: Center Point Large Print edition. | Thorndike, Maine :
    Center Point Large Print, [2018]
Identifiers: LCCN 2018004527| ISBN 9781683247951
    (hardcover : alk. paper) | ISBN 9781683247999 (pbk. : alk. paper)
Subjects: LCSH: Murder—Fiction. | Large type books. |
    GSAFD: Western stories.
Classification: LCC PS3553.O5547 S47 2018 | DDC 813/.54—dc23
LC record available at https://lccn.loc.gov/2018004527

"out of the mud grows the Lotus"

James Hughes

ONE

McAllister Sims sat on the express office porch and patiently watched the thermometer rise, and when the red reached ninety-four, he unbuttoned the collar of his shirt and rolled his sleeves to the elbow. Often he cast squinted eyes at the lead-colored sky and wondered how so much heat could drift down through such an overcast. The promise of rain was heavy, had been so since he got up, which was as near to dawn as a man could get without lighting a lamp.

Sims studied the town for he had little else to do. Gunlock was always quiet in the morning. The school bell clanged and this was followed by a noisy rush of children trying to be on time and yet enjoy the last moment of freedom.

Sims yawned and looked down the road toward the lime-hued flats. Beyond, mountains looked dismally gray and half hid by the overcast. In the other direction, foothills lay broken and jumbled, and coming off that last rise before town was a rider; Sims gave his attention to this man, holding him in view as he entered the town. The rider came on, saw Sims and veered for the hitch rail in front of the express office.

"You're early, Mr. Buck," Sims said. "The

7

others ain't showed up yet. Neither has the stage with the money."

"This is my day to loaf," Harry Buck said and stepped from the saddle. He was a young man, thirty some, and he moved carefully, as though his energy was limited and he didn't want to waste any of it. Harry Buck's clothes were old and much patched, and he gave a man the impression that he would have a hard time remembering his last good meal. He cuffed back his hat, revealing dark, unbarbered hair. "The stage is late, ain't it, Sims?"

"Yup," Sims said. His wrinkled face wreathed into a smile. "How long since you seen a dollar, Mr. Buck?"

After a pause Harry Buck said, "Too damned long."

Sims was a gnomelike man, with a face that was age-weathered and time-wrinkled. He wore a pair of bib overalls with one strap missing, and his outsized shirt had been a gift from Doctor Reichstad, who had taken it from an itinerant drunk who happened to choose Gunlock as a place to die. "Looks like rain comin'," he opined.

Buck glanced at the sky, then said, "Looks like hell's about to bust loose." He wiped the back of his hand across a cheek. "You know whether Lovering's place is open or not?"

"He's open," Sims said. "Why the hell not? Today we get some money."

"Yeah," Buck said softly. "Today we pay our debts."

He walked up the street toward the saloon on the next corner. When he passed Haskill's store, he paused and looked through the fly-specked window. The saddle he had been thinking about for nearly a year was still on the tree and would likely stay there, according to his arithmetic. There was the feed bill to pay, and the groceries, and the last payment on his bank loan, all of which left him with enough for two good drinks and grub for another year.

He studied the saddle. Not too fancy, he decided. At least no silver work. Just a plain, working roper, the kind any man ought to be able to afford, and the fact that he could not afford it made him slightly angry. By training and economic necessity, Harry Buck had never considered himself an extravagant man, and his purchases had always been limited to necessities. Yet a man had to have a luxury now and then, something he bought just because he had a yearning, nothing more.

Moving on, he walked to the next corner and mounted the porch of Lovering's saloon. Muggy heat lay stale in the big room and Lovering stood alone behind his bar. Buck wiped his hands on the legs of his pants and then leaned against the bar. Lovering looked at him for a moment, then said, "Beer weather," and drew a stein, placing it on the bar in front of Buck. "On the house," Lovering said.

"Fixin' to rain," Buck said. He raised a finger and cleared the foam from his upper lip. His face was clean-shaved, as though this had been his last chore before leaving his own place.

"You pass Temple Manly's place on the way in?" Lovering asked.

"Yep. Didn't stop."

"I guess he ain't left yet. The stage is late. Maybe it rained on the other side of the mountains."

"Maybe," Buck said. He finished his beer. "Thanks. I got some business to take care of."

He stepped out to the edge of the porch and looked at the sky's threatening color. No breath of air stirred, yet Buck felt as though he were standing in front of an open furnace door. From a side street half a block away a man emerged. He came toward Harry Buck, a smile on his melon-shaped face. "First come, first serve, huh, Harry?"

"I got up too early," Buck said easily. "Habit."

The fat man hitched up his sagging trousers. He wore a pistol on his hip and the weight of a nickel-plated star pulled down the front of his vest. "Was headin' for breakfast. Join me?"

"Already had mine, Harms. Thanks anyway."

The sheriff's face wrinkled and the flesh around his eyes bunched. "Hell, you can hold a stack of cakes and some eggs." He took Harry Buck by the arm and steered him down the street.

Since the best food in Gunlock was found in the hotel dining room, Sheriff Harms ate there. He motioned Buck into a chair, then sat down across the table. The cook thrust his head out and Harms said, "The usual, Jerry, and make it two." Harms turned his attention to Buck. "You been cuttin' it mighty thin this summer, ain't you?"

"I get by," Harry Buck admitted.

Harms grunted and pawed his mouth out of shape. "We all get by, Harry. Temple Manly sees to that. Be some sad faces around here without Mr. Manly, that's for sure."

"My face wouldn't be sad," Harry Buck said. He looked out through the open door; a horseman was coming down the street. Even Harms was curious enough to shift his bulk around for a look.

The rider came into view briefly, a tall young man, splendidly mounted. When he passed beyond their vision, Harms turned around again. "Well, that's one half of the Manlys. Jim likes to ride alone, don't he? He's a strange kid, not at all like the old man."

Buck said, "He may be lucky there."

After some time the cook came with their breakfast, and when Buck saw the wheatcakes and eggs he tried not to appear hungry. He was long ago sick of his own cooking, and the lack of variety in his diet whetted his appetite for things he couldn't afford. Harms upped the syrup pitcher and poured what Buck considered a week's supply over his cakes. Buck couldn't recall the last time he had used sugar or cream in his coffee, but the taste lingered in his memory.

They had almost finished when Jim Manly came into the dining room. He sailed his hat onto an empty table and hiked a chair around to the left of Sheriff Harms. The cook poked his head around the door again and Jim Manly said, "Coffee, Jerry."

Jim Manly was E. Temple Manly's son, and he dressed like it. Harry Buck decided that the price of Jim Manly's coat would have kept him in grub for two months. Jim Manly was a brash young man, full of confidence born of the fact that his father had money, and although Jim was rarely allowed two nickels of his own to clack together, the money, the power, was still there behind him.

"You ought to get married, Buck," Manly said.

Harry Buck glanced at him. "I can hardly feed myself as it is."

"Two can live as cheap as one, they say, but only half as good." Jim Manly smiled and leaned back in his chair. "I was over to Betty Cardigan's for supper the night before last."

Buck's glance came up, quick, hard, resentful;

his feelings unhidden. "Don't get your hopes too high," he said. "If I ever get some money together, she won't stay single long."

"Then I won't worry about it," Jim Manly said, smiling.

"Ain't you got sense enough to take a warning?" Buck asked. He wanted to leave and thank Harms for the free breakfast, only without letting Jim Manly know that he had sponged a free meal. *First a drink, and now a free meal:* this was Buck's thought.

"Your father still home when you left?" Harms asked.

"I don't keep track of him." Manly swiveled around in his chair and looked out the door. "What the hell's wrong with this weather? If it's going to rain, then why the hell don't it just rain?"

"Not my jurisdiction," Harms said, rising. He signaled the cook. "Put this on my tab, Jerry." He indicated them with a sweep of the hand. "I'd better check the express office. That stage ought to be here any time now. If it don't bring the money, Manly can't pay us."

He went out then and Buck sat idle and ill at ease.

"Tough year, huh?" Jim Manly asked.

"Tough enough," Harry Buck said. He stood up. "Some business I got to attend to. See you, Jim."

13

"Sure," Jim Manly said and watched Buck leave.

The livery and feed store was two blocks east and Harry Buck walked over. Hardison was sitting in the archway, dead pipe locked between his jaws. He was studying the sky. "Don't the color of that beat all? Was I in Kansas I'd be headin' for the cyclone cellar." He pulled his attention away from the sky and looked at Harry Buck. "The holy one is here." He jerked his thumb toward the interior of the barn and Buck saw E. Temple Manly's four-hundred-dollar buggy out there, traces down.

"Come in fifteen minutes ago. He's over to the bank now." Hardison grinned. "The stage must be gettin' close. Mr. Manly can smell a dollar."

Harry Buck blew out a breath; with the money so near, he felt strangely light-headed. "I'll be in and pay you as soon . . ."

"Scratched it off already," Hardison said. "Bring it over later."

"Thanks," Buck said and walked back toward the center of town. He had a grocery bill to settle up, and an order to leave, so he stopped at the store. John Kohler was there, settling his account. Kohler was big and blond and forty some, and had lived enough years to salt a dollar or two away, which made him less dependent on E. Temple Manly than some of the others who lived around Gunlock.

Kohler turned as Harry Buck came up to the counter. His blunt face was accustomed to smiling and there was gentleness in his pale eyes that said he had never hit a man or whipped a horse in his life. "Payday," Kohler said and patted his back pocket. "Not much, but still payday." He took Harry Buck by the arm and led him away from the counter. "Where the hell have you been? You used to come around once in a while."

"The place keeps me hoppin'," Buck said and hoped that John Kohler would accept this without question. Yet he wondered how much Kohler would guess, for a man with less than a hundred and fifty head of cattle couldn't be too busy. The trouble was, every time Buck visited Kohler there was a couple of free meals and a bunk for the night, which was all right when a man was in a position to pay it back, but Buck wasn't in that position, so he stayed away.

"I didn't see any dust on the road," Kohler said. "You don't suppose the stage got held up? That's our money he's carrying. . . . Well," he added, "the day's unusually hot and I've got a thirst. Let's go over to Lovering's and . . ."

"Thanks, no," Buck said. "I've got some chores . . ."

"You've got, hell!" Kohler edged him toward the door.

Over his shoulder Buck said, "I'll be in later, Mr. Haskill."

A small crowd lined Lovering's bar. Sheriff Harms was there, talking to Jim Manly, and at the far end stood Hank Wilson, the thin-faced deputy, and his cousin, Indian Reilly. Buck and Kohler edged up and Lovering drew two beers, sliding them down the bar. Buck waited until Kohler picked up his stein before hoisting his own.

"I'll stand this round," John Kohler said. Then he turned to Harry Buck. "My wife's been asking why you don't come to supper, Harry. How about Sunday night?"

"Why, I guess that would be fine," Buck said softly.

Someone on the street yelled, "The stage is coming! The stage is coming!"

The men left the bar and went outside to line up on the porch. From the end of the street a cloud of dust boiled up behind the racing coach, then it wheeled by, braking to a halt in front of the express office half a block down. The driver and guard dismounted and hoisted a strongbox to the ground.

John Kohler took a cigar from his pocket, bit off the end and said, "Gents, there is the last money from a stone-dead cattle market. Hard times are upon us."

From across the street, E. Temple Manly emerged from Gunlock's one-room bank and walked toward the saloon. He was a firm-bodied man in his early fifties with invading streaks of gray in his hair. His hat was from Dallas, and worth two months' wages to a working hand. His nod was short and included them all. He said, "It will be a time before the money is counted, deposited and checked out to you."

"Deposited?" Harry Buck asked. "Mr. Manly, why can't you just pay it out over the express company counter?"

"Because business is conducted properly, or it is no business at all," Manly said. He spread his hands. "Gentlemen, I only ask you to wait awhile."

"How long?" John Kohler asked.

"Perhaps an hour or so," Manly said. "Come on inside. I'll stand drinks all around."

There was nothing to do but follow him inside. A wind was beginning to show signs of strength; it whisked an old newspaper down the street. John Kohler paused for a glance at the sky. He said, "I want to be home when this lets go. Be a hell of a storm."

He went inside with the others and bellied against the bar. With E. Temple Manly buying, the drinks were whiskey, and out of the good bottle. Lovering went out to slam the storm shutters for the wind's velocity had increased alarmingly.

Sheriff Harms, who stood at E. Temple Manly's right elbow, said, "Was I you, sir, I'd

17

take a saddle horse home. A wind like this can upset a buggy mighty easy."

"I believe you're right," Temple Manly said. "See to it that a horse is saddled and waiting for me, Harms." He looked around him, his glance settling on Harry Buck. "You've never been to my place, Buck. Why is that? In four years you've never once been to my place."

"I mind my own business," Harry Buck said evenly. "You and I never had business, that's all."

"Oh?" Temple Manly's eyebrow went up. "Buck, there isn't a nickel in credit given out in this town but what I put my approval on it. I suppose you didn't know that?"

"I knew that," Harry Buck said. "But I didn't know you wanted to be thanked for it."

The silence turned to molasses and E. Temple Manly set his glass down, a magnificent frown forming on his forehead. "By God, I don't know whether I like that or not, Buck."

"Harry didn't mean . . ." Kohler began, but stopped talking when Temple Manly slapped his hand on the bar.

"Let him talk." He turned and faced Harry Buck. "Before you start shooting your mouth off, remember that it was my connections in Kansas City that found a market for your cattle, and keep in mind that they were shipped in my cars, and don't forget that my credit kept your

18

belly from banging against your backbone all summer." He paused. "Now go ahead and shoot off your mouth."

There was anger in Harry Buck, but it burned like a deep-banked fire. He spoke, and his voice was even. "Mr. Manly, if everybody kissed your butt, it would be mighty sore, wouldn't it?"

"Say what you mean," Temple Manly snapped.

"I'm gettin' there," Buck said. "I never asked you for a damned thing. Not credit, not to find me a buyer, or to use the space in your cars. You offered those things, to me, Kohler, and to Wes Cardigan. And I recall we thanked you for it. Maybe you didn't hear, so I'll thank you again, but by God I ain't going to do it every time we meet."

"You made that plain," Manly said. The planes of his face were stiff as though they were hardening clay. His fingers toyed with his whiskey glass, then he downed what was left and turned to the front door. He opened it to a raw push of wind, then paused there. "I'll let you know when the money's ready to pay out. Until then, don't bother me about it." His eyes switched to Sheriff Harms. "Get a horse saddled for me. I'm going home."

He slammed the door and Harry Buck looked at the varnished bar top. Finally Harms said, "Guess I'd better get a move on. Mr. Manly don't like to wait."

19

After Harms left there was a short silence. "Wonder why Wes Cardigan didn't come in?" Buck finally asked.

"Maybe he thought he wouldn't get his money," John Kohler said. He kicked the bar and added, "God damn it all! Manly can run fine on what he's got salted, but we need cash."

Kohler consulted his watch. "Getting on toward noon." He walked to a window and looked out. Gloom invaded the room until it seemed like approaching nightfall. "A miserable goddamned day," he said.

"Hell, I'm leaving," Jim Manly said.

"Ain't you going to wait for the old man?" Kohler asked.

"He's never waited for me," Jim said. "Anything you want me to say to Betty Cardigan for you, Harry?"

Buck frowned and Jim Manly laughed once before slamming the door. With a sigh John Kohler turned to the bar and leaned heavily. "You damned fool, Harry. You're going to lose that girl if you don't get off your butt and go see her."

"Takes money to court a woman, John. I couldn't afford to buy a clean shirt."

"Jesus, she ain't going to look at your shirt," Kohler said. "Why, when I married, I had to sell my saddle for enough to get the license."

"Times were different then," Harry Buck said.

"Different, hell!"

"You didn't have Temple Manly," Buck mentioned.

John Kohler sobered. "Yeah, I didn't, for a fact." He remained quiet for a time, then said, "If you need money, borrow on your place. You paid cash for it, didn't you?"

"Yep. But I don't borrow from the Manlys."

"See what you mean," Kohler said. "You hungry?"

"Haven't done enough to get hungry."

"Well, I'm hungry," Kohler said. "I'll toss you for the meal." Before Buck could protest, he pulled a quarter from his pocket, flipped it and slapped it on the back of his hand. "Heads or tails?"

"Heads," Buck said.

Kohler peeked, then made a disgusted face and put the quarter away without letting Buck see it. "Hell, I can't win a damned thing today." His nod turned Buck toward the front door, then they paused on the porch, braced against the blasting wind. Kohler put his lips close to Buck's ear; it was the only way he could make himself heard. "Christ, will you look at it blow!" He clutched his hat in one hand and coat in the other, which still blew away from his body like the tail of a kite. A swirl of dust stormed down the street, cutting visibility to half a block. Then the first pelting rain fell. There was no first gentle fall,

21

just a sudden deluge, and they ran across the street for the hotel overhang.

The hotel dining room was deserted, except for two men eating at a corner table.

Buck laughed softly and John Kohler looked at him. "What the hell's funny, Harry?"

"The weather," Buck said. "Damn it, it's the kind of weather you'd expect when Manly comes to town. The ground ought to tremble and the wind ought to blow. Sort of like a theatre orchestra playing loud as hell when the villain comes on stage."

After Kohler and Harry Buck had blunted their appetites, Buck said, "John, you're a smart man. Tell me, have we got any right to the money that's in the express office?"

"Not until Temple Manly puts it into his account at the bank." Kohler leaned forward. "You see, the cars were consigned to Manly; his bank has handled all the paper work. Stop sweating, Harry. You'll get your share. Hell, Temple Manly's as honest as they make them."

"I know that," Buck said, "but I've got something to worry about. I'm broke and against the wall, and I'm too stubborn to ask for any more credit."

"You ought to be able to hang on for a few more days," Kohler said. "Hell, Manly will get over his mad and settle up."

"You don't understand yet," Buck said. "I've

figured things out to the letter. John, when I rode into town today, I'd already eaten the last of my flour and cooked the last piece of backfat. A man can get damned hungry in two or three days."

"I never looked at it that way," Kohler said, adding, "I'm going over to the express office." He gathered his hat and coat. Buck eased away from the table.

When they gained the hotel porch, they turned shoulders to the wind. The rain rattled on the roof and drove, slanting, along the street, dimpling it, mixing a river of mud. They splashed across, then hurried along to the express office. Most of the business houses sported lamp-bright windows for the darkness was nightlike.

When they entered the express office, McAllister Sims looked up, startled; he flourished a pistol at them until he recognized them. Then he grinned sheepishly and tucked it beneath the counter.

"Makes me nervous, all this money," he said.

"Did Manly say anything about taking it to the bank?" This was Kohler's question.

"Mr. Manly told me to stand here with this pistol until he wanted the money," the express agent said. "I guess Mr. Prentiss, the banker, will come after it."

"When? Did he say when?"

"No, Mr. Buck, he sure didn't." Sims scratched

his head. "I'd as soon pay off you fellas, you know that, but Mr. Manly said . . ."

John Kohler waved his hand. "Yes, I know. Mr. Manly said to wait." He took Buck by the arm. "Let's go home."

"That's a long ride, just to turn around and come back tomorrow," Buck said.

"Jesus, I ain't going to stay in town tonight," Kohler said. "Are you ridin' part way with me or not?"

"All right," Buck said. "Sims, where the hell's my horse? I had him tied out in front."

"When it started to blow, I took him to the stable. Is that all right, Mr. Buck?"

"It's fine. Thank you, Sims."

They went out, crouching as they walked against the wind and rain. When they approached the saloon, they ducked onto the porch. Sheriff Harms and Hank Wilson were standing there. Indian Reilly stood against the wall, shrouded in his habitual silence. He was a ghost of a man; if a man didn't look often he could forget that Reilly was there.

"Givin' up?" Harms asked.

"Hell yes," Kohler said, very disgusted.

Harms nodded and looked at Harry Buck. "You talked out of turn to Mr. Manly. You shouldn't have done that. It don't kill a man to be pleasant. And it's as easy to compliment as it is to cuss. You ought to learn a lesson from this."

"I know my lessons," Buck said flatly.

Without another word they walked to the stable and went to the rear stalls where Kohler saddled his horse. Buck drew the cinch tight on his own mount and swung up, pausing there, looking at his hands folded across the saddlehorn. "This is a hell of a country, John."

Kohler was about ready to mount, and as he put his foot in the stirrup, a shot hammered on the wind, distorted so much that it was hardly recognizable. "Hey!" Kohler said. Then three more shots made a cluster of sound, fading instantly.

"By God!" Kohler forgot the horse and ran for the stable door.

Buck followed him, mounted. They looked up the street, trying to see through the rain-smeared gloom. The door of Lovering's place banged open and Sheriff Harms came out. Another man was running toward the express office; Buck recognized the deputy, Hank Wilson.

Gigging his horse, hoofs flinging mud, he stormed up the street. Behind him, Kohler was trying to mount and keep up at the same time. Buck almost caught Hank Wilson as the deputy stopped on the express company porch; he flung off and helped lift McAllister Sims to a sitting position.

The man was dead. Blood leaked from two bullet holes in his chest, then Hank Wilson thought of the money. He dropped Sims like an armload of unwanted groceries and went inside. Buck followed him and one look into the express box was enough to show both of them that it was clean.

When they returned to the porch, Harms and Kohler were there. A crowd of townsmen braved the rain to cluster about.

"The money . . ." Harms began.

"Cleaned out," Hank Wilson snapped.

"What the hell's this?" someone asked, then pushed through. He handed Hank Wilson a pistol and the deputy looked at it carefully. To Buck he said, "I've seen this gun, but I want someone else to identify it."

"Whose is it?" asked Kohler. "Buck, do you know?"

"Yeah," Harry Buck said. "It belongs to Wes Cardigan."

A murmur rippled through the crowd, but Harms quieted them easily. "Now we don't want to go off the handle here. I'll get my horse and we'll get up a posse. Buck, Kohler, I'll ask you to come along. This was your money too, you know. Hank, you and Reilly get your horses." He saw someone in the crowd that he trusted. "Whitney, get a couple of the boys and take Sims over to Doc Reichstad's house. There ought to be a medical examination made."

"All right, Sheriff." A burly man collared

two of his friends and placed Sims on a coat. Grabbing the corners, they carried him along the walk.

"This sure as hell happened fast," Kohler said. "Harry and I were saddling up when the shots sounded: Wham! Wham! Wham! Like to scared me out of my growth . . ."

"I saw it from the porch," Hank Wilson said.

Had he dropped a bomb he would have had no less an effect. Harms looked at him sharply. "Is that so, Hank?"

"I said it was," Wilson said. "Reilly had gone in: I was turning to follow him when I saw Sims run out. That is, I thought it was, then I saw that it wasn't. He moved too fast to be Sims. Then the shooting started. Sims went down and the other fella rode out of town like all hell had broke loose."

"Can you swear it was Wes Cardigan?" Harms asked.

"Well, the light was bad—yes, it was Cardigan all right."

"Be damned sure," Harry Buck said softly. "We've got to arrest the man."

"I'm sure," Hank Wilson said. "As sure as I'll ever be." He turned to Indian Reilly. "Get the horses."

"We'll ride to Manly's place first," Harms said importantly. "He has a right to know about this."

"To hell with Manly . . ." Kohler began, but Harms held up his hand.

"I don't mean to argue this. We're going to Manly's place." He hitched up his trousers, then pawed water from his face. "This is a posse and Mr. Manly's authority won't do us any harm."

"Harms is right," Hank Wilson said. "Hell, if Manly behaves himself we'll even let him slap the horse from under Cardigan, when we catch him." He turned away then, and John Kohler looked at Harry Buck, a large question in his eyes. Lovering was standing on the porch in front of his saloon and Hank Wilson yelled at him. "Hey, Lovering, let me have a quart! It's goddamned cold and wet out where we're going!"

"Maybe you ought to leave Hank, your deputy, here in town," Kohler suggested. "Sort of to keep the peace until you get back, Harms."

The fat man looked uneasy; he wouldn't meet Kohler's eyes. "I guess Hank will want to come along," Harms said. "Besides, it ain't my place to stop him."

"Then whose is it?" Harry Buck asked.

"Why, I guess it's yours," Harms said. "If you feel up to it."

They gathered on the porch in front of the express office while Indian Reilly fetched the horses. John Kohler slapped his hands and stamped his feet, making grunting sounds in his

28

throat. He looked at Harry Buck, who stood in silence.

Finally Kohler said, "Tough on you, Harry. I mean, you feeling the way you do about Betty."

"There ain't going to be any hanging," Buck said softly. "I mean that, John."

"Sure. Sure, there won't be," Kohler said, without conviction. "Christ, I knew when I got up that this day was going to turn off rotten!"

Sheriff Harms came up, his fat face grave. "We ought to have some gear. Buck, go to Haskill's store and tell him to give you ponchos to go around." He looked around, counting silently. "Hank and Reilly have their pistols. You two?"

"Mine's at home," Kohler said. He looked at Harry Buck's bare hip. "Better get a couple, Harry."

"All right."

"And tell Haskill I'll be responsible," Harms said as Buck walked toward the store.

Haskill was standing in the shelter of his doorway. "Dirty business," he said. "You going after him?"

"Yep," Harry said. "Ponchos all around, Mr. Haskill." He walked over to the glass counter where Haskill kept his guns. "Mind if I look at these?"

"Help yourself," Haskill said. He sorted through the oilskins. "Wonder what the hell can get into a man to make him rob and kill?"

"Maybe he was tired of being poor," Harry Buck said. Haskill came back, laying the ponchos on the counter. Buck had a pair of guns laid out, both long-barreled .44's.

"Got some good leather to put those in," Haskill said. He opened a drawer and laid a half dozen holsters on the counter. Buck looked at the new, stiff leather, then stuffed a gun into one.

"Better fill two shell belts," he said. "Mr. Haskill, you got anything that's used?"

"A couple. Look in the second drawer." He got two boxes of cartridges off the shelf and began to fill the belt loops. Harry Buck was trying on an old belt and holster. He tied the tip of the holster down and dropped the gun into it, testing the feel of it. Suddenly he whipped his hand up and cocked the .44 when it came hip high.

"Well now," Haskill said, a little surprised. "I didn't know you could do that, Harry. You've had some practice, ain't you?"

"Some," Buck admitted. He began to load the cartridge belt, and when it was full, he loaded five of the chambers and let the hammer down on the empty.

"I'd hate to be Cardigan," Haskill said. Buck raised his head and looked at him. "Well, you figure it, Harry. The money he took belonged to all of you, money each of you needed damned bad. That adds up to a pretty determined posse,

Harry, and if Cardigan gets hung a little sooner than usual, I guess we can understand."

For a moment Harry Buck just stared at Haskill, then he gathered the ponchos under his arm and hurried out. The posse was mounted and waiting in front of the store.

Harry Buck passed out the ponchos, then went back into the store.

"Forget somethin'?" Haskill asked.

"Well," Buck said, a little ill at ease, "I meant to square up my account today and buy a few things. Hate to ask, but can you see your way clear to let me have a pound of bacon and a sack of Arbuckle's coffee?"

"Sure," Haskill said. He went behind his counter and put the provisions in a flour sack. When he brought these to Buck, he stuffed two sacks of cigarette tobacco into Buck's jumper pocket. "Tobacco is a comfort to a man sometimes. Wouldn't want you to run out, Harry."

"Thank you," Buck said and went out again.

Harms was irritated by the delay and Hank Wilson wore a scowl. Harry Buck stuffed the food into his saddlebag, and swung into the saddle.

"The quicker we start, the quicker we get this over with," Harms said and turned out of town, the posse bunched up behind him.

TWO

During the late afternoon Lila Manly stood on her back porch and watched the storm develop. Wind-driven water thundered against the roof and lashed the shuttered windows, searching out unsuspected openings. The ceiling and wall plaster began to show widening circles of moisture. All ranch work ceased and the hired men stayed within the security of the bunkhouse. Out in the west section, cattle lowed in misery, their tails to the blasting wind. The horse herd huddled in the lee of the barn, their coats dripping.

A rider poked out of the gloom, splashed across the yard and dismounted in the dubious shelter of the barn. He moved about carefully, a poncho draping him to the ankles. A tall-crowned hat with a huge brim funneled water away from his face. As he lit a lantern, one of the hands braved the storm to dash the short distance from the bunkhouse. He paused in the barn doorway, the glow of the lantern bright on his rain-slick hair. "Put him up for you, Mr. Manly?"

"Thank you, George," Manly said. "Everything all right?"

"Yes, sir. If you can call this damned rain all right."

"Well," Manly said, "it can't last forever." He handed the reins to the ranch hand, then sloshed across the muddy yard. On the porch he stopped to remove his poncho, then went quickly inside.

He was tardy in closing the door and the sudden blast of wind whipping down the hall extinguished the wall lamp. Very patiently he dug through his pockets for a dry match, for he was not a man to be disturbed by weather or anything he couldn't control. With the lamp going again, Manly turned to hang up his poncho and hat, then bent to tug off his soggy boots. He was tall and firm-bodied except for the slight paunch that insisted on drooping inelegantly over his belt. Manly was exceedingly conscious of this evidence of his physical decay, and made every effort to disguise it by standing straighter, carrying his chest higher. He was approaching fifty and loathed every day that brought him nearer to it. His face was blocky and still retained much of his earlier handsomeness. He had a long, straight nose and rather thin lips, pulled thinner by habit. His eyes were dark and steady; stern, some people said, but Temple Manly thought of them as assured. Events along the forty-nine-year track of his life had endowed him with what he regarded as an acute perception. Manly could feel a genuine compassion for a thief, because in his own youth he had wanted many things he was never destined to have. And the man who lied no longer remained an enigma to him, for he could recall times when he was reluctant to face the truth about himself. This knowledge had its effect on Temple Manly, and although he continued to walk among men, he was always aware that he possibly walked a little above them too.

A framed mirror hung between the lamps and he made it a habit to study himself critically each time he entered the hall. Gazing at his own reflection, Temple Manly unconsciously straightened his string tie and shrugged the shoulders of the dark suit to a better fit. With increased anxiety he regarded his receding hairline. The gray at his temples, which a few years before had caused him moments of worry, he now considered an asset for it gave him a gracious maturity without making him seem perceptibly older.

Thoughts of growing old disturbed him, so he shook out his sack of tobacco and sifted some into a creased paper. He could easily afford those factory-made cigarettes he'd heard about, but a practical part of his mind told him it would look best if he went on rolling his own. It gave him a common touch that linked him with the workingmen, let them know that money and position hadn't gone to his head. That was why he always wore Levi's instead of the pants to his suit—as sort of a bond with his men and the people in the county. Hard to beat, the common touch, Manly decided, and drew again on his smoke.

While he stood there, steps rapped across the porch and the door whipped open, then quickly closed. Jim Manly flogged water from his hat and said, "Hello. I thought you'd change your mind and settle up." He nodded toward the yard. "Coming down to beat hell."

Temple Manly looked at his son and saw himself some twenty years before. "Get out of those wet duds before you come down with the pip," he said. "And you let me worry about the money. Waiting never hurt any man, especially smart ones like Buck and Cardigan."

"Forget I said it," Jim Manly said. "Ma in the kitchen?"

"That's the only room in the house she likes," Manly said with a trace of irritation. "Ten rooms and she prefers the kitchen."

Gathering up his soggy hat and coat, the young man passed his father and went to the end of the hall. There he stopped and said, "I've been over to Cardigan's."

Manly made an impatient gesture with his hand. "We'll talk about it later, Jim." After the young man disappeared, Temple Manly walked to the kitchen. His wife turned with a start. "My, you scared me, Temple. Did you get your business all settled?"

"No," he said. "It won't kill them to wait a day or two." Seeing her working over the stove caused him a mild discomfort. "Can't see why you don't hire a cook, Lila. It isn't that we can't afford it."

"Just try to think of it as a common touch," she said lightly.

He looked at her quickly, suspicious, as he usually was, that her remark was more than it seemed to be. But she had turned her back to him, a most annoying habit; he liked a person to look at him when he spoke. Yet he said nothing, merely scraped a chair around and exposed his wet feet to the stove's heat. The house shivered as a strong gust nudged it, and the dripping of water in the pans on the floor began to annoy him.

"I'll get George to fix the roof as soon as the storm lets up," he said.

At forty-three Lila Manly was still slim and shapely and the roughness of the land hadn't put its mark on her. Her hair was flaxen, her skin smooth, and there was still enough of the coquette in her to make going to bed an adventure.

He said, "Jim came home. He was over to Cardigan's place again."

"I know. He left early this morning before you went to town."

"Lila, he's seeing too much of that girl. I'm

going to have a talk with him after supper."

She was not a woman who argued. Going to the hall, she called Jim to the table, then took her chair on his left. Jim Manly came in and sat down, smiling as though he didn't have a care in the world. Looking at him, Temple tried to recall if he had been that carefree at twenty-three, but that was too far back to remember clearly.

"You sore at me for going to Cardigan's, sir?"

For a moment Temple Manly didn't answer. He looked at his son and decided that it wouldn't make much difference if he said yes or not. Control had somehow slipped away. "I'm not a monster, Jim, and I don't like to tell you how to live, but you're smart enough to profit from my mistakes. I just don't want the girl in the family."

"That's all right," Jim said easily. "If we get married, I was figuring to find a place of my own."

Temple Manly began a hurried loading of his plate; he had no intention of being pulled into that kind of discussion. Then he changed the subject. "How was Cripple Creek? Last storm we had it ruined twelve acres of bottom land."

"Still down when I crossed," Jim Manly said. "Hell, sir, if it rises, it rises. You aren't Moses; you can't hold back the water with your hands."

"Now see here . . ."

"Temple, eat your supper," Lila said. "Jim didn't mean to be disrespectful."

Temple Manly ate in silence, looking now and then at his son. Jim had his mother's fair hair and his father's ranginess. He was tall, and his shoulders were heavily muscled. Manly felt uneasy about the boy for Jim lacked perspective, and judgment as to what was of value and what was not. Like that time the bull broke loose and took a bone-snapping fall in the breaks to the north. Jim had calmly shot him, completely ignoring the five-thousand-dollar loss and the open gate that had caused it all. True, the bull had been insured, but there was the principle of the thing to consider; to an orderly man these strokes of misfortune just did not happen. Like his mother, Manly reflected, Jim placed an idiotic trust in providence.

"Takes money to get married," Temple Manly said. "I suppose you've thought that all out. And a job? You have to make a living."

"I guess I'll get by," Jim said casually.

Manly frowned, a thundercloud of wrinkles forming on his brow. Lila saw this and touched him on the arm. "I baked a peach pie this afternoon. I'll cut you a piece."

"Thank you, my dear." He looked at his son. "Jim, when I was your age, I . . ."

"How big a piece do you want?" she asked.

"Huh? Oh, you . . ." Then he recalled his expanding stomach. "Not large, my dear." He turned away from her. "As I was saying, Jim, I . . ."

"Would you like some whipped cream on it?" Lila asked.

Manly jerked his head around to present his annoyance, knowing full well what she was doing. Shoving back his chair, he said, "Hang the pie!" He stomped into the living room to read.

A fireplace spread heat through the large room and Temple Manly began to roll a cigarette, his heavy brows bunched with displeasure. While his fingers patiently formed paper and tobacco, his mind groped for a way to make his son understand the importance of being a Manly. Because he was a Manly, certain things were expected of him. Not that he had anything personal against Betty Cardigan; she was a good enough girl. But marrying her was out of the question; it opened up too many ugly possibilities. First thing you knew her brother would come borrowing, gear at first, or the loan of a wagon, or a spare hand to help him at the gather. Then a tight winter would come along and it would be money. Manly shook his head and puffed on his cigarette.

When he was fourteen, Texas had just survived an economic tragedy; the war had left everything in chaos. His father, in desperation, had shot himself, and from that moment on, E. Temple Manly's one aim had been to climb so far out of poverty that no one would ever dare hint at his humble beginning.

Now he had so many horses that he left it up to one of his four foremen to keep count. And his land holdings extended to a little over a quarter of a million acres of Texas. In any good year he would ship eleven thousand steers wearing the Manly brand.

Finally Lila came in, her work finished. She glanced at him, then patted his arm. "He's young, Temple. Weren't you ever young?"

"I suppose I was," he said. His easy chair was invitingly close to the fire and he sat down in it, his legs outstretched. His wife sat across from him, her ever-present sewing on her lap.

The babble of the wind had become a background sound, then he raised his head slightly. He looked at his wife, so calm, so unconcerned; she seemed to grow more so every day. "Did you hear anything?" he asked.

She did not take her eyes from her sewing, nor did her fingers cease their deft movements. "The wind makes all kinds of noises on a night like this, and the conscience magnifies them."

"What's that supposed to mean?" Manly snapped. He turned and faced the porch, then moved quickly into the hall and flung open the front door.

Lila looked up in surprise as her husband invited four men into the room. Their ponchos rustled and they huddled together so as to concentrate the dripping water on the heavy hooked rug. Removing their hats, they slapped them against chap-covered legs.

Manly said, "If it's the money you're after, you've chosen the wrong way to get it."

"It's not that, exactly," said John Kohler. Manly looked at him; the others he merely swept with a glance for they came into a certain category in Temple Manly's thinking. He classified all people. Some were the speaking-to class, while others were lumped into the nodding-to class, as were Buck and Hank Wilson. Other people he merely looked at and there were some folks around Gunlock who considered themselves lucky to rate that much.

Lila put her sewing aside, stood up and said, "You're soaked. I'll make a pot of coffee."

Ponchos were peeled off and the men stood uneasily, conscious of the mud on their boots. Temple Manly walked to the fire, indicating that they were welcome to share it. He opened a small cabinet and brought out bottle and glasses. When each man had one, Manly waited for them to make the first move.

John Kohler nursed his drink with care while he backed to the fire to steam. No one spoke and Manly wondered what held them silent. He knew that the money was on their minds; what else did they have to think about? He watched Kohler, trying to fathom the man's thinking. Kohler was a simple man, living in his original house and driving a ten-year-old buggy. Because of this, Manly felt a twinge of pity for him; he felt that way about all the easygoing men. People took advantage of men like that.

The others stood close together in the clannish way inferiors have: this was Manly's judgment. But Sheriff Harms must have felt that his badge elevated him slightly, for he stood alone. When he brushed his vest aside to get at a handkerchief, the star gleamed dully in the yellow lamplight. Harms was heavy and old and tired. His years had left him with only a residual bitterness; he still seemed to embrace a small hope for mankind.

"Been some real trouble, Mr. Manly," he said. He had a round, simple face. The years in a soft job had added many inches to Harms's waistline and flesh hung in loose sags beneath his chin.

"It seems that you people are always in trouble," Manly said. "If it's the money, I told you I'd get around to it. The trouble is that you expect everyone to jump when you want something."

"We said it wasn't the money," Harry Buck said.

Manly looked at Buck, then at Hank Wilson standing behind Harms. He leaned against the fireplace, drinking his whiskey in preferred solitude. He was a lanky man, basically unfriendly and tough, even when he didn't have to be.

Harry Buck had finished his drink and set the glass aside. He did most things in a hurry, whether it was a job at hand or judging another man. Manly found the young man vaguely disturbing, but then, people like Harry Buck had always bothered him. Probably because they never let go of anything, a piece of land or an idea. A man had to kill them to whip them, and this marked Buck as a leader, a man to fear.

Lila came back into the room, blonde and smiling, a coffeepot in one hand and cups balanced precariously in the other. "Why not take off your wet things?" She put the load down. Chap buckles jingled, then they backed close to the fire again. Manly stood back and observed them, a small uneasiness in his manner.

Harry Buck said, "You'd better come along with us, Mr. Manly."

"Tell me why," Manly said.

Harry Buck glanced at Harms, then had another cup of coffee. Hank Wilson amused himself with polishing his deputy's star and watching Harms. John Kohler realized that Harms wasn't going to put the problem into words. "This is a posse, Mr. Manly. The express office was held up."

"The money stolen?" Manly asked.

"All of it," Harms said. "You can see why we need you along."

"That was your money," Manly said. "I was just handling it through the bank for you." He

44

turned as Jim came into the room, his eyes going from man to man. Harry Buck nodded to him; they were slight friends, but no one spoke.

"A man was killed," Kohler said evenly. "Sims."

"I recall the man," Manly said noncommittally. He shook out his tobacco and built a smoke.

"We'd sure like to have you along, Mr. Manly," Harms said with some hesitation. His fat hands came up to his vest front, then dropped back to his sides. "The killer was seen leaving town, so we can identify him." He looked around at the others, then lapsed into silence.

Manly's patience, always thin with those who held back, snapped, "Well man, out with it, or is it some secret?"

"Hank here says it was Wes Cardigan," John Kohler explained.

Jim Manly's reaction was instantaneous. "What kind of a lie is this?" He was angry and wanted the men to know it.

Temple Manly shot a warning glance at his son, but the young man ignored it. "Mind you," he said, "I'm not doubting Wilson's word, but this seems a little thin to go on."

"He dropped his gun," Hank Wilson said. There was brightness in his eyes, the kind a man gets when he sees a long-sought-after goal in sight. "One of those altered cap-and-ball Colts. He must have lost it while gettin' on his horse."

Jim Manly opened his mouth to speak, but a

45

wave of his father's hand silenced him. "A lot of people own those relics," Manly said. "I believe I still have one stuck away in a trunk."

John Kohler, more direct than either Harms or Wilson and less impressed by Manly's personality, said, "We don't intend to debate the matter. We know this was Wes Cardigan's gun. He tried to sell it last winter when things got tough. I was in the saloon the day he tried to get thirty dollars for it." His glance switched to Jim. "You spend considerable time at Cardigan's, so I'll describe it to you. Engraved, with ivory grips. Some Union officer had it during the war; his name was on the backstrap."

For a moment no one said anything. Finally Jim Manly nodded and said, "That was Wes's gun all right. I've seen it many times."

Harms pulled at his lip. "I give this a lot of thought, Mr. Manly, and I guess it's enough to go on. Old Sims wasn't much but he was human and he's dead. The light wasn't too good and Hank says he wouldn't want to swear it was Wes, but the gun sort of ties it up, far's I'm concerned."

"I see," Manly said. "Well, you have a job to do; it seems odd that you'd waste time here."

"We got to make this hanging official," Hank Wilson said flatly. This drew a deep frown on John Kohler's forehead and Harms stirred his feet nervously. Temple Manly looked at each of them, more particularly Harry Buck, who stood loose and idle and apparently unconcerned.

"Buck," Manly said, "you're a neighbor of Cardigan. What kind of a man is he?"

"Hell," Wilson snapped, "who cares what kind of . . ."

Temple Manly's eyes skewered the deputy. "When I want your opinion, I'll ask for it by name."

An amusement came into Harry Buck's pale eyes and pleasure wrinkles formed around the ends of his lips. "Don't know what to say," Buck admitted. "If you was to ask me whether I'd loan him fifty dollars, I'd say he was good for it. He never seemed a killin' man. Just quiet and tended to his own business like a man ought to."

"I see," Manly said. He considered this briefly, then said, "Tell me, Buck, are you for hanging Cardigan when you catch him?"

That he had scored was obvious. Harry Buck's angry pride made his eyes shine and color came into his face. "Why, goddamn you, Mr. Manly, you got no call to think I'd . . ."

Temple Manly waved his hand, his glance swinging to John Kohler, who understood that the question was silently being put to him. "I think the man ought to have a fair trial if and when we catch him," Kohler said.

"I don't have to ask you," Manly said to Hank

47

Wilson. "Or Harms either." Then his manner changed and he smacked his hands together. "All right, I'll go. Jim, go to the bunkhouse and have George saddle two horses. I'll take the bay and you'd better ride your roan. He's steady on his feet and can keep on the move."

Like most of the orders Temple Manly gave, these were phrased to tolerate little debate. When Jim grabbed a poncho and dashed out, Manly took Harms by the arm and led him to one side while Lila kept the others occupied with the coffeepot.

The fat sheriff was vastly relieved and had so little pride that he didn't bother to hide it. "Was afraid you wouldn't come, Mr. Manly. John and Harry I could count on, but Hank'd like my job, and he's got Indian Reilly with him."

"Reilly? Where?"

"Outside on the porch," Harms said softly. He took out a handkerchief and wiped his thick lips. His teeth were yellowed and stained from years of cut plug; there was the odor of horses and sweat and damp woolens about him. He put his handkerchief away and shook his head, making his plump cheeks quiver. "I ain't much, Mr. Manly, and I got you to thank for my stayin' in office, but I want to see justice done. You can see how important that is, can't you, Mr. Manly?"

What kind of an answer did the man expect?

Not the truth surely. This was the price a man paid when he fooled himself, even for a moment. There always came a time when a man was faced with his own lack of worth and if he couldn't find a place for himself, then he was forced to make the last fatal blunder, or ask someone to make it for him. He supposed that Harms knew about that. For years now Harms had worn the star, throwing drunks in jail, breaking up fights on Saturday night, and in this feeble way trying to convince people that he was an able lawman. But now he would have to act beyond his ability and he was not up to it. Harms wouldn't be the first man Manly had let fall and never given a second thought.

I suppose it's because of Jim, he thought. He had to help the young man now, or lose him. Whether or not he caught Wes Cardigan was of little importance; he just didn't want the lad's faith destroyed by not going along. Even when a man didn't want to help, it was best if he put up a show anyway.

Jim came back in a few moments, and Manly went into the hall for his oilskins and rifle. The others were buckling on their chaps, bundling into their foul-weather gear and Lila went with them to the door.

By the time they had trundled out, Jim reappeared, a poncho draping him to the ankles. His expression was troubled and grave. Temple

Manly said, "Go on. I'll be along as soon as I say good-bye to your mother."

When the door closed, blocking out the storm's fury, Manly put his arm around his wife's shoulders and led her back to the fire. "This is a terrible thing," she said softly. "Do you believe Wes did it, Temple?"

He shrugged. "Not being there when it happened, I couldn't say."

"But he just isn't the kind! And to kill for money, Temple!"

"Men have done it," he said flatly. "Lila, you met the man once when he came here after his sister. How can you say one way or another? A man can need money badly. The bank could have refused a loan. We don't know."

She looked at him steadily. "Temple, haven't you ever believed a thing without proof?"

Buttoning his slicker, he said, "I don't think this will take long. The storm will drive him to shelter." What he did not say, but meant, was that he never made a concession to weather, or much of anything, and because of this would find his man when others might fail.

"And when you find him, Temple, will it be Hank Wilson's way or John Kohler's?"

He grew impatient and very much in a hurry, surprised that she understood him so well. "They're waiting," he said and gave her a quick kiss. Then he opened the door and stepped onto the storm-scuffed porch. The others turned to him. In the darker shadows, Manly saw Indian Reilly, silent and stone-faced. George was there with a lantern, and at Manly's nod, started for the barn.

THREE

Walking ahead of the others, George and his lantern cast a moving circle of brilliance in the rain-puckered mud. High over the mountains, lightning jabbed a crooked finger across the sky, illuminating the yard and buildings with a burst of bone whiteness. A ponderous chord of thunder followed.

Harry Buck helped George fight open the door. Temple Manly lifted a pair of elkhide shotgun chaps from a wall peg, then opened his slicker to buckle them on. As he bent over to fasten the snaps, he asked Harms, "Where do you propose to start?"

Harms was more than a little flattered by this deference; he removed his soggy hat and scratched his thinning hair. "Well, Mr. Manly, it's my guess that Cardigan will head for the sulphur sink country, if he ain't there already." He went on in his high, droning voice, explaining that Cardigan would probably take the valley road and what he figured they ought to do to head him off. Manly closed his ears to this rambling flow of words and broke open a box of cartridges. He dropped the bulk of them in his coat pocket. The remainder he fed through the loading gate of his Winchester.

Hank Wilson, who was inclined to be curious, picked up the discarded box, turning it over in his hands several times. "Figure to meet a grizzly?" He pointed to the illustrated caliber. "I never knew they made a rifle that big." Then he grinned with a touch of insolence. "Course, I ain't got the money to buy every newfangled gun that comes out either."

For an instant Manly pondered whether to crush this impertinence or ignore it. In his coolest voice he said, "As long as you don't have to carry it, don't worry about it."

George and Harry Buck came to the front of the barn with the horses and the barn door was muscled open again. For a moment they stood in the rain like squires standing to horse but not daring to mount until the king mounted. Finally Temple Manly swung into the saddle. George hovered near Manly's stirrup. "When do you expect to be back, sir?"

"When we catch our man," Manly said heavily. He glanced at his son, a dark, round-shouldered shape, then down again at George. "See that Mrs. Manly is driven into town on Saturday."

Harms swung his horse around to side Temple Manly. "No use stopping at Cardigan's place, Mr. Manly. We checked and he ain't there." Water ran in a continuous stream from the V crease in his hat and he pawed it from his face. A shaggy mustache was hanging limply along the ends of his lips and water dripped from the pale hairs. Manly clung to his aloof silence, creating in the minds of these men the illusion of self-sufficiency.

Manly pivoted in the saddle and looked at his son. "Side me, Jim." For a moment he thought the boy was going to exhibit an open defiance. Finally Jim edged close and sat in stubborn silence. Manly put out his hand and touched him briefly, trying to transmit his understanding, but he felt the young man stiffen and dropped his hand away.

Leading out, Manly took them from the muddy yard; the posse lumped loosely behind him. Rain dashed against them in smashing sheets, cold and stinging before the pushing wind. The horses moved reluctantly, heads down, trying to edge away on the lee quarter. The bulk of Manly's range lay in this high valley, a scooped-out bowl nestled between a horseshoe of timber-carpeted hills. Toward them the posse moved, led by the inscrutable Temple Manly.

They rode for an hour with nothing but the sloshing of hoofs to puncture the monotony of drumming rain. Body heat dissipated quickly in the chill wind and Manly had to set his teeth to keep them from chattering. He would like to have blown on his hands or flailed his arms but he dared not for fear the others might construe it as a sign of weakness. From his right, Jim Manly said, "Why did you come? I could have made it alone."

The sound of his son's voice startled Temple Manly and he turned his head. "I can turn back," he said. "But I thought you needed me, Jim." He knew the young man would never argue this, yet the checkmate solved nothing.

"I'm here because I'm Wes's friend," Jim said. "Wes is nothing to you."

"That's right," Manly said. "He's nothing at all to me."

Men like Wes Cardigan were no mystery to Temple Manly; he could almost guess Cardigan's moves since the robbery and shooting. Panic would rule the man for a time, driving him to familiar ground, which would be the Cardigan home place. Then realization would come to him and he would flee; the problem then became, where? Manly conjured up a mental picture of the country for a radius of fifty miles. Mountains in three directions, with one hell of a desert blocking the fourth side. No choice for a desperate man, according to Temple Manly's thinking. The main road could be eliminated since there was a telegraph office in each town. Cardigan's only chance lay in getting across the desert.

There was a run of talk behind him, then Harms, who rode directly behind, said, "Indian Reilly wants to know whether you want him to lead or not, Mr. Manly?"

"Thank him," Manly said civilly, "but tell him that I know the terrain on my own land." The word went back and Manly settled uncomfortably. He didn't like the idea of the Indian coming along in the first place, but if one man was forced to endure another, he did it best by keeping that man in his place.

Jim Manly said, "Wes didn't do this, sir."

Manly sighed inwardly. Just like his mother; got his mind locked on something and you couldn't shake him loose. "I'm glad you think so," he said aloud. "Faith in a man is a nice thing to have, when it's properly placed."

"Don't treat me like a fool," Jim said hotly. "I can make up my own mind."

"I've always treated you as you deserved," Manly told him. "Jim, don't let your feelings for the girl color your thinking." He jerked his head toward the procession strung out behind him. "Do you think they wanted me along because they like me?" He shook his head. "Every man here has an ax to grind, and if hanging Cardigan will put a sharper edge on it, then they'll stretch his neck. Do you think Harms really cares what happens as long as he looks good afterward? Or Harry Buck? What's this to him, besides the hunt? Cardigan could have the money on him, and if he has, how much of it do you think will get back to the express company? Kohler's along because he feels he has to come; the man has a conscience and he wouldn't sleep well if he thought he hadn't done his duty. So he's not really concerned with Cardigan, but himself."

"And you, sir?"

Temple Manly paused a moment. "Jim, I'm the biggest man in the county. Because I get the most out of it means that I have to accept the most responsibility, and give the most. You're a Manly too, Jim. Just forget Wes as an individual and do a job."

Someone in the rear cursed the weather in a nasal voice; Manly recognized it as Hank Wilson's. "I could sure do with a drink of whiskey," Wilson was saying.

Harms swung quickly around in the saddle. "None of that now!" he warned in a loud voice. Harry Buck, who trailed Harms, swung out of line and dropped back to Wilson's place and rode thereafter on the man's left flank.

"Damn a man that can't leave a bottle alone," Harms was muttering. He leaned forward to peer through the wall of darkness that enveloped them, then settled again in the wet saddle, letting his reluctant horse follow Manly's mare.

Several times Temple Manly swung around for a backward look but he could see nothing except the indistinct blobs that were horses and men. The thought of Hank Wilson swigging a bottle disturbed him, for among other things, the man had a weakness for drink.

The land rose in ragged sweeps. Jagged boulders and glacial residue buttressed the winding trail. Manly called back, "Single file through here! Better stay close up!"

The riders began to separate until they rode head to tail, cautious and clinging to the black, bobbing shape of the rider ahead. The trail was narrow and the going slow, with a hundred-and-eighty-foot clean drop for the first man who made a mistake.

At last they broke free, topping a small rise, and Manly led them into thickening groves of trees. Finally he dismounted and began to stamp circulation into his legs before he caught himself. A man ought to be tougher than this, he thought, but the cold was making him numb.

Kohler swung down and began groping forward to where Manly stood with his son. "I guess you know where you're going," he said, "but the town road would have been easier. We could have cut off to Cherry Basin. A little longer, but not as damned rough."

"These things are always rough," Manly said. He glanced around and saw Harms huddled in his poncho. Opening his slicker, Manly bent over to use it for a shield while he rolled a cigarette. The sudden flare of the match was a shocking brightness in the dark. From somewhere off Manly's left, Hank Wilson whipped his hat in an arc, slapping the match out.

"What the hell you tryin' to do, give us away?"

Slowly Temple Manly turned. He spoke with ominous softness. "Don't ever do a thing like that again." Then he waited, letting his silence weigh heavily on the man's courage. Like wax long held in the hand, Hank Wilson's manner softened and he spoke in a voice that was resentfully apologetic.

"I'm just jumpy, that's all."

"Make sure you don't jump at me," Manly said and struck another match. "Light up," he said to the others. "We'll remain here a few minutes."

Indian Reilly moved about with his usual restlessness. He was a lanky, nervous man with few good habits and a manner that bred instant distrust. He was some remote kin to Hank Wilson, Manly recalled; perhaps a third cousin. Trouble was, so many of his kind were born on the wrong side of the blanket that a man could hardly keep track. Reilly shuffled up to Harms and said, "No track on night like this. We go back?"

"Mr. Manly knows what he's doing," Harms said, as though he had been offered a personal insult. "Get on back there and mind the horses. We need you, we'll call you." When Reilly moved away, Harms looked at Manly and smiled. Manly stifled the impulse to reach out and reward the sheriff with a pat on the head; the gesture would not have been out of place.

Turning to his horse, Manly mounted, and this silent signal sent them all into the saddles. Without a word, Manly moved off into the slanting rain.

A miserable hour passed before they halted again, then Harms bumped into Manly and cursed, but he was quick-witted enough to blame his own clumsiness. Ahead, in a nest of dark trees, lay the black outline of a cabin. Manly said, "Buck, put the horses in the lean-to." He dismounted then and toed the door open. After a moment's fumbling, he found a lantern and put a match to it.

The woodbox was filled with dried wood, and John Kohler, after a nod from Manly, built a fire. Slickers and ponchos were shed and the men began to crowd around the growing blaze. Hank Wilson stood in one corner with Indian Reilly, plainly indicating where his allegiance lay. The lantern light made deep hollows in their cheeks and gave Indian Reilly's face an ominous cast.

Wilson said, "Can't see why we're wasting all this time."

"You've got a lot of it to waste," John Kohler said with some sarcasm.

Harms was rubbing his plump hands before the fire. His cherub face was thoughtful and composed and he said little, trying to convey the impression that he and Temple Manly knew what they were doing. Working with important men was one of Harms's pleasures for he fancied that some of their quality rubbed off on him and, carefully used, the luster lasted a long time. This would be good for a lot of cracker-box talks. By mentioning his name often enough with Manly's, he could swing votes come election time.

Harry Buck came in, flogging water from his hat. He looked at the fire, then stripped off his poncho. "I should have brought some coffee," he said. His glance touched Manly and the latter read a boldness in his eyes, or was it independence? Buck was obviously not a man who leaned on anyone; he stood alone by preference.

"All right to look in your stores?" Kohler asked. Manly nodded and Kohler went to the packing-box cupboard and commenced to rummage. He found a waxed bag of Arbuckle's coffee and an old pot, bringing both to the fire.

"I'll fill that up," Buck said and took the pot outside. He held it under the dripping eave for a few moments, then brought it back in and set it on the stove. When Kohler poured in the coffee he had ground with a hand mill, Buck said, "Don't be stingy with it. I like it strong."

Jim Manly's next step took him to the cupboard, where his hand explored a moment, then came away with a silver dollar.

To Harry Buck he said, "Do you know Wes Cardigan's handwriting?"

"Seen it a couple of times," Buck said. "Don't you know it?"

"Yes, but I want someone else to identify it too."

"Let me see that," Temple Manly said. He took the bag and read: *I took the bacon and two cans of beans and the .44 shells. A dollar ought to cover it. Wes.*

"That sounds like an honest man trying to do the right thing," John Kohler said.

"Any man can afford a dollar's worth of honesty," Hank Wilson said. He edged Harms out of the way and lifted the note from Temple Manly's fingers. Harry Buck lifted his head sharply and watched with a fine-honed anticipation, his glance focused on Manly's suddenly hardened expression.

Without warning, Manly lifted his hand and whipped the back of it across Hank Wilson's face. The blow was sudden and didn't suffer for want of power. Wilson's feet eased off the floor and he was flung backward into the pole bunk. The bottom rail split under his weight and straw ticking sifted onto the floor. Manly's tone was conversational. "I told you once to watch yourself." He looked at Wilson while the deputy pawed at the slight trickle of blood oozing from his nose.

No one spoke. Rain dribbled on the roof with its monotonous murmur. Hank Wilson stayed on the floor, his eyes flat and expressionless. Against the far wall, Indian Reilly shuffled his feet until he was clear. He carried a Spencer carbine in the crook of his arm and he kept looking at Temple Manly as if mentally taking aim.

Harry Buck touched Reilly lightly with his finger and said, "I wouldn't mix in this, was I you." There was a quiet warning in his voice and it held Indian Reilly. Buck's face was bland but there was nothing mild about the .44 tied to his thigh. Indian Reilly sagged back, his eyes dark and glittering.

Without looking at Buck, Manly said, "I can blow my own nose."

"Why sure," Buck said, smiling. "I was just pickin' out a partner in case the music started. Or did you want to be a hog about it and have all the fun yourself?"

John Kohler chuckled, then broke off quickly. Manly waited a moment longer, then turned his back on Wilson. The coffeepot was rocking on its heat-warped bottom and he pulled it to the edge of the stove.

The fire was thawing them out; steam rose from Kohler's clothes, so closely did he hug the stove. The tension eased, leaving them loose and easy, all except Manly, whose face remained coldly impersonal, as though he were surrounded by strangers. Hank Wilson got up off the floor and brushed the straw from his clothes.

In the corner lay a heap of discarded cans and Harry Buck cut the tops away from two with his jackknife. The cans were slightly rusted, but after washing them in rain water, they served well enough to hold coffee. The heat was rising in the cabin, turning the air stagnant with the effluvia of horses and men.

Impatient with waiting for the cans to make the rounds, Buck drank from the pot after cooling it in cold water. He shared it with Harms and Kohler who strained the grounds through their teeth.

Finally Jim Manly spoke. "Did you guess Wes would come here?"

Everyone looked at Temple Manly. He set his can down and rolled a cigarette before answering. Somehow this made his reply more dramatic. "A man on the dodge needs help," he said. "The towns are out, so he'll head for Rynder's place on the edge of the sink." He paused to draw on his smoke and drink some more of his coffee. "This is the closest way and the most dangerous, but obviously our man is daring enough." He picked up the note and waved it. "A cool man wrote this. Whether that coolness stems from innocence or . . ."

"An innocent man don't run," Hank Wilson said darkly.

Manly's unfriendly glance touched him. "You have difficulty in learning, don't you, Wilson?" Then he went on, completely ignoring the man,

". . . or whether he believes he can outrun us, remains to be seen."

"Wes wouldn't run if he thought he had a chance," Jim said hotly.

Manly's brows drew together. "Son, under certain circumstances any man will run." He said it, but still left the impression that this applied to all save himself. "A man's flight has always been construed to be an admission of guilt. We have to assume that Wilson is right and that Wes is our man."

"I don't like to be called a liar," Wilson said. "I'm a law officer in this county and . . ."

"You're an incompetent tough who drinks too much," Manly said flatly. "And if I ever call you a liar, I'll do so in such a way that you can't mistake it."

Harms inserted his whining voice into the argument. "I agree with Mr. Manly. Wes will head for Rynder's place."

"If he's not there already," Manly said evenly. "He's moving fast, yet he doesn't seem to be in too much of a hurry." He fished out his watch and popped the lids. "At the rate we're traveling, we ought to raise Rynder's place by daylight—if there is such a thing any more." He put his watch away, then looked squarely at Harms. "I want this man taken back to Gunlock alive, Harms."

With that, Manly gathered his slicker and rifle and stepped outside. In a moment they gathered by the door while Indian Reilly went for the horses. Mounted, Manly led them up a thin trail through the timber, following the faint break that would lead them eventually to the thirty-mile-wide sulphur sink to the northeast.

Again Harms fell in close behind Manly and his son. After a while Harms edged forward to say, "Mr. Manly, I intended to bring Wes back for trial."

"What you mean to do, Harms, and what you usually do are often two different things." He nodded toward the rear of the column. "Hank would like to see a man hang. That star you pinned on him has gone to his head. Indian Reilly is shirttail kin of Wilson's, so they'll side together." He bent sideways in the saddle to peer into Harms's face. "You've set around on your butt too long. It's time to get off or get out. When we catch Cardigan, I'll expect you to have made up your mind."

Harms sulked back to his place and mulled this over. Jim Manly edged closer to his father and said, "We all know what Harms is; you didn't have to rub his face in it."

"When I need your criticism, I'll ask for it."

"Yes, sir," Jim said, his tone full of sarcasm. "And of course I'll come in on bended knee, sir."

Temple Manly flipped his head sideways. "You act like a man who wants to learn something the hard way, Jim. You may be too old for the woodshed, but I can still double my fist."

"I'm not going to fight you," Jim said flatly. "I would if I thought it would do any good."

"That's your mother talking," Manly snapped.

"No, she's given even that up." He lapsed into a brief silence. "Don't you feel anything for Wes? Can you imagine what it's like, alone and running?"

"What he feels is not my concern," Manly said evenly. "But to get back to Harms. Do you think I should lie to him, give him a pat on the head and tell him what a good man he is, and then watch him mess up the next thing that comes along? Would I be doing him a favor that way?" He reached out and took the young man by the arm. "I don't fool men and I don't want them fooling me. You're here because of Cardigan's sister and you resent the fact that I attach no feeling to the man whatever. Jim, what do the others feel for him? Do you think Buck and Kohler can stop Reilly and Hank Wilson? Hank's killed two men in a stand-up fight; he's fast and there's a mean streak in him. But I can stop both of them, Jim. I can speak and because I'm Temple Manly nothing will happen. People are always in awe of power, son; that's why you have to learn to use it wisely."

"I never wanted power," Jim Manly said quickly. "I'm Wes Cardigan's friend; that's why

I'm here." He paused and looked at his father. "Didn't you ever do anything in your life just because you wanted to, and for no other reason?"

"I could never afford that," Temple Manly said. "And neither can you." He raised his hand and wiped water from his face. "Your mother would think differently; she'd share her last crust of bread with a stranger. But I'd eat mine so I could grow stronger. The weak die off, Jim. If you stopped to feel sorry for them, you'd wear your eyes out crying."

"Sure," Jim Manly said. "But the fact remains that I love Betty Cardigan and I'm going to marry her. And it's her brother Harms is after." He wheeled his horse and fell out of the column, rejoining it near Harry Buck.

The young rancher was riding head down, his shoulders rounded in discomfort. When Jim Manly sided him, Buck said, "You and the king arguing again?"

"Who says we argue?"

Buck's laugh was a musical bubble over the rattle of rain. "You two go together like off-size boots. He surprised me by even coming along."

They topped a ridge and paused in a small pocket of rock and scrub pine. Temple Manly dismounted and fashioned a cigarette while the others swung down to walk circulation into their cold legs. John Kohler's teeth chattered and he glanced toward Manly, but the tall man stood alone, apparently unperturbed by discomfort. Jim Manly did not go forward but remained near Harry Buck, who was having difficulty getting his smoke going in the wind. At the rear, Hank Wilson uncorked a bottle and tipped it up.

The gurgle attracted Buck's attention and he knocked it away from Wilson's mouth. "Stay sober," Buck said evenly. "You getting drunk now is all that we need."

The bottle broke with a loud tinkling and Wilson swore heartily. He doubled his fist and swung at Buck's head, but the young man raised his knee and caught Wilson in the groin. Harms was surging back, bellowing, "What's goin' on here?"

John Kohler took a small storm lantern from his saddlebag and lit it. Then he came back, casting the faint glow ahead of him. Hank Wilson was sitting on the ground, his legs doubled up. He had vomited on his slicker and was just recovering from another seizure. Harry Buck stood still, watching Indian Reilly while Kohler and Harms bent over Wilson. The lantern's glow caught the fragments of the bottle and reflected them like distant stars. Harms toed over a shard of glass bearing a familiar label.

To Wilson he said, "Get up! I warned you to leave the damn bottle at home."

"I can't!" Wilson said, groaning. "God, I'm ruined!"

Temple Manly stepped up then, moving Harms aside. He looked at Wilson, then at Harry Buck. "You're rough and you don't waste time."

"I give people what they have coming," Buck said. "Surely you ain't going to argue that attitude, are you?"

"No," Manly said, and returned to his horse.

Indian Reilly was helping Wilson to his feet. When Harry Buck moved away, Jim Manly went with him. "You don't like my father, do you?"

For a moment, Buck stared at him, then smiled. "I don't like this goddamned rain either, but there's nothing I can do about it."

Harms had gone back to stand by Temple Manly; he seemed to draw a comfort from the tall, stern man. Manly looked toward a sheltering rock overhang to the right, then he tipped his head back and studied the night sky, finding no break in the storm. He hunched his shoulders and pulled his slicker tighter around him.

Out of the darkness a small alien sound broke into the pelt of the storm. Manly was instantly alert, the muzzle of his .40-82 Winchester poking from the folds of his oilskins. The metallic ring of a rifle's action being worked rang out, alerting each man.

"Who's there?" he shouted. "Sing out! Who's there?"

The shifting came again, deep in the brush beneath the overhang. A shod hoof struck rock, clearly discernible. "Kohler, bring that lantern!"

There was a rushing movement from the rear and Kohler passed Manly, keeping well out of the man's line of fire. Harry Buck had his .44 exposed, a nickeled, probing snout. Manly moved forward with them while the others tagged along, nervous and ready to shoot anything that moved.

Then John Kohler swore and laughed in a relieved voice. Harry Buck's hand darted out to grab the mane of a skittish horse while his other pawed beneath his slicker to re-holster his revolver. They all gathered around the animal, Kohler holding the lantern high.

"That's Wes's horse," Jim said. There was a hint of fatalism in his voice and a touch of despair.

The men looked at each other, one thought uppermost in their minds; a dismounted man couldn't get far in this weather.

FOUR

Temple Manly was vaguely amused by the diverse effect the single discovery of the horse and its attending possibilities had on the men about him. On Harms's fat face there was an unabashed anxiety, for he had an almost child-like inability to face the reality of his own personal weakness. He fretted about on his short, fat legs, breathing noisily through his nose like a wrestler pinned inescapably to the mat. Hank Wilson's eyes held a bright glitter and he stood near Indian Reilly as though he wanted to share this moment with another who understood the dark and twisted avenues of his thinking. Hank moved with studied tenderness for he was still feeling the discomfort of Harry Buck's driving knee. And Harry seemed more concerned about the horse than he was with its absent owner: he paced slowly around the animal.

Only Kohler seemed completely undisturbed; he set his lantern on a rock and, at Manly's nod, followed with the light as Manly made his inspection. Bending down by the horse's forefeet, Manly discovered the hobbles there. "Grass," he said. "Cardigan wove a pair of Indian hobbles, but what for?" He realized that he was conducting this mental speculation aloud and stopped lest the others think him a victim of indecision.

He moved about the mare, rubbing his hands over the wet coat. At last he said, "Sweenied shoulder. I guess Cardigan figured we'd come through here—in fact, he must have counted on it." He raised a hand and pawed his mouth out of shape. "He obviously wanted us to find the horse."

"Fair shelter," Harry Buck said in his idle voice. "Braiding those hobbles took time, Mr. Manly. Is the man out of his head? He doesn't have time to kill." He turned his head and looked at Indian Reilly, who stood in the shadows, his penny-complexioned face expressionless. "How long has this horse been here, Reilly? You're an Injun and supposed to know those things."

"Can't tell," Reilly muttered. "Too much rain. Big storm."

"He's as useless as tits on a boar," Kohler said disgustedly."

"Seems to me," Harry Buck said evenly, "that the man was more concerned about his horse than he was with his own hide." He scratched the budding stubble on his cheeks and looked at the others, as though seeking agreement to bolster his opinion.

Temple Manly grunted. Jim Manly said, "Wes is a kind man." The words fell flat and he was instantly sorry he had said them.

"Do you think he struck out afoot, Mr. Manly?" This was Harms's question.

"We're dealing with an intelligent man," Manly said. "I had some saddle horses pastured up here. Cardigan could have cut one out and made a trade."

"Trade you say?" Hank Wilson limped forward, then stood with his legs slightly spread. "Seems that you're determined to lean over backward for Cardigan just because your kid's hard up for the girl."

Temple Manly's eyes flicked to his son, expecting the young man to act, but the moment passed while the lad floundered in his usual trough of indecision. Harms, however, puffed his bulk between Manly and Wilson and shook his finger under Wilson's nose. "Here, now," Harms snapped, "you watch how you talk to Mr. Manly!"

Harms's interference annoyed Temple Manly to the point of anger. He opened his mouth to blast the sheriff, then closed it with a snap. Standing in the rain to argue about a man as low on the social scale as Wilson seemed a little foolish. He turned his back on the deputy to speak to the others. "Since there were horses in this section, I believe it would be extremely foolish to assume that Cardigan's on foot." He fumbled through the folds of his clothes to bring out his watch, holding it to the light to read the hands. "A quarter after three," he said. "Buck, cut the hobbles on that horse. Likely she'll drift down the valley to the home place within a week or so."

He turned to his own horse and Jim followed him. Before Manly could mount, the young man took his arm and said, "I'm sorry, sir."

"Yes," Manly said, "I suppose you are." He meant to let this go but something goaded him to add, "You're short weight, Jim. I suppose I'm to blame."

"You couldn't ever be to blame for anything," Jim said, his tone openly sarcastic.

Temple Manly's blocky face seemed to grow more solid, but there was no anger in his voice. "Jim, I've never belted you for your sass because I've always believed that you were entitled to an opinion, even when it wasn't worth listening to. Why don't you go home, Jim? What good are you here?"

"That's what I keep asking myself," Jim snapped and wheeled to his horse. Manly waited a moment, troubled by the young man's tone, then he swung into the saddle. The others followed and Manly waited while Kohler blew out the storm lantern and stowed it. Indian Reilly pressed forward with his horse and Manly took the bridle.

"Where the hell you going, Reilly?"

"Find way down," Reilly said in his flat voice.

"Get back where you belong. When I want to blow your whistle, I'll pull the chain." He nudged his horse into motion, leaving the pocket for a narrow trail that would take them out of the mountains.

Jim Manly came back to ride on his father's right. After a time he said, "If I was a horse, you'd have shot me a long time ago."

"Be glad you're not a horse," Temple Manly said. "Jim, never waste time on self-pity. Fools do and suffer for it. You're not a fool."

"At least I'm something," Jim said. He lapsed into a long silence, then said, "Wes left his horse in trade, so you can't accuse him of horse-stealing. He's honest. Are you so stubborn blind you can't see that?"

"A Yankee storekeeper in Illinois once created a reputation for honesty by walking a few miles to return some pennies. Some years later he parlayed that into a slogan that helped put him in the Presidency." Manly looked at his son. "Give me ten dollars and I'll walk among strangers and make them believe I'm honest. Jim, forget the dollar and the hobbled horse. They don't prove a thing."

"You're just supposed to catch him, not judge him!"

"Is that possible?" Temple Manly asked. He settled down to the discomfort of the ride. The pace was telling on him. His legs ached and shooting pains deviled the small of his back, bringing to his attention the indisputable evidence of his physical deterioration. Yet weariness worked on them all, and had he bothered to look, he would have found the other men lolling in the saddle.

Hank Wilson was riding cockbilled and Manly heard Harry Buck laugh. "Acorns swelling up on you, Wilson?"

The deputy cursed and fell silent.

Manly found his trail and let the jaded horses pick their way to the lower levels. An hour inched by with agonizing slowness, and the darkness all but blotted out the faint trail that at times clung like ladder rungs against the sheer side.

From the rear Harry Buck said, "Kohler, do you have the time?"

There was a pause, then a match flared and was immediately killed by the rain, but not before Kohler read his watch. "Half past four in the morning," he said.

"You don't have to pin it down," Buck said. "I can tell it's night."

Then abruptly the rain ceased. There was no break in the sky's boiling swarthiness, but water no longer engulfed them. Temple Manly stopped in a small glen and dismounted. He took off his hat and flogged it against his leg, then stood with his head bare. From the nearby timber, water dripped onto the squaw carpet, but the night was strangely silent. The chill seemed to lift and Kohler removed his poncho, rolling it to stow behind his saddle.

"Buck," Manly said, "see if you can find some fairly dry branches. We can have a fire."

Harms came up, his boots making soft slushings in the earth. "Mr. Manly, it can't be far to Rynder's place." He longed for the comfort of four walls and a good roof; Rynder's held the promise of these things.

"Then twenty minutes won't make the difference, will it?" He shed his slicker as Harry Buck came back with an armload of dead branches.

Buck got the fire going, then stood before it, the flames outlining him blackly. The horses stood with lowered heads, almost too tired to move. Indian Reilly was in the shadows; he seemed to prefer them. Hank Wilson faced the fire, standing to the left of Harry Buck. He looked around finally and rubbed the side of his face. "Be careful the next time you come into Gunlock, Harry."

"Of you?" Buck smiled quickly. "Don't scare me, Hank."

"You should have gone on home," Wilson said softly. "Harms don't need you and neither do I." He scuffed at the soggy ground with his toe. "Don't butt in when we catch Wes Cardigan, Harry."

"Depends on you. I wouldn't stand by and see Wes pushed into anything that wouldn't wipe off." He grinned. "Harms'll fold, which leaves John and me. Manly I don't know about yet." Buck took out a soggy sack of Durham and creased a paper. After the cigarette had been built, he bent forward and lifted a glowing faggot, and when he was finished, tossed it back on the fire. "Did you really see Cardigan, Hank?"

The deputy whipped his head around quickly, his eyes narrowed. "I said I saw him. You want to call me a liar now?"

Buck's glance dropped to the bone-handled Remington carried cross-draw fashion on Hank Wilson's hip. "Not here," he said. "I'll make it plain if I do though."

He heard Manly come up behind him and turned away from the fire. Kohler joined him, and Harms, who always made it his policy to cling to the pace-setters. Jim Manly remained near his horse, half hidden from the others. Harry Buck sided him and drawled, "Feeling real unsociable tonight, ain't you?"

Jim Manly opened his mouth to speak, then shook his head instead. After a short pause he asked, "Got any tobacco on you?" Buck handed over sack and papers, then took them back when Jim Manly had his cigarette made. The young man cracked a match on his belt buckle and cupped his hands around the flame. His face was drawn with fatigue and worry; the barest hint of a whisker stubble fuzzed his cheeks. He glanced at Buck over the flame, then said, "If we catch Wes, and someone breaks out a rope, Hank Wilson is mine."

"You'd never be able to handle him," Buck said softly. He tipped his head forward and studied the dark ground. "Ever shoot a man, Jim?"

"You know I haven't."

"Well, Hank has," Buck said. "He won't hesitate to draw, but you will. That will make the difference." He looked at the younger man. "You want to go home across your horse?"

"No," Jim said. "But I'm not going to stand by and watch Wes hang."

"Not my intention either," Harry Buck said. "Jim, if you have to fight, if that's what it's going to take to make you feel like a man, then you keep Indian Reilly off my back. I'll take care of Wilson."

"Can you?" Jim Manly asked.

Harry Buck paused for a moment. "Before I came to this country, I raised my share of hell. Some of it not good, Jim." He blew out his breath. "I think I can beat Hank Wilson, and I won't hesitate, because like Hank, I know what it is to face a man across a gun."

There was no more time for talk; Temple Manly was stomping out the fire. They swung up wearily and fell into single file, following Manly's lead off the long slopes.

The absence of rain was a vast relief, and without the wind to push it down their collars, they now had some measure of comfort. Harms still rode directly behind Temple Manly; Jim was again silently siding his father for appearance's sake. After an hour's endless winding, Manly pulled his horse to a stop. He turned to speak to Harms. "I don't know if I like this or not."

He pointed below. In the distance, a single lighted window winked like some far star, faintly oscillating in the storm-cleared air. "Rynder's," Harms said softly. "Cardigan must be there now or they wouldn't have a light at this hour."

The posse crowded close behind Manly. "How far?" Kohler asked.

"As the crow flies, two miles. The way we'll go—closer to three and a half." Manly's voice was matter-of-fact.

"You have a plan, Mr. Manly?" This was Harms's question and Harms's eagerness to shove responsibility onto someone else. But not so far that he couldn't take a little of the credit if everything worked out all right. And if it didn't, he could always say that Mr. Manly had been helpless. Everyone would agree that when the day came that Mr. Manly couldn't do anything, the situation could well be considered hopeless.

"Yes," Manly said simply. "Go down there and get him."

With that he gigged his horse with his heels and moved out. They covered another mile before the clouds parted, allowing a pale moon to cast an aluminum sheen over the land. They put the timber behind them, entering a sparse, rocky section. The ground turned sandy beneath the horses' hoofs, and in spots, sticky mud. To the right, a runoff of water made a thrashing gurgle as it boiled down to meet a creek below.

There was a faint gray cast to the eastern hills and the clouds rapidly dissipated; a warm breeze ghosted across the sink, carrying with it the rotten odor of sulphur seeps. The land was no longer etched in jagged hummocks but lay level. The sulphur flats shimmered under the faint, growing light, and beyond, another ring of mountains loomed darkly.

The light in Rynder's window grew more distinct. A dog barked in the distance and Temple Manly did not slacken his pace; he had never for a moment entertained the hope of sneaking up on this isolated ranch. The light still glowed in the window and when it failed to go out, Manly guessed that Wes Cardigan had already started across the thirty-odd miles of sink.

They rode into the yard with no attempt at stealth and dismounted wearily. John Kohler and Harry Buck came up to stand near Harms.

Temple Manly walked directly to the door. He banged his knuckles against the door and listened to the sound boom through the low cabin. Then the door opened and Rynder stood there, his old face composed. He was near seventy, his cheeks darkened to the color of mahogany. His whiskers were white and so long that he wore them tucked.

He looked at Temple Manly, then briefly at the others. "Been expecting you gents," he said, stepping aside so they could enter. He watched them file past. Then when Hank Wilson stepped to the threshold, Rynder blocked the doorway with a stiffened arm. "You ain't welcome here. Neither is that Injun."

Temper crowded into Hank Wilson's expression and he surged against Rynder's arm, but Harry Buck, already inside, turned back. "Wait outside," he said sharply. He put his left hand flat against Wilson's chest and stood that way. Danger swirled in Harry Buck's eyes and played around the loose ends of his lips. He seemed almost eager to challenge Hank Wilson as though this were a pleasure he had long put off and could scarcely restrain himself any longer.

"You kiss my . . ."

"Better mind now," Buck said softly. He locked eyes with Hank Wilson, and after an additional moment of this, Wilson wheeled away and went over to where Indian Reilly waited with the horses. The two men seemed united by a common anger and a mutual impatience.

Temple Manly had been standing in the center of the room, closely observing this play. When Buck shut the door, speculation pulled Manly's eyes nearly shut; there were facets of Buck's personality that the older man only half understood. Buck had strength and an almost savage will, and he had no hesitation about laying it on a man.

The inside of the cabin was small and divided by a heavy blanket that served to shut off the sleeping quarters from the main part which contained a stove, a table, and scattered pieces of homemade furniture. As Manly turned to speak to Rynder, the blanket moved and Betty Cardigan stepped out. She was a tall girl, golden from the sun, with her hair bleached to a pale wheat. Her eyes were a startling shade of gray as she studied them.

Jim Manly stared at her in shocked surprise for she was the last person he expected to find here. "Betty," he said and stepped toward her. Temple Manly reached out and fastened his fingers in his son's sleeve to hold him back, but Jim flung off the grip without so much as a glance at his father. Instead of angering Temple Manly, this manifestation of independence seemed to quietly please him.

Without doubt, Betty Cardigan was relieved

to see Jim, for she touched him lightly as he put his arm about her, and gave him a small smile. Jim stood quite straight, facing the posse, silently declaring his allegiance to the Cardigans, guilty or innocent. He seemed a trifle pompous and theatrical; perhaps his youth made him unsure, or his inexperience. Instead of lending her strength, he appeared to be drawing it from her.

Harry Buck said, "What are you doing here, Betty?"

"I came with Wes," she said. "If he was caught, I wanted to be here." She glanced at all of them, and there was accusation in her eyes.

"To keep Wilson from hanging him?" Buck asked. He shook his head. "Hank wouldn't let a woman stop him."

Temple Manly watched the girl with eyes pulled into narrow slits. She was, he judged, much stronger than the man who stood beside her. Strange that he hadn't seen her in exactly that light before, but then it took trouble to bring out the characteristics of a person. He said, "When did your brother leave here?" Judging from the tone of his voice, he could have been asking the time of day, or a direction.

She glanced first at Jim Manly as though seeking his assurance, but he had none to give. "Two hours ago," she said. Worry was etched into her expression but she was not a woman who broke easily; Temple Manly could see that.

86

Must run in the family, he thought. Wes Cardigan had proved to be a cool one once the first driving surge of panic had ebbed.

Harms released a ragged breath and tried to make a helpful suggestion. "We made a long ride for nothin', it seems, if he's skedaddled across the sink." He hitched his pants higher on his bulging stomach. He was eager enough to give up the whole thing but hesitated to offer the suggestion for fear it might cast a later shadow on an already shaky reputation. "Girl, you been with Wes all night?"

She nodded. "Since late afternoon when he came home from town."

Manly spoke. "Did your brother shoot Sims?"

Betty Cardigan looked steadily at Temple Manly, then tears began to form in her eyes and she turned to Jim Manly, unable to answer for a moment. His arm tightened around her and he spoke to her so softly that the others couldn't hear.

Temple Manly spoke impatiently. "That was a simple question; we'll find the answer sooner or later."

Finally she brushed her eyes with the back of her hand and said softly, "Yes, he shot Sims. He admitted it as soon as he came home." She clasped her hands together and fell silent.

"Seems pretty clear-cut then," Harms said. He slapped his palms against his thighs and looked at the others. John Kohler was frowning; Harry Buck was studying the tips of his muddy boots. Their disturbed thoughts were not hard to guess, Manly decided. By admitting his guilt, Wes Cardigan had in a way betrayed the men who had faith in him. Now the job of bringing him back would be very difficult.

John Kohler eased himself out of the group and stepped up to Betty Cardigan. He stood there hat in hand, with a great dignity about him. "A man just does not shoot another without reason," he said gently. "How it happen?"

"Will it make any difference?" she asked. "You've already made up your minds to hang him!"

"I have no rope," Temple Manly said solemnly. "Guilty or not, it makes no difference to me. As long as I live, the man gets a fair trial."

She wanted to believe him; that much was mirrored in her eyes. And because he was E. Temple Manly, his words had force and substance; his simple statement was as good as an oath. Yet still she looked from face to face as though she wanted to will open their hearts to read the darkness that lay in each of them. Finally she said, "It was an accident. Wes said that he heard Sims yell. A man ran out, then Sims. There was some shooting; Sims thought Wes was someone else. Wes didn't know what was going on so he shot back. Sims fell and Wes ran."

"Does Wes admit dropping his gun?" John Kohler asked.

For a moment Betty Cardigan's face remained blank, then she looked genuinely puzzled. "Gun? Wes was carrying his gun when he came home."

Harms cleared his throat and wished he could make sense of this. "Wes's cap-and-ball was picked up in the street outside the express office." He looked apologetic. "That's got to be explained away, Miss."

She frowned. "Cap-and-ball? Sheriff, he traded that a month ago for a .44-40 Winchester and twenty dollars."

Harry Buck's head came up quickly and he looked carefully at the others. Temple Manly shook his head. He liked a thing simple, uncluttered; the girl was complicating this. "Assuming that's the truth, you won't mind telling me who he sold it to."

"I don't know," she said, a touch of desperation in her voice. "He never said. All I know is that he took it to town and made a trade. Brought home ten dollars' worth of groceries and gave the rest to me."

"He was seen leaving the express office," Manly reminded her gently. He felt pity for this girl; she was battling a near hopeless thing and he could offer nothing to ease her trouble.

"If he was," she said, "then your witness was

the man who ran because Wes said there wasn't anyone else on the street."

Harms looked at Temple Manly who turned to Harry Buck. "Ask Hank to step in here."

Rynder, who had made a point of staying out of this, snapped, "I don't want that varmint in my house!"

Manly glanced at him briefly but said nothing, just gave Buck the final nod that sent him to the door. He flung it open and said, "Wilson, come on in."

A moment later Hank stepped inside, squinting against the bright light. Temple Manly eased Harms and John Kohler aside and faced Wilson. "You say that you saw Wes Cardigan leave the express office?"

Wilson paused a moment, looking steadily at Betty Cardigan. "That's what I said."

"And where were you standing?" Manly asked. His voice was even and cool, almost disinterested.

"Near Lovering's saloon." He glared at Betty Cardigan. "She was trying to make me out a liar?"

"Lovering's is half a block up the street from the express office," Manly said firmly. "The storm was coming up; it was pretty dark all afternoon. You could be wrong, Wilson. How many drinks did you have?"

"I ain't wrong," Hank snapped, "and I wasn't

drunk!" He looked at Harms, for of all these men, Harms was the easiest to push around. "What the hell you all standin' here gabbin' for? Christ, Harms, I've done your dirty jobs while you sat around on your butt and shot off your mouth. Ain't you going to stick up for me?"

"We're trying to get at the bottom of something," John Kohler said. "Miss Cardigan claims that Wes traded his gun a month ago."

"She's lyin' to save his skin!" He whipped around to face Kohler. "I don't like this, everyone tryin' to make me out a liar. By God, I was in the saloon when the shooting started and I can prove it." He flung a careless hand toward Betty Cardigan. "You trying to tell me that Cardigan ain't the killer? Why this little bitch is lying her head off."

Jim Manly made the distance to Hank Wilson in two jumps. Wilson half whirled, his hand crossing his body for his gun. He flipped it clear of the holster as Harry Buck's nickel-plated .44 flashed in the lamplight. He brought the long barrel down across Wilson's gun, sending it kiting into the corner. Temple Manly caught his son around the throat and held him while Wilson made a lunge for his fallen gun, then stopped rock-still.

"Let's not start to quarrel," Harry Buck said mildly. He put his gun away and smiled with disarming innocence.

Watching him narrowly, Temple Manly said, "You're pretty fast with that, Buck."

"Tolerably," Buck said. He looked at Wilson, leaning against the wall. "Maybe you ought to apologize," he said.

Keeping his head tipped forward to hide his deep resentment, Wilson said, "Lost my temper."

Rynder retrieved the gun and handed it to Wilson who wheeled and slammed out. After he had gone, Temple Manly released his son. The young man shrugged his shoulders, his face still darkly angry.

"I expect we'd better get on with this," Manly said. He flung the door open and stepped outside. Dawn flushed a smoky gray light over the land, turning the desert floor a sickly green, then a pale cream. Harms followed Manly outside, then Kohler and Buck. Jim came out last, talking gently to Betty Cardigan, trying to give her assurance that he lacked himself.

Near the horses Indian Reilly stood with customary taciturnity. He wore a red shirt and a belt festooned with silver; smaller coins were sewn into the band of his hat; he seemed proud of his primitive vanity.

"Fetch the horses," Manly said. He stood there, his fingers working over paper and tobacco. After the smoke was drawing, he stared out across the sulphur sink and the distant mountains standing so clear in the bland light.

"I'm going with you," Betty Cardigan announced unexpectedly.

Temple Manly looked at her, understanding the impulse but rejecting it immediately. "You've come too far already," he said. "Rynder, why don't you take her home?" Then some touch of kindness made him alter that decision. "Take her to my place. Lila will be a comfort to her." And she might even be a comfort to Lila, he thought.

"I thank you for that," she said, "but I have to come with you. Can't you see that?"

Hank Wilson led the horses up and each man took his own. Wilson looked at Betty Cardigan, then at Manly. "You ain't going to take her, are you?" His glance switched to Harms. "If you don't do somethin', I will."

Harms had already settled himself in the saddle, but Wilson's tone, which he had grown to hate, goaded him into action. He roweled the horse around so that he towered over the deputy. "Hank, I'll admit that I'm fat and lazy, and I've let you run my office to suit yourself while I played cards and drank beer. But, by God, I'm still sheriff of Buckeye County and I'll tell her whether she can come along or not." His burst of self-assertion went to his head, even to the point where he made a decision without silently seeking Temple Manly's approval. "Fetch up a horse, girl, we'll wait for you."

Harry Buck was filling all the canteens from

the trickling water pipe and he turned to look at Harms, a brief admiration in his eyes. Then he glanced at Temple Manly, but the man had his back turned again and was staring out across the sulphur sink. Kohler was standing near his horse, his long face composed and unreadable. Finally Hank Wilson turned away in disgust and mounted, while Rynder went to the small barn for the girl's horse. He came out a few minutes later, leading a calico pony.

As soon as Betty Cardigan came back out of the cabin, the others mounted, Temple Manly once more in the lead.

FIVE

Temple Manly had difficulty remembering when he had been so tired. His back seemed plank-stiff and a pestering headache set up a small throbbing in the veins at his temples. He thought of dismounting and walking a while to ease the tightness of his thighs; this would have been a help, but he clenched his teeth instead and rode on. He considered with a marked degree of envy the several hours of sleep Wes Cardigan must have enjoyed; he could almost hate the man for the comfort he had known.

With the addition of Betty Cardigan, the posse's number had grown to eight and his problem had increased tenfold. He should have insisted that she stay behind, but he had been too tired to protest strongly and now the damage was done. Nature had endowed this girl with a surplus of feminine charm and Temple Manly was certain that she would use every bit of it to woo the posse from its purpose.

Mentally he measured each man, holding them up to the cold, critical eye of his emotionless inspection, and found them all wanting. Harms could be eliminated as not worth worrying about; the girl was smart enough to understand that once her brother was caught, Harms would assume the role of fretful spectator, lending only a quasi-legal status to the events.

Harry Buck was another matter. In his bone-poor way he was likeable enough, and as dangerous as a wounded bear; because of this, she would work on him first, Manly decided. John Kohler was a married man with three half-grown children, but he didn't expect that would stop her. With Buck and Kohler on her side, she could destroy his control.

Then he wondered if she would have the gall to approach him; the prospect was oddly exciting until he erased it with angry concentration.

By eight o'clock there was enough heat in the day to drive Temple Manly out of his coat; he rolled and stowed it behind his saddle. The others soon followed his example. Sweat began to bead Manly's forehead and upper lip; he raised his sleeve frequently to wipe it away and his white shirt soon became grimy. Being sensitive to uncleanliness, his annoyance increased gradually to unbearable proportions and finally he rolled the offensive sleeves to his elbows, thereafter allowing the sweat to drip from his face. The longing for enough water to wash his face became a minor fixation in his mind for the stubble on his cheeks itched intolerably.

By nine the sun was a molten gong suspended in the electric blue of the sky, and his shirt clung moistly to his perspiring shoulders and chest. The light danced against the grayness of the sink, nearly blinding him. Finally he turned in the saddle and said, "Reilly, go on ahead and read sign." He motioned to the ground and the tracks he had been patiently following.

The Indian spurred forward, his bronze face expressionless. He rode a few yards in the lead, his body bent over the horse's neck. Cardigan was leaving an obvious enough trail; too obvious, Manly suspected. This was another confusing aspect of the problem. If it were true that Wes had unwittingly become involved in someone else's crime, then why was he running? This would have been the last solution Manly himself would have sought. There were so many disturbing factors in Cardigan's behavior; the man simply didn't act like a criminal. Temple Manly liked men to fit into easily defined categories; he found it extremely difficult to base any decision on these illogical vagaries.

By midmorning, Manly had to stop for a drink of water. He raised his hand to signal the others before dismounting. He looked at the posse, all of whom were bleary-eyed and unshaven. Their shell belts were draped over their saddlehorns; the heat had made them uncomfortable. Each man broke out his canteen, shook it to measure mentally its contents, then tipped it up carefully. Hank Wilson drank with a noisy gurgle, then complained to Harms about the loss of his whiskey bottle.

Manly pulled his hat low over his eyes and from beneath the brim quietly observed the others, particularly Betty Cardigan. She saw John Kohler standing alone and walked casually up to him. Jim, who had been with Harry Buck, looked up with pinpointed attention.

Only Manly was within earshot, for she kept her voice low. "Mr. Kohler, do posses really remain indifferent to the man they hunt?"

No fool, that girl; Manly smiled thinly. She had lost no time in going after Kohler, and in the right way too, digging into his pride first, making him sound his principles.

Kohler thought the question over a moment, then said, "I don't really know your brother. Saw him a few times. Spoke to him once or twice. I can't judge any man on such short acquaintance. However, I've spent the most miserable night of my life chasing him, and, in spite of myself, I can't help but hold that misery against him."

"A man is innocent until proved guilty," she said firmly. "What about that? Are you going to forget that?"

"No," Kohler admitted. He cuffed his hat back and mopped at the sweat on his forehead. "Girl, I guess any man could walk across the street to arrest someone and not have any feeling toward him one way or another. But if catching him's a bit of work, then by the time he's caught, a man's sympathy can be plumb wore out." He sighed and replaced his hat. "What's the fuss now? Wait until we catch him, then ask me how I feel."

She knew when to quit; Manly had to give her credit for that. But that also made her dangerous. A cool-headed woman was always a menace. As soon as she walked away from Kohler, Jim intercepted her. She stopped when he took her arm. "Betty, why won't you let me help you?" he asked.

Her eyes regarded him quite frankly and then she glanced quickly at Temple Manly, but he had been anticipating this and swung his head down in time. "Let me be, Jim. You can't help me."

"But I can," he insisted. "I believe in Wes."

"Perhaps you do," she said. "But Wes is running, Jim. A thing he has never done before in his life. I don't understand why, but I'm going to find out." She moved slightly, freeing herself from his grip.

Temple Manly swung back into the saddle and this was the signal for the others to follow him. The talk gave him something to study as he rode along; the troubled feeling he had had about Wes Cardigan was eased slightly by what Betty had just said. Manly believed her. Wes wasn't the type that ran; a dull, frightened man did that, but everything Cardigan had done so far pointed to an intelligent, thinking man, not one who plunged in panic to escape.

He had been trying not to weigh Cardigan's guilt or innocence; a jury would have to do that, yet he could not avoid forming an opinion. There was no getting around the fact that the man was an enigma; it was his nature to stand his ground, yet he was in flight. Why? To Manly's way of thinking, the answer to that question would undoubtedly prove more interesting than the chase.

Noon came and went and the hours wore on. The heat was intense, almost smashing. The sulphur flats shimmered and danced and mirage lakes appeared invitingly to remind them of the water sloshing so temptingly in their canteens.

At the point, Indian Reilly stopped suddenly and dismounted. His moccasins scuffed the crystalline sulphur bed, stirring up a small rank cloud. Manly rode up and Reilly handed over a piece of blue cloth. Harms expended the extra effort necessary to drive his mount forward with an increase of speed and joined them.

Manly spoke to Harms. "A piece of shirt." He pressed it to his cheek experimentally, feeling the lingering moisture. "Blood on it too." When Harry Buck edged up, Manly handed it to him. "What do you think?"

The blocky-faced young man made a thoughtful examination of the cloth, then said, "Wes must be pressing his horse pretty hard, Mr. Manly. Looks like he bathed her mouth and nose."

"Damned free with his water," Harms grumbled. "If he's got that much to spare, he could leave a canteen for us."

"He had only one canteen," Betty said flatly. "He's as thirsty as any of you."

"Let's close this thing up," Manly said, moving forward again.

Each man dropped back to his own interval. Hank Wilson was silent, riding hunched over. Harry Buck eased out of the column and dropped behind Wilson. The deputy frowned at this and said, "What the hell's the idea?"

"Don't want you gettin' lonesome," Buck said dryly. He stared at Wilson until the man shrugged and wrapped himself again in his somber thoughts.

Both Manly and Kohler were riding with their heads tipped forward, eyes closed as though asleep. Betty Cardigan rode slouched sideways in the saddle, looking back often. By moving forward two paces, she left Jim Manly and sided Kohler. For a moment he rode on, then spoke without lifting his head. "Your brother's a strange man, Miss. We don't understand him."

"He's a confused man who feels he has no friends." She looked around at Hank Wilson, her expression uneasy, then she turned back. "I don't like these odds, Mr. Kohler. Harms is undecided;

he'll go where the wind blows. Harry Buck is cautious. And Mr. Manly, I don't think anyone really knows. But this is Wes's life you're playing with."

"I don't have to be told that," John Kohler said softly. He smiled to reassure her, then fell silent. After a moment, she dropped back in her usual place behind Jim Manly.

He turned in the saddle and looked at her. "You left me out, Betty. Any reason?" He had the look of a boy who has just seen himself cheated out of a piece of cake.

Her voice was troubled. "I don't know how strong you are, Jim. I've never had occasion to ask before, or to find out." She was trying to be honest with him, but he misunderstood, whether from deliberate intent or lack of perception she had no way of knowing.

Ahead of Temple Manly there was no movement at all. Nothing save the trail stretching across the flats. The sun was half down when Indian Reilly stopped again. Manly halted and dismounted; the others followed his example. Leaning forward, Manly asked, "What is it this time, Reilly?"

"He walk," Reilly said tersely. "Some time now, he walk."

"His horse is probably tired," Manly said. He was too weary to discuss it. He turned, slightly annoyed as Harry Buck came up, his blunt face alive with interest. Manly found that he could resent the young man's strength and obvious resistance to this bone-wracking fatigue.

"Don't mean to butt in," Buck said gently. "I couldn't help but overhear. You mind if I look at them tracks, Mr. Manly?"

"Help yourself," Manly said and uncorked his canteen.

Harry Buck walked on a few yards and knelt to study the faint imprint on the powdery ground. Then he came back, the answer in his smile. "Wes's horse has gone lame on him." He jerked his thumb toward the cool-looking mountains less than seven miles away. "Probably holed up in there, ready to pot the first man who steps in range."

"You get all that from the prints?" Manly asked.

"Sure," Harry Buck said. He shook out his tobacco and made a smoke before answering further. "Wes has bound his pony's foot with his coat. You can tell by one light print every time she steps." He drew a deep breath and slapped his rib box as if to encourage breathing in this thin, bodiless air. "Beats the hell out of me why he didn't just shoot the horse instead of leading her."

"The man poses a good many problems," Temple Manly said. "We'd best get on."

His nod sent them into the saddle again. Harms

made it only on the second try. Saddle leather protested and he swung in line as the column moved out. Betty Cardigan remained silent but watched each of them closely. She knew when to talk and when to hold her peace.

The sun died slowly, painting the sky in violent hues. The timber-studded foothills loomed closer and Manly kept them at a slow walk until they were well into the wooded fringes. Dismounting, he said, "A fire is in order; I'm damned hungry." His tone was peremptory, his manner brusque. He asked for no opinion and did not offer to share his own.

Thirty some hours in the saddle had taken their toll on men and horses. Harry Buck picketed the mounts, then gathered wood for the fire. Wilson seemed unusually nervous and Indian Reilly kept searching the thickening shadows. While Buck built the fire, Manly, Harms and Kohler stood in a tight knot, silent, yet each seemed bound by a common thought.

Finally Hank Wilson rubbed his hands together and said, "Jesus, this is a hell of a place to stop."

Manly turned slowly and looked through the gloom at the man. "There's wood for a fire and a creek up the trail," he said. "Can you ask for more?"

The fire was beginning to cast off light now and Wilson's face was drawn with concern. Betty Cardigan sat alone, observing these men with a growing sense of helplessness; she pressed her hands together, working her long fingers rhythmically in a kneading motion.

Jim Manly approached her and spoke softly but she sent him away with a curt shake of her head. The young man's expression turned fretful and he stood with his back to her while he sulked in silence. Manly observed this with some displeasure which was further aggravated when he saw Harry Buck taking it all in.

Harms stretched out his plump bulk on the ground and shut his eyes. John Kohler clung to his silence a while longer, then said, "Mr. Manly, what do you think?"

"About what?" Manly asked.

"Wes Cardigan."

"I think we'll catch him," Manly said, knowing full well how frustrating was his answer to Kohler.

But the man's even temper held. "I mean, what's going to happen when we catch him?"

"Likely we'll tie his hands and take him back to Gunlock," Manly said. Then, because he felt a twinge of conscience for treating Kohler thus, he added, "The more I observe about the man, the more puzzled I become, and I still can't understand why he ran." His glance indicated Wilson and Reilly, once again sharing a mutual solitude. "Reilly can read sign better than he lets on. And Wilson's as nervous as a whip-broke horse. Seems to me that he doesn't really want us to find Cardigan, yet he can't wait until he gets a rope around his neck." Manly shook his head in bewilderment. "I thought this was going to be just a manhunt. A simple manhunt." He blew out his breath in exasperation and turned his attention to the manufacture of a cigarette. The passing moment of explanation had embarrassed him, for the long habit of silence was hard to break. But Kohler did not presume to comment and Manly enjoyed his cigarette.

On the ground, Harms snorted through his nose and sat up. "Dang ground's too hard," he complained. Glancing into the deep shadows of the timber, he let his eyes carry up to the high ridge outlined against the lighter sky. "Wonder where he is."

"Looking right down your throat," Manly said evenly, his cigarette making a red dot as he drew deeply.

Harms gave a start. "What's that?"

"I agree with Mr. Manly," Kohler said. "Harry, come over here." When Buck drew close, Kohler asked, "Where do you think Cardigan is now?"

Manly watched Buck as he had his look at the ridge. He picked out a pinnacle of rocks and pointed. "Around there." He laughed softly. "Gents, his horse is lame and he's as tired as you or me. How far can a man go?"

This was, Manly had to admit, just about the

way the scales were set. The thought floated around in his mind that they could go into the rocks and smoke Cardigan out, but his common sense told him that this was impossible. They were all too tired to spend the rest of the night beating around in the darkness, taking a chance on getting their heads blown off.

"We'll camp here tonight," Manly said briefly and went to his horse for his blankets. Wilson was watching but said nothing when Manly tossed his soogans down quite a distance from the fire. Harry Buck still stood by Kohler.

Finally Kohler said quietly, "I just don't understand him, Harry."

"Manly?" Buck shrugged slightly. "Just a big man, John, who's trying to walk without stamping his feet."

"And the boy?"

"Scared," Buck said. "But then, I was scared at twenty-three."

"Like hell you were," Kohler said. "Manly interests me. Is he really that hard, or does he have two sets of rules—one for himself and the other for everyone else?"

"Anyone ever tried asking him?"

"You don't ask the Manlys of the world a lot of questions, Harry."

"I would," Buck said, "if I wanted to know anything." He left Kohler then and got his blankets, spreading them by the fire. He was a little amused at the others, for they shunned the light, figuring that if Cardigan was close enough to see them, he was close enough to shoot, and no one was willing to present an inviting target. Yet Harry Buck boldly crossed and recrossed in front of that fire. From his saddlebag he took a small frying pan and a wrapped packet of bacon. Cooking a few slices crisp, he laid them on the brim of his hat while he mixed flour and water for his pancakes. The aroma of his cooking caused all eyes to turn his way, for none had thought to bring food along, certain that the chase would be a short one.

The pancakes joined the bacon on the hat and then Buck boiled a little coffee in the skillet. Hank Wilson could take no more of this. He got up and came over. "That's a lot you've fixed," he said. "You wouldn't share it with a man, would you?"

"Nope," Harry assured him. When the coffee bubbled to the strength he liked he took the whole thing over to Betty Cardigan. "Help yourself," he said and began to eat.

Hank Wilson lingered by the fire a moment longer, then stomped back to his place and sat down. Betty Cardigan looked at him, then at Harry Buck. "You've made an enemy there."

"Not my first," Buck admitted. He motioned toward the pancakes and bacon. "Go on, help yourself."

"I don't feel right . . ." Then she smiled. "All right." She took one of the cakes, folded it around three strips of bacon and ate. Buck leaned back and waited for his coffee to cool. The sky was clear and bright with stars.

A lifetime under them had given him a crude knowledge of the solar system, although he had only the names he had given them to tell one from another. "That's the old man leading the calf," he said.

"What is?" She looked at him sharply.

"Those stars there," he said, pointing them out to her. "See him and the calf behind him?"

For a time she stared, then laughed. "I do! It is an old man with a calf!"

He swept his arm through a short arc. "That's the Injun squattin' by his waterhole. No, you're lookin' too far to the left. There. See him?"

The skillet had cooled enough to handle with bare hands and he let her drink first. With no sugar or cream, Harry Buck's coffee was pretty powerful, but she made no complaint. Finishing it off, Buck dumped the grounds, then went to his saddlebag. Taking the remainder of the bacon and flour, he put them in the skillet and took it to where Temple Manly sat.

"That'll hold you until you get to Red Rock," Buck said.

"I made no mention of Red Rock," Manly said evenly. He looked almost contemptuously at the

109

skillet of food, then at Harry Buck; he thought he could feel an insult in the gesture.

"Wes will have to get a horse," Buck said. "Red Rock's nearest, about fifty miles. With luck, he'll make it by tomorrow noon." Buck was no fool; he understood that Manly was deliberately trying to ignore him, letting him stand there with his offer of food while he made up his mind whether or not to accept it. Buck knew this was Manly's way, but that didn't make it any easier to take. Casually, he tossed the skillet on the ground, spilling a little of the flour from the sack. Hank Wilson groaned slightly while the others waited.

Temple Manly said, "You have a high-handed way that I don't like, Buck."

"Who the hell cares what you like?" Buck asked softly. "I offer you food and you act like you'd be doing me a favor to accept it."

He turned on his heel and walked back to Betty Cardigan. Temple Manly regarded the skillet for a moment, then lay back on his blankets, his hands folded behind his head. Jim got up and walked over to where his father lay. His face was stiff with resolution and he stood braced with his feet apart, like a man readying himself for a storm of trouble.

"Are you going to pick it up?" There was an odd challenge in his voice, but only half given.

"No," Temple Manly said. "And neither are you."

"Goddamn it, I'm hungry! My belly's touching my backbone."

"You'll live until tomorrow," Manly said. "If the others want it, there it is."

Hank Wilson didn't need a second invitation; he stood up immediately and walked over. When he picked up the flour and bacon, Jim Manly said, "Don't be a hog. I want some of that."

"You'll wait until tomorrow," Temple Manly said. He reared up suddenly and glared at all of them. "Do you think I'm a fool? Can't you see what Buck wants? He wants us to fight over his handout, like a bunch of dogs. . . . Well, I wouldn't eat it if I was starving." He waved his hands in disgust. "You want it, take it. I'll do without."

Wilson took the skillet to the fire and commenced frying the bacon. Harms, whose appetite was always enormous and whose pride was small, joined the group to sniff the flavors. "I ain't too proud to eat," he said firmly.

Neither were the others, with the exception of Temple Manly, whose iron will forbade it, and Jim, whose fear of his father was stronger than his hunger. Buck leaned on his elbow, gently drawing on a cigarette while he watched them eat. Betty Cardigan asked, "Why, Harry? You must have had a reason." Her tone was gently probing; she sensed that people did not demand answers from Harry Buck.

"Yep," he said gently. "A man usually has a reason for what he does."

"You could have offered it to him in a different way," she said. "He was offended." Then she paused, a new thought coming to her. "Or was he supposed to be?" She took him by the shoulder and pulled him around so she could look into his eyes. "He was supposed to be, wasn't he?"

Buck's long lips pulled down briefly, then he took a final drag on his smoke and butted it into the ground. "I knew what Manly would do, but I wasn't too sure about Jim. Now I am. He ain't growed up enough to spit in the old man's eye yet."

"If you did it to show me what he was," Betty Cardigan said, "then it was wasted, because I already knew his shortcomings."

"You're smarter than I gave you credit for," Buck murmured. He turned his head and looked at Temple Manly; the man looked asleep but Buck was sure he wasn't. He wondered if the man ever slept. Jim Manly sat on the ground, his arms around his knees, his forehead resting on his wrists. "The kid's cussing himself now," Harry said softly. "Cussing and telling himself that maybe the next time he'll stand up to the old man." His glance touched Betty briefly. "You didn't pick much."

His bluntness stunned her for a moment, making her slightly angry. "What are you trying to do, Harry?"

"Keep you from betting your money on a poor hand," he said. He stood up and walked over to the fire. Hank Wilson looked up at him and smiled, the first sign of friendliness the man had shown to anyone since the posse left Manly's place. Kohler was licking the bacon grease from his fingers and reaching for a cigar. He stood up, grunting at the pain this movement caused in his legs.

"I'm too damn old for this. After forty, the ground gets hard." He put a match to his cigar and locked eyes with Buck over the flame. "Don't get Manly down on you, Harry. You can't afford it." He took Buck by the arm and moved him a little away from the others. "The Manlys always run things, Harry. We nod, speak when spoken to, and hope to hell they never decide to put the knuckles to us. You've got a good place started. Don't throw it away because you want to bump heads with Temple Manly."

This talk disturbed Harry Buck; that much was mirrored in the blunt planes of his cheeks. "You on his side, John?"

"Yes and no. I mind my own business, Harry. I leave Manly alone and give him no call to get sore at me." He smiled to ease the edge from this advice. "Be smart and do the same."

"What right has Manly to decide what's good for me?"

Kohler was not stupid; he knew what Buck was

leading up to. "Manly's a big man, Harry. Why do you think Harms wanted him along?" He took Buck's arm and shook him slightly. "This is Manly country. Don't try to change that."

"What about that man up there?" Harry Buck asked, indicating the rocky pinnacle. "John, don't you feel anything for him?"

This was pressing the matter to an uncomfortable point and Kohler paused before answering. "Harry, there's a lot of things I feel and never let on about. Hell, a man'd be spending all his life wiping somebody's nose if he let himself get soft. Wes made this mess for himself and it's up to him to get out of it. I won't stand for seeing him hung on the first tree we come to and I think Manly feels the same way. But that's as far as I go. Wes's fight is his own."

"All right," Buck said. "All right, John, you've made it plain enough, I guess."

Kohler shook his head sadly. "I haven't convinced you of a damn thing, have I?"

"No," Harry Buck admitted. "Hell, do you think Manly's the first of his kind I've run into?" He blew out a disgusted breath. "Pa settled in Kansas when I was a kid. I watched him take off his hat to the 'Manlys' and smile and speak soft when he wanted to yell. I watched it eat into him until he wasn't worth a damn thing. Sure, there's Manlys in this world, a son-of-a-bitchin' lot of 'em. And they ride high, push your face in the

114

dirt, making their own rules as they go along—one set for you and one for them. And because they're big, everyone smiles and pretends to like it."

"What are you going to do about it?" Kohler wanted to know. "Tell me, Harry."

"Stop sucking up to him," Buck said flatly. "Hell, look at you, John, if Manly stopped quick, you'd run your nose up his hind end!"

John Kohler stiffened as though he had been slapped. Finally he said, "You're tired, Harry. I'll forget you said that." He turned and stomped to his blankets to stretch out.

Buck remained motionless, turning his head to look at the fire. Indian Reilly was eating alone, and since he was at the bottom of the social scale, even to Hank Wilson, Reilly ate the leftovers. That was, Buck decided, another sample of Temple Manly's kind of living; every dog to his own kennel.

Finally Reilly finished up the scraps and sought a dark spot where he curled up to sleep. The fire was a bed of red coals and the camp very quiet. Betty Cardigan left her blankets and joined Buck. Jim Manly raised his head and looked in her direction, then sat still and watched. "Aren't you tired?" she asked.

"Dead tired," Buck admitted. "Betty, what did Wes do with the money?" He asked the question easily, as though he were remarking about the size of the new moon or the promise of rain.

For a heartbeat she just stared at him. "Money? What money? Harry, what are you talking about?"

He smiled then and his severe expression eased, like he had suddenly seen a sunset after days of rain. "You really didn't know, did you? It's all right. Someone robbed the express office and it's really the money the posse's after."

"How much money?"

"About eight thousand," Harry Buck said softly.

"Oh," she said, a sob in her voice. "Oh, Wes— Wes."

"They don't give a damn about Sims—Kohler hardly remembered his name. It's the money, Betty."

"Wes didn't rob anyone," she said. "Harry, please believe me."

"Don't make much difference what I believe," he said. "If Wes ain't got it on him, they'll get rough with him. And if he does have it on him, Wilson's got a new rope along." He turned his head slightly and looked at the dark shape of Temple Manly, lying motionless in sleep. "And there's a man who won't give up until Wes is caught, Betty. Me, I'd rather have the devil after me than Manly."

SIX

Temple Manly discovered that his extreme fatigue made sleep nearly impossible. That, coupled with the fact that someone seemed always to be making a trip into the bushes. Each time one of the posse moved, the attending noises woke him. Twice he rolled a cigarette to occupy his time; this was better than sitting idle while sleep eluded him. No one else seemed disturbed and this annoyed him. The fat Harms slept on, snoring blissfully. Kohler, who lay ten feet away, rolled over once, then pulled his blankets up around his neck. He grunted as though troubled by a dream, then lay quietly.

Jim Manly was unduly restless; he awakened his father twice, and the third time Temple Manly spoke with considerable irritation, "Can't you hold your water?" Instead of answering, Jim stalked away, increasing his father's vexation. Manly checked his watch in a match flare and found that it had stopped; he had forgotten to wind it.

This accumulation of petty annoyances made him swear; he clamped his teeth together and fumed in silence. Sitting up carefully to favor his sore muscles, he became aware of the vast stillness. In the brush, the horses stirred slightly on their pickets and he turned his head to pick up these sounds more clearly.

On the other side of the dead fire, Hank Wilson moved before sitting up; then he left in the direction of the horses. A moment later Jim Manly returned, and when he saw Wilson's blanket empty, took his pistol in hand and again left the camp. Temple Manly frowned, unable to see the need for all this stirring about.

After waiting for what seemed an interminable time, he threw his blankets aside and got to his feet, still cursing gently to himself. From the direction of the picket line came a brief crashing of brush, then the unmistakable sound of a fist colliding against bone. Someone grunted, and this was enough to awaken Kohler and Buck.

"What's goin' on?" Kohler wanted to know.

"Get your lantern and we'll find out," Manly said, picking up his rifle. Harry Buck was settling his gunbelt in place. He joined Manly, as did Kohler as soon as he had the lamp going. Indian Reilly was awake but he did not leave his blankets. As the trio trooped by Betty Cardigan, she sat up, a silent question in her eyes. Harms slept on; thunder wouldn't have awakened him.

The noise of a struggle grew more pronounced as Manly approached the thicket. He crashed through like a determined bull; Kohler's high-held lantern splashed light on Jim Manly and Hank Wilson. Young Manly was on the ground but trying to get up. Blood made a dark streak below his nose and both eyes were beginning to puff.

Hank Wilson flipped his head around as Temple Manly said, "Who started this?" When neither spoke, his face hardened. "Goddamn it, when I speak, I expect an answer!"

A quick caution filled Wilson's eyes. "I thought maybe he was Cardigan, sneaking down to steal a horse." He waved his hand in a half-plea for understanding. "In the dark, you can't tell one man from another."

Getting to his feet, Jim Manly brushed at his clothes. Then he daubed at the blood oozing from his nose. He'd made his mark on Wilson too; the deputy's lips were swelling and raw. "I guess we both thought it was Cardigan," Jim said. "Sorry to have disturbed you, sir."

"I'm getting sick and tired of this goddamned faunching around," Manly said, his voice sharp-edged. "First Wilson goes into the bushes, then Reilly gets up to look for Wilson, and now you got to go looking for both of them." He waved his hand. "This monkey business has got to stop so we can all get back to sleep. You been out of your blankets four times tonight, Jim. I've had enough of it, understand?"

"Yes, sir," Jim said, with unusual meekness.

With this speech out of his system, Manly felt some relieved and walked back to his blankets;

Kohler and Harry Buck followed him. When they had pulled out of earshot, Jim Manly picked up his fallen revolver and said, "Keep your damn hands out of my saddlebags, Hank. That goes for Reilly too. If you don't, I'll kill you."

"I was just checking the horses; you heard me tell your old man," Hank muttered.

"Like hell. The old man might swallow that, but I don't!"

"I tell you I thought you were Cardigan." He waited a moment, then added, "Aw, to hell with you, Jim. I don't give a damn if you believe me or not." He wheeled and stomped back to camp, crashing boldly through the brush. At his blankets he flung himself down.

Indian Reilly stirred and spoke softly. "What you find?"

"Nothin'," Hank said. "Not a goddamned thing." He pulled the rough blanket around his neck and lay there, his eyes closed. He heard Jim Manly come into the camp, but did not bother to look at him.

Betty Cardigan was wide awake; as Jim passed, she sat up, startling him. "Can't you sleep, Jim?" Her voice was gentle, barely above a whisper.

"I thought I heard someone foolin' with my horse," he said. "Turned out to be Hank." He was in no mood for questioning. His head ached and his nose was agonizingly tender.

"Did you really think it was Wes?"

"Well, he needs a horse," Jim said. The soft murmur of their voices reached Temple Manly; he reared slowly, menacingly from his blankets, and this was enough to send Jim to his own. Betty lay back down and the camp once more was quiet.

Sleep seemed still out of the question to Temple Manly; try as he might to attain it, he remained exasperatingly awake while the others slumbered until dawn. He was the first up, stamping about, impatient to be on the move. No need of a fire with the food gone; the thought brought stabbing pangs to the pit of his stomach.

The first gray light began to spread down the shanks of the mountain, brightening the flats behind them. Manly faunched about like a foot-sore bear while the others hurriedly saddled and made ready to mount. He was the first on his horse and Harms voiced a protesting groan as he swung up. As the edge of the sun began to show, they were pushing toward higher levels, trying to break away from this trail and across the ridge to the main road beyond.

Temple Manly did not expect to see any sign of Wes Cardigan, and when he found the young man's camping spot barely a yard off the trail, he exhibited some surprise before catching himself. Be best, he decided, if the others figured that he was aware of Cardigan's presence. Judging from the sign, Cardigan must have left around dark, which would give him a nine-hour lead, at least. This caused Manly a fretting moment. He hated the thought of losing ground; suddenly he became obsessed with the desire to make it up. The horses were in poor shape; a night's forage had done little to restore their waning vigor. Yet he began to drive even harder, pushed by an inflexible will that seemed stronger than himself.

By ten o'clock Manly felt that the posse had made good time, but a glance at Kohler and Harry Buck told him that they heartily disapproved this wearing pace. They didn't speak, but their expressions drove him to an unaccustomed explanation. "What the hell, don't you want to catch him?"

"I ain't wantin' to kill my horse," Buck said flatly. He hooked one knee around the saddle-horn and looked squarely at Manly.

"If that's your worry, I'll give you another when we get back," Manly said in a voice that closed the matter, and pushed on.

He was forced to stop from time to time and he resented each lost moment. It was such a hopeless waste as far as he was concerned, those lost intervals while Betty Cardigan searched out a dense thicket for privacy, or Wilson dallied over something that should have been taken care of in a hurry.

At noon they topped a rise and looked down at a small cabin nestled in a green valley. Manly directed the posse toward the place, cutting onto a narrow trail that led them to a fenced section. He bent from the saddle to open a gate, then rode on to the house, leaving Wilson, who was bringing up the rear, to close it. As they approached the yard, a man stepped out, a rifle held in the crook of his arm. A woman appeared in the doorway, her expression dry and aloof. The man was in his forties, workworn and dirt poor. A cud of tobacco swelled one cheek and he spat often.

"Howdy," he said. "Care to sit a spell?"

"No time for that," Manly said, his voice brusque. "We need food, for which we'll gladly pay. And fresh horses; we'll buy those too."

"No horses," the man said. "Had a nice mare mule, but sold her this morning right after day-break." He squinted at Manly, his head cocked sideways. "Posse, huh?" He saw the star on Harms's vest.

"Our business is no concern of yours," Manly said shortly. "Are we welcome to dismount?"

"Do," the man said. "Ma, rustle up somethin' for these gents to eat."

"Ah, thank you, no," Manly said hurriedly. "Just something to take along. If the gentleman we seek has a fresh mount, we'd best not dally."

"Don't take long to eat," the man insisted. He turned toward the house, the matter settled so far as he was concerned.

"Stop now or stop later," John Kohler said. "I can't see the difference, Mr. Manly." He was tired and longed to rest, but pride forbade his showing his fatigue more openly.

"Perhaps you're right," Manly said and stepped from the saddle. He saw that Reilly watered the horses and led them to the barn, then paused at the watering trough to remove his shirt and chaps. His shoulders were heavy and dark with hair and he was very conscious of the soft roll of flesh around his middle that sagged abominably when he bent over. He splashed water over his head and shoulders, and for a final rinse, bent at the hips and immersed himself. He let himself drip dry as he washed out his shirt. He wrung the shirt as dry as he could and put it back on. From the cabin came the enticing odors of cooking food and his hunger became almost unendurable. Kohler and Hank Wilson had already disappeared inside with Harms. Indian Reilly sulked about the barn, inspecting the jaded horses.

Harry Buck lounged against the hitching rack in front of the cabin, his fingers idly creasing a cigarette paper. His head was tipped forward but his attention was fixed on young Manly, who had Betty Cardigan by the arm and was speaking to her in a low, earnest voice. Temple Manly could not hear the words, but he could see her expression with its touch of anger. Finally, Betty went into the cabin, leaving Jim standing there, her anger now transferred to him.

He watched the young man as he had done so often, trying to predict what he would do next; it was increasingly difficult of late. Jim stalked over to the watering trough and stripped off his shirt with little regard for the buttons. Then he slobbered water over his face. Temple Manly said, "I wouldn't quarrel with the girl now, boy; she has enough trouble to fight as it is."

Jim raised his head quickly, letting water cascade from his cheeks. He gave his father a flat-eyed stare. His nose was swollen and discolored; there was still puffiness around both his eyes, giving him an odd, bloated appearance. Flipping the water off his hands, he hitched up his shell belt and then put on his shirt. "Do you suppose I'll ever reach the age when I can have a little business to call my own?"

Temple Manly frowned and flogged his mind for a method to reach this young man. He was dogged by the feeling that he could no longer communicate with him; apparently they no longer shared a common language. "I'm not against you, Jim. God, boy, if you'd let me, I'd help you."

"You've done too much already," Jim snapped. "I'm sick of being Temple Manly's son. Sick of having people smile when they don't want to, speak when they'd rather ignore me—all because I'm Temple Manly's boy. Can't you understand that I'd rather have people hate me for myself than to pretend to like me because I'm a Manly?"

"I didn't know the name was that distasteful to you," Temple Manly said softly. He waved his hand. "Go on into the house, Jim. Go on."

After the young man entered the cabin, Temple Manly sat on the edge of the watering trough and contemplated his greatest failure. He supposed that every man's son harbored a certain amount of resentment toward his father, but Jim's feeling extended beyond that; he acted like a man who had been brutally cheated.

From behind him, Betty Cardigan said, "Mr. Manly, you have to eat something." He turned and saw her standing there, a full plate in her hands. That she could think of him with kindness at all was a minor miracle.

He took the plate and began to eat. "Very good," he said. "It was nice of you to think of me."

"I've thought of you often," Betty said. She moved around and sat down beside him. Her hands smoothed the wrinkles from her faded jeans.

"Have you really?"

"Yes," she said, smiling slightly. "I've tried to figure out what kind of a man you are. That seemed important to me since Jim has so often asked me to marry him. I don't mean to be unkind, Mr. Manly, but if I married Jim, we'd have to live in your house; he couldn't make a go of it himself. So you can see why I wondered about you."

"I see," he said softly. "You're a frank woman; I like that."

"There is a difference between being frank and being unkind, isn't there?"

"I suppose there is," Manly said. "But I've never tried to differentiate. A man's better off if he calls a spade a spade." He mopped up the remaining gravy with his bread, then said, "You and Jim ought to settle your quarrels before you're married."

"I never said that I was going to marry him, to either of you," Betty said. She looked at him, at his surprise, and the quick mistrust in his eyes. "Don't you believe me?"

"From the way Jim talked . . ."

"That was Jim's talk," she said. "Can I be frank? Even a little brutal?" He nodded slightly. "I could never marry Jim, Mr. Manly. And it's not because he is a Manly; neither of you scare or impress me at all. Jim simply isn't a man yet. Perhaps that's his own fault, or maybe it's yours, but he blames you for it. If he was more of a man, he wouldn't do that, because he'd understand himself better. He says that he loves me; he says a lot of things. I don't love your son, Mr. Manly. And I never told him I did. Perhaps

I feel sorry for him because he is your son; it must be terrible to grow up in the shadow of so big a man. I doubt that Jim has ever stood in the sun by himself on account of that." She caught her lower lip between her teeth and held it that way for a moment while she rubbed her palms together. "I wanted to tell you this so you'd understand how it is between us. I don't want Jim for a husband, and if there was any way to tell him to stay away from me, I'd do that. But he's the kind of person who can't face the truth."

Temple Manly had continued to eat while she talked; he was afraid to trust his expression if he stopped. He put the plate aside, drank his coffee, then washed the cup in the trough before filling it from the water spout. After he had rolled a cigarette, he said, "My son is lost to me. I can no longer talk to him."

"Could you ever? Mr. Manly, you've spent the main run of your life being powerful and important. But there's a price to pay for that. People are always a little nervous around men like you. Perhaps you mean them no harm, but the threat, or the possibility of it, is always there. You have no common touch, Mr. Manly. All you'll ever get out of most people is a polite mention of the weather."

"Then why are you bothering with me now?" he asked.

"I think I feel a little sorry for you," Betty Cardigan said. "You must get tired of being so alone."

He snubbed out his smoke and looked at her. Habit made his expression inscrutable, but this girl's honesty chipped that away. "I am," he said. "But I'm afraid that I've gone too far now to change anything."

Buck and Kohler came out of the cabin then and Betty took the plate and cup back to the settler's wife. Harms eased his bulk through the door and stood there, picking his teeth. He squinted at the sky and the molten sun, then said, "If the rain don't drown you, the sun fries you." He turned as Temple Manly approached; his manner changed to one of concern. "Mr. Manly, what we going to do about the horses? With Wes on a fresh mount, it seems to me that we'll never catch him."

"We'll catch him," Manly said. "Kohler, what time is it?"

"Quarter after two."

Temple Manly wound and set his watch. "Get Reilly and Wilson out here. We're leaving." He swung his head and looked at the faint scar of the road twisting to the higher levels. This country was not to his liking. Too much brush and rock up there, which put all the odds in Wes Cardigan's favor if he ever tired of running and decided to make a fight of it. And Manly did not forget the fact that Cardigan was equipped to fight, he had taken that full box of .44 cartridges from the line shack.

Harry Buck spoke without glancing up from the cigarette he was manufacturing. "Wes will head for Red Rock, Mr. Manly."

Turning his head to look at him, Manly said, "That's twice you've mentioned that."

"May mention it again if the notion strikes me," Harry Buck said and snapped a match with his thumbnail.

"We'll go to Red Rock," Manly said, somehow leaving the impression that this was his lone decision, unaffected by Buck's mention of the town.

He stomped around impatiently while Reilly and Wilson brought up the horses. The settler and his wife stood near the door of their cabin, watching. When the posse was mounted, Temple Manly fished through his pocket for a five-dollar gold piece. He offered it to the settler, but the man shook his head.

"Can't take money for being neighborly," he said.

"Five dollars will feed you for a month this winter," Manly said firmly, a little offended by the man's attitude. "Don't be a fool now."

"I ain't," the man said, looking squint-eyed. "Hope you get your man."

"We'll get him," Hank Wilson said flatly.

Kohler turned and looked at him, as did Harms; the others ignored the deputy.

Manly returned the coin to his pocket and wheeled his horse; the others followed him from the yard. Ten minutes later they were high on the road and the settler's place was only a small scar on the clearing's face.

Through the remainder of the afternoon they moved at a slow, steady pace, broken only by reluctant housekeeping stops. Temple Manly continually studied the country around him, not liking any of it. The timber slopes were growing barer by the mile and jumbled rock offered countless hiding places for Wes Cardigan. Manly had trouble ridding himself of his apprehensions, for the man had been on the run long enough to get angry, and an angry man was capable of anything.

He spent a good deal of time observing the men with him and the girl who spoke to no one. Jim was riding toward the rear of the column near Hank Wilson, and Manly noticed that Wilson had an uncommon interest in young Manly. Harry Buck sat his saddle slack-bodied, as though he was in no particular hurry. Kohler and Harms were both feeling the effects of the pace, but Indian Reilly's expression remained stonily indifferent. Manly wondered if the man ever felt anything.

When the sun touched the rim of the mountains,

Manly stopped and dismounted. He motioned Indian Reilly forward to take the horses, then stood there, hands on hips, wondering if he should camp for the night or push on to Red Rock. For hours now he had been anticipating trouble, and when it failed to materialize, his relief was almost overpowering. The posse gathered around him, except for Indian Reilly, who, as usual, kept himself apart.

John Kohler said, "I'm wearing out, Mr. Manly. You may be made of iron, but the rest of us are damn tired."

"You'll feel better once you've had a bath and shave in Red Rock."

"Maybe the law there could take over," Harms suggested, still hopeful of an easy out.

Temple Manly turned and coolly stabbed Harms with his eyes. "We need no outside help to clean our house. Try to keep that in mind."

"Sure. But I only meant . . ."

"I'm quite aware of what you meant," Manly said. His glance touched Harry Buck and he read amusement in the tall man's expression. "Something strike you as funny, Buck?"

"You," Harry Buck said easily. "You're so stiff it's a wonder you don't break when you bend. Why don't you just take the star off Harms's vest and be done with it? We know who's wearing it."

Easing Kohler aside, Temple Manly stepped up

to Harry Buck. "One of these days, I'll teach you a little respect."

"Always eager to learn," Buck said. "But I'll tell you something, Mr. Manly: you'll get farther leading a man by the hand than you will kicking his butt all the time."

Jim suddenly whirled away, running toward Indian Reilly and the horses. "What the hell you think you're doing there?" He sent this question ahead of him as he ran. "By God, I said I'd kill you and I meant it!"

His shout was almost frenzied; everyone turned to stare at him. Reilly jumped and faced Jim Manly, his expression guilty. Hank Wilson said, "Watch him, Reilly!"

This seemed to be a signal, for the Indian whipped his rifle around, working the lever as the weapon swung level. Temple Manly caught his breath sharply and tried to lift his own gun but Harry Buck slammed his hand down on the barrel and held the muzzle to the ground. Even as Temple Manly struggled to free his weapon, Jim's hand dropped to his holster and he shot as soon as the muzzle came hip high. The bullet caught Indian Reilly flush in the breastbone, slamming him back into Kohler's horse. The animal skittered about, frightened, and Reilly wilted, striking on knees and shoulder.

The echo of the shot rattled through the hills like dice in a leather cup; Jim Manly looked down at Indian Reilly without expression, then holstered his gun. Harry Buck released his grip on Temple Manly's Winchester and stepped back, his eyes pulled into thin slits. Kohler and Harms seemed too stunned to move.

"Jesus!" Wilson said. "Reilly!" He ran forward and lifted the dead man for a moment, then let him sag back. Turning, he faced Jim Manly. "All right, now it's time to pay up." Wrath made a bright shine in his eyes.

"That's enough!" Temple Manly said loudly.

"Keep out of it," Harry Buck cautioned. He spoke so quietly that Manly doubted his ears for a moment.

"What did you say?" Manly shot him a brief glance, but he dared not do more.

"You lift that rifle to interfere and I'll draw on you," Buck said. "He made this for himself so let him finish it."

Hank Wilson was standing spraddle-legged, his right hand hooked into his gunbelt near the buckle; he had no more than a six-inch reach to his holster. "You didn't have to kill Reilly, Jim."

"Keep your mouth shut, Manly," Buck warned. "I mean, keep it shut tight." He stood quartering toward Manly, his arms loose and idle by his sides. Manly shot him a darting glance, then whipped his attention back to his son and Hank Wilson.

Jim Manly was saying, "Go ahead, Hank.

134

You're just shootin' off your mouth. You don't want to gun me."

This was a possibility that Temple Manly hadn't considered, but there must have been truth in it, for Hank Wilson pawed a hand across his mouth and restricted his anger to a glare. That Wilson could actually be afraid of the young man seemed preposterous, yet the boy had got into action fast enough. But surely Jim was not fast enough to be a threat to Hank Wilson, who, some said, was one of the best guns in Texas.

"I'm waiting," Jim Manly said coolly. "Hank, move now or back away."

"This isn't the place," Hank Wilson said, suddenly evasive. "But there'll be another."

When Hank turned away, Temple Manly realized that he had been holding his breath. Jim stood still while Hank lifted Indian Reilly and carried him into the rocks. This meant another delay while Wilson built a cairn over the dead man.

Kohler stirred and touched Harms on the arm, drawing the fat man's attention. They walked to one side and stood together, clearly out of this. Harry Buck waited, for he had spoken harshly to Temple Manly, and he would now have to answer for it.

Finally Manly said, "Buck, don't ever interfere with me again."

"I will if I think it's necessary."

"I've said it; better believe me."

"And you better believe me," Buck said, then shook out his smoking tobacco. Betty Cardigan, who stood slightly apart, was studying Jim Manly.

She said, "You did that almost too well, Jim. I didn't know you could kill a man, even in self-defense."

"A lot none of you know," he said and walked to his horse, fussing with his saddlebags and then the cinch, as though he suspected Indian Reilly of foul play.

Temple Manly stared at him. Was this man his son, or a stranger? He had killed Indian Reilly without hesitation, and obviously without regret; this troubled Manly, for here was a facet of the lad's personality that he had never suspected.

He walked over to a lone rock and sat down. Betty Cardigan looked at him, then at Harry Buck. "Would you really have drawn on him, Harry?"

"I don't suppose we'll ever know now," he said, drawing deeply on his smoke. He glanced around, first at Hank working on his mound of rocks, then at Jim Manly, standing alone now, for this act of violence had isolated him. "Came on sudden-like, didn't it?" He paused, his brows furrowed. "Old Manly's smart, and he's thinking about that now. He's seen his share of shootings and watched how they usually build up slow to

136

the point where a man has to be killed to satisfy the other."

"What are you trying to say, Harry?"

He shrugged. "Don't rightly know, except that there wasn't any build-up at all; it just exploded." He turned his head and looked at her, a genuine sympathy in his eyes. "Your man could be a real killer, Betty; he's sure got the instinct for it."

"Harry, that's not . . ." She closed her mouth and looked back at Temple Manly. His face was set stone-solid and he was concentrating on a spot on the ground a few feet ahead of his boots. The tired lines in Manly's face seemed to be etched there permanently. His despair was a weight rounding his shoulders. "I'm sorry for him," Betty said softly. "Real sorry."

"Be worth watching to see what Manly's going to do about this," Harry Buck murmured. "Be interestin' to see if he's got two sets of rules, one for us common folk and another for the Manlys."

"That's damned unfair," Betty said stiffly.

He laughed and ground out his cigarette under his boot heel. "Who the devil said it was fair? This is Manly country; I've been told that by men who ought to know."

Hank Wilson finished his chore and came back. He mounted immediately and sat his horse, impatient to move on. He showed no real remorse over Reilly's death; perhaps he even slightly resented the labor the killing had cost him. The others mounted wordlessly and waited for Temple Manly. Finally he sighed and stepped into the saddle.

He looked at no one, just turned his horse toward the climbing road and entered the early evening shadows. Just ahead lay a rocky slash and when he was seventy-five yards from it, a rifle coughed unexpectedly and a bullet plowed into the ground in front of Manly's horse. The animal reared and Manly fought him back to docility. The surprise attack was almost a relief; Manly had begun to think of Cardigan as a figment of his imagination rather than a flesh-and-blood enemy. The shot reestablished relations between hunter and hunted.

"That's far enough—*far enough—enough!*" Wes Cardigan's voice and its mocking echo died.

"I thought you'd soon get tired of running!" Manly shouted. He waited until the reverberations died out, then added, "Better give up, Cardigan!"

"Let me go up there and get him," Wilson said, edging forward. "I can circle the rocks and . . ."

"Stay where you are," Manly ordered. "You damned idiot, that shot could have emptied a saddle if he'd wanted to do that." In a louder voice he called, "Cardigan! You can't run forever!"

"Don't intend to," he called back. "Betty? Betty, go home!"

"No! Wes, no harm will come to you!"

"Yeah?" His derisive laugh floated down. "I saw what happened to Reilly. Quick, wasn't it?"

"I give you my word . . ." Manly began.

"Save that!" Cardigan interrupted. "I've got to slow you people down." The .44 banged and Manly's horse grunted and immediately began to spit blood. Manly felt the animal's knees bend and jumped clear as the horse fell. Even while he rolled on the ground, the rifle layered the hills with another echo and Harms's horse reared, mortally struck. The fat sheriff was almost caught when the horse fell, but the others had had enough; they wheeled and dashed back out of rifle range. Cardigan fired once more, killing Reilly's horse, which Wilson had been leading.

Temple Manly got to his feet and brushed casually at his clothes; boldly he stood in Wes Cardigan's sight. "Try shooting a man!"

"Shot one by mistake and some of you are set on hanging me for it," Cardigan replied. "You got lots of horses."

Manly's anger choked him and he thought of flinging a random shot into the rocks, then realized he would only be wasting ammunition. Harms was on his feet, badly frightened, but he dared not run until Manly gave permission.

"Mr. Manly . . ."

"Shut up. Cardigan! Cardigan? Can you hear me?"

There was no answer. Manly waited a few seconds longer, then walked back to where the others waited. Harms trotted along behind, looking back repeatedly over his shoulder.

John Kohler's face was gray in the thickening darkness. "Mr. Manly, we've got to get horses."

"We'll get them in Red Rock," Manly said. "Girl, give Harms your pony. You can ride double with someone."

This was a windfall to Harms, who dreaded even the short walk from his Gunlock office to Lovering's saloon. Yet he had to register a token protest. "Mr. Manly, what about . . ."

"Get on the damned horse," Manly snapped as Betty swung down.

Jim Manly eased his horse forward and freed a foot from the stirrup so she could mount. But instead she looked at Harry Buck and asked, "Would you give a footsore friend a ride, Harry?"

He grinned and slid back on the horse's rump. "Sure."

This left Temple Manly dismounted, but without a word he turned and started walking up the trail. One by one, they eased after him, at a reduced pace. Speaking softly, Harry Buck said, "Got to hand it to old Iron Butt; he's all man."

SEVEN

The town of Red Rock lay on an expanse of dun-colored flats that formed an ell-shaped sweep between two small mountain ranges. Reaching out to the east, the Texas-Pacific railroad tracks disappeared into the horizon, while in the other direction, they sliced through a gorge, driving west and south. This was a railroad town, built by railroaders and populated by them. Unlike the cattle towns, which were mostly flung together, Red Rock showed careful planning. The main street was wide and smooth, flanked by tall adobe buildings with their boardwalk overhangs and painted woodwork. The hotel sat on the far corner, a huge, three-storied building convenient to the roundhouse and switchyards at the southern edge of town.

Toward this Temple Manly led his posse. Ten hours of walking had played havoc with his feet; he knew that the mushiness within his boots was due to blood from broken blisters. Yet none of this discomfort was evident in his rigid expression. In a conversational voice, he said, "Wilson, take care of the horses. See that they're rubbed down and grained." His glance swung to his son. "You come with me. Harms, Kohler, be where I can find you." He looked at Buck.

141

"I know better than to tell you what to do." He slapped his stomach and contemplated a bath and shave. Somehow these things seemed more important now than catching Wes Cardigan.

"I'm going to put up my horse," Jim said evenly. He wheeled away and rode down the street before his father could protest.

Temple Manly looked after him briefly, then said, "Kohler, there ought to be some local law around here. See if you can find him and send him to my room. Perhaps Wes has been seen in town." The chairs on the hotel veranda looked inviting; he longed to sit down but his pride held him. He dared not acknowledge this weakness even to himself.

"After I get a room of my own," Kohler said. He was not a contrary man by nature and felt a compulsion to explain. "I'm as dirty as you are, Mr. Manly; an hour more of waiting won't make a big difference."

"Have it your own way then," Manly said tartly and swung onto the hotel porch. A few men loafed in the evening's last light and they observed Manly and the others curiously. Because Manly was a man very sensitive to the opinions of others, he exerted a strong-willed effort to walk without a limp. Harry Buck was helping Betty Cardigan down; the others had already dismounted and were standing slack-bodied and weary.

By the time Manly stepped inside, the clerk had the register turned around and the pen wetted in the inkwell. Temple Manly scrawled his name with a hurried flourish and took his key. "You have a bath here?" His manner implied that if they didn't, they'd better get one.

"Fifty cents extra," the clerk said. The others were trooping across the veranda, flogging dust from their clothes, stamping it from their boots.

"Send up a boy with water right away," Manly told the clerk and went up the stairs. He could hear Kohler talking to the desk man as he moved along the hall, searching for his room. Inserting the key, he went in, then closed the door and leaned against it. It was a relief to be alone, a relief just to lean against something. He admitted the torture of his aching muscles and the fatigue that lay like a weight on his back.

The room was small but clean; that in itself was an oddity for western hotels of his knowledge. The bed was simple, cast brass affair with huge knobs and a high headboard. Manly eased over to it and lowered himself with gratitude. He tugged off his boots with great care, gentling as much as he could the soreness of ruptured blisters. He had been right about the dampness; it was blood. He peeled off his ruined socks and flung them in the far corner. Free of confinement, his feet felt chilled, yet inflamed. He poured the wash basin full of water and soaked them, leaning back with a sigh at the soothing coolness.

While he sat there, someone knocked on the door and Manly wondered if he should remove his feet from the basin in the event that it was one of the posse. Then he resigned himself to the fact that comfort was more important than appearance and said, "Who is it?"

"The water, sir."

"Well, fetch it in; the door's unlocked." He took the towel and gently dried his feet.

A fifteen-year-old boy came in, a pewter bathtub balanced on his back and a heavy wooden bucket in one hand. He set the water down then righted the tub. When his glance touched Manly's tender feet, he asked, "Horse go lame on you, Mister?"

"Fill the tub, please."

"I was goin' to," the boy said. "How come you walked while the others rode, Mister? They make you walk?"

The questions aggravated Manly. He quickly gave the boy a quarter and shooed him out of the room. With the door safely locked, Manly stripped off his clothes and lowered himself into the tub, then slowly added the water.

With his bath completed, Manly dressed carefully, recoiling slightly at the touch of his filthy clothes. Pulling his boots back on presented a major problem, but with set teeth he managed the task and walked back down to the lobby.

To the clerk he said, "Have the tub and water removed from my room."

He went out and down the street to the clothing store. This was a workingman's town and the selection, he found, was limited. He made enough purchases to cover him from the skin out and paid for them. The clerk provided a back room and Temple Manly went there to change. Redressed, he walked through the store to the alley and threw his old clothes in a trash barrel. A handy barbershop gave him a few minutes' ease in the chair and he emerged clean-cheeked.

Once again on the boardwalk, he speculated on whether or not to seek out the local law. He decided to wait; it would be better to send for the constable. The man who summoned another always had the psychological advantage. At the hotel he met the sweating boy, still lugging water.

"Gosh, but you're a dirty bunch," the boy remarked in passing.

Temple Manly reached out and seized the boy by the ear, hauling him back. "Since you like to talk so much," he said, "go and tell the marshal that I want to see him."

"Got to deliver this water," the boy said.

"Sonny, I just told you to do something." Manly's tone was easy but the boy was no fool; he understood an order when he heard one, especially an order that canceled out any previously given to him.

Setting the bucket down in the hall, he turned promptly enough and headed for the stairs. Manly said, "Where was this going?" He indicated the water bucket.

"To the lady in number twelve," the boy said. "Gosh, any more baths around here and the rain barrels'll be empty."

"Get on with what I told you," Manly said and hefted the bucket. He found the room across from his own and knocked on the door. Betty Cardigan's voice invited him in.

She was by the bed, clad only in her bloomers and thin shirtwaist. When she saw Manly she gasped with surprise and grabbed her jeans to hold in front of her. "I expected the boy," she said lamely.

"The boy's busy," Manly said. He backed out of the door and closed it quickly.

In his own room again, he took off his boots and new socks before the leaking blisters ruined them. He had bought some salve and a small section of cloth. With these he doctored and bandaged his feet, then lay back on the bed, his hands propped behind his head.

He felt a slight craving for a smoke, but getting up to roll one seemed not worth the effort. He switched his thoughts to Wes Cardigan, who, by now, was probably heading north on a good horse. The young man's unexpected action from the rocks had been audacious enough, and he had succeeded in slowing the posse down. But Cardigan was smart enough to know that he hadn't really stopped them by shooting three horses. Just delayed things a little, bought a few more hours of time for himself. He knows I'll never give up, Manly thought. He knows, so why didn't he raise the sights a little instead of shooting my horse?

There was really only one way to stop a man, he decided. Like Jim had stopped Indian Reilly. The thought brought an unpleasant picture to Temple Manly and his forehead wrinkled slightly. All that time the boy had been banging away at tin cans to practice his draw, Temple Manly had regarded as merely a phase through which most young Texans passed. Now he could see that the whole business had had serious undertones which had escaped him completely, and being the man he was, he had to assume full responsibility for them now. Of course it was self-defense; there would be no legal action.

Knuckles tapped lightly against his door and Manly said, "Come in."

A tall, thin man in a dark suit entered, then closed the door. He had a long, hound dog face, and drooping mustaches. "My name's McKitrich. Marshal of Red Rock." A star gleamed on his buttoned vest, but he wore no pistol, or at least none that was visible.

Manly sat up and introduced himself. "I'm with a posse from Gunlock."

"You with the law office there?" McKitrich asked easily.

"No," Manly said. "But Sheriff Harms is taking a bath now so I thought I'd better talk to you for him."

McKitrich was stripping the wrapper from a cigar. While he searched for a match, he said, "Know the man you're after. But he ain't here."

"I figured that," Manly said. "But perhaps you can give me some idea of where he was heading." Civility, he told himself, would go farther here than a peremptory manner.

"Tell you exactly," McKitrich said. "Fact is, he came to my office, told me you fellas were behind him, and what he intended to do about it."

"Where is the man?" he asked. Suddenly all of his aches and pains seemed personally inflicted by this elusive fugitive, and he felt that he must make Cardigan pay for them in full.

"Took the four-fifteen train to Gunlock," McKitrich said calmly.

Unmindful of his feet, Manly stood up. "What's that?" Somehow this answer made the situation even worse.

McKitrich was smiling slightly through his cloud of cigar smoke. "Sort of surprised me too, a man going back to where his trouble began.

But he bought his ticket and got on the train; I was at the depot and saw him."

"When's the next train out of here?" Manly asked. He felt the same now as he had the day the horse had bolted with Lila half in, half out of the buggy; he hadn't known what to do then either.

"Six-five in the morning," McKitrich said. "Takes you to Willows. From there you can catch the stage to Gunlock. Should put you in town around midnight or one in the morning."

Manly turned to the window and looked out; he didn't want this marshal to witness his new concern. His mind groped for the answer to Cardigan's unexpected move. He could find only one that began to make any sense. Wes Cardigan had deliberately played him for a fool—led him on, then left him holding an empty sack like some green kid on a snipe hunt. Seen through his fury, only one fact seemed logical; the others were unimportant; Cardigan had aimed for Temple Manly and hit him hardest where he was weakest, in his pride! A deep surge of anger shook him, for this was something that would be talked and laughed about for years: how Wes Cardigan wore down a posse led by Temple Manly, then stood back and laughed at them. Manly clenched his fists; whatever compassion he had formerly felt for the man dissolved before this new realization.

The marshal was saying, "This fella was worried about his health, Mr. Manly. He said there was some of you who had a new rope they wanted to use." He scratched his cheek with his little finger. "You a proper deputy, Mr. Manly?"

"Deputy? What the hell are you talking about?" He was impatient to be alone so he could think.

"A posse ought to be deputized," McKitrich said evenly. He shrugged and turned to the door. "Course, the man's gone now and it ain't my responsibility, but if he'd stayed here, there wouldn't have been any hanging."

Temple Manly faced the man. "Marshal, if we ever decided to hang anyone, I doubt that you'd be able to stop it."

"But I'd try," McKitrich said. He smiled briefly. "It's a nice town we have here. Enjoy it. You got a while until train time."

After the door closed, Manly stood with his head tipped forward, his thoughts turning again to Wes Cardigan and what the man's return to Gunlock would mean. No doubt he was attempting to arouse public sympathy by portraying the posse as a group of bunglers led by a fool. But Temple Manly felt that he alone was the real target; everyone with a lick of sense would understand that. Harms was a fat dolt, and beneath everyone's easy tolerance, he was considered thus. Kohler and Buck were really little men; they would suffer no actual humiliation. No, this was directed at Manly, and gathered on Cardigan's side would be the countless people Manly had stepped on. How many were there in Gunlock, he wondered, who would seize this opportunity to ridicule him? Too many, he supposed, and momentarily regretted his lifetime pattern of ruthless self-achievement. A little consideration, spread out over the years, would have neutralized Wes Cardigan's maneuver. But he hadn't been considerate and people relished the spectacle of an unpopular man being dethroned, or knocked down to pint size. He would have to return to Gunlock, his own town, and face them all; his pride would permit no other decision.

He had a sudden realization of his hunger and decided that food would make him feel better. Cautiously he slid into his boots; the bandages and salve made a soothing pad when he put his weight on his feet, and walking, he found, was not too difficult. Leaving his room, he went down to the street and found a small restaurant wedged between the butcher shop and the shoemaker's place. John Kohler and Harry Buck were already there, seated at a table near the east wall. At any other time, Temple Manly would have merely nodded and taken a table by himself, but he felt a compelling urge toward companionship; he walked over, placed his hands on the back of an empty chair and asked, "Do you mind?"

John Kohler was visibly surprised but he masked it quickly. Harry Buck looked up, then said, "Sit down, Mr. Manly." He caught the waiter's attention and brought him over.

"Steak and potatoes," Manly said, adjusting his silverware. "Any kind of vegetable, and pie." When the waiter moved away, he added, "I spoke to the marshal here. Wes Cardigan took the train back to Gunlock."

Kohler looked at Buck for a moment. Then he said, "Well, that makes us look foolish enough. I didn't give him credit for being that smart."

"Kohler, you could never look foolish," Manly said. "Just me."

Kohler frowned, not understanding exactly what Manly meant, but Harry Buck understood. He said, "Mr. Manly, you could just tell folks not to laugh. They wouldn't dare then, would they?"

"I didn't expect you to understand," Manly said.

"Why not?" Buck asked. "You're mad at Wes because he made you look like a tin-plated sucker. Maybe you're mad enough now to side with Wilson and stretch his neck. Wouldn't be the first time a big man reared up and got nasty because someone suggested that both of them pulled on their pants the same way. Wes pulled a handful of your tail feathers and stuck 'em in his hat. You ain't the kind who likes being laughed at. Few men are, but a big man like you would like it a lot less than me."

Temple Manly looked squarely at Harry Buck. "Are you after me? Is that it, Buck?"

"You don't have a damn thing I want," Buck said. The waiter came with their meal and until the dishes were set in place there was no more talk. While Buck cut his steak, he said, "Knew a fella near Matagorda Bay once who built himself a boat. Couldn't stand it to be a boat like everyone else owned. No, this one had to be special. Built it big, and he built it heavy. Took ten mules to drag it to the water. Floated fine too, until he poked a hole in it, then it sank so damned quick he didn't have time to jump overboard. Drowned, poor bastard." His glance was somewhat amused. "You're like that boat, Mr. Manly. And you'll sink quick once a hole's punched into you. Now you take me, I got no money or position in the world, but I can stand to be laughed at. You got money and position, but when folks start makin' you the butt of a joke . . ."

Manly interrupted; he didn't want to hear Buck say it. "That's a hard-nosed opinion to have of a man!"

Harry Buck shrugged. "Look, I didn't make the damned rules; you did. All I'm waitin' to see is if you live by the ones you set up for others, or do you have a set for yourself."

"I think," Kohler said brusquely, "that we're getting off the subject. We started out to catch a man who robbed the express office. I'd as soon we finished up doing what we started."

Betty Cardigan entered the restaurant as Manly was finishing his pie. She started for another table, but he suddenly got up and offered her his chair. The move was so unexpectedly courteous that she was startled; experience had taught most people who knew Manly that generosity was alien to his nature.

"I'm through here," he said, and seated her before she could think of an argument. Kohler also was sliding his chair away from the table.

"Join me in a smoke, Mr. Manly? I've got a few good cigars left."

"Thank you," Manly said. "I'd enjoy it."

He and Kohler walked out to sit on the porch. Betty turned her head to watch them, then the waiter came over and she gave him her order. "Is it true that Wes went back to Gunlock?" she asked. "Why would he do that, Harry?"

"He's innocent, ain't he?" The waiter puttered about, lighting lamps to lift the sooty darkness of evening. Harry Buck's blunt face was shadowed; his whisker stubble made him seem grim.

"Guilty, innocent—that's not the point now, Harry. Wes had no reason to go back. No reason at all." Her brother's action upset her; she couldn't decide whether it was good or bad.

"Wes isn't the kind who'd do anything without a reason," Harry Buck said. He rolled a smoke, then leaned back in his chair to enjoy it. "Betty, Manly's taking this manhunt damned serious; he seems to take everything that way. And when he started out, he meant to get Wes, even if he had to chase him to hell and back. Now if you was Wes and had a man like Manly after you, what would you do?" He spread his hands. "Remember that getting caught ain't the answer. I don't think Manly would let harm come to Wes, but he'd bring him back roped hand and foot. Innocent or not, he'd look guilty as hell when Manly brought him in. No, Wes had to take the lead away from Manly and make him look foolish."

"Is that why he went back?" she asked.

"That's my guess," Harry said softly. "He went home and left Manly out on a limb. After leading him through a storm and across that stinkin' sink, and then shooting three of the horses, Wes just calmly takes the train home as though it's been a picnic." Buck leaned forward. "Betty, you want to know who's going to get laughed out of Gunlock when he gets back?"

"Manly?"

Buck nodded. "E. Temple Manly, the big man. And the bigger you get, the tougher it is to be the butt of a joke. Laughing with Manly is all right, but laughing at him is something else. You think he don't know what he's in for?" He snubbed out his smoke in his saucer. "Manly's mad, Betty, clean through. He's got a reason to hold a grudge now. Something to get even for. The next thing that occurs to me is, just how E. Temple Manly's going to settle the account. Now, you wouldn't laugh at Jim. I guess you know what he'd do."

"I don't think I'll ever forget the way Jim shot Reilly. If he inherited those instincts from his father . . ." She closed her mouth suddenly, unwilling to put the thought into words. The waiter brought her food and went back to the kitchen. Harry Buck looked past her shoulder and his glance drew her attention around. Jim Manly was walking toward them; he sat down without invitation. His face was bloated and his eyes bright. He had washed his face but forsaken a shave because of the tender bruises.

"Some town," he said derisively. "Dies at sundown."

"I guess the men here work hard," Buck said softly. "Maybe they like their sleep." He watched young Manly and understood him. These men could never share friendship; they were organisms destined to clash.

Jim Manly glanced at Buck and his empty dishes. "If you're through here, we won't keep you, Harry." There was a native sarcasm in the man; he seemed to enjoy being insulting, yet always kept it restrained, making it difficult for a man to take open offense.

"You ain't. Betty and I were having a conversation before you stuck your bill in."

Color climbed quickly into Jim Manly's face. "You got a blunt mouth that I like less and less all the time." He looked around. "Where's the damned waiter? Hey! How about some service here?" The cook thrust his head out, showing irritation. "Bring me something," Jim said. "What's the matter with you? You got a woman back there?"

When the cook disappeared, Harry Buck said, "One of these days you're going to talk like that to the wrong man and get your head mashed out of shape. You may have the Manly manner, but you lack your old man's muscle."

"That's what Indian Reilly thought," Jim said. He looked pointedly at Harry Buck. "Things have changed some since we started out; I've killed a man."

"You killed a stupid Indian who couldn't think very fast," Buck said. He pushed back his chair and stood up to leave, but Betty reached across the table and took his arm.

"Stay, Harry."

Jim Manly looked first at the girl, then at Buck. "What the hell is this? I've driven some stakes into this claim."

Buck frowned and darted a glance at Betty

Cardigan, who was trying to attach a proper meaning to this remark. Buck said, "Jim, be careful now."

"Careful?" Jim Manly grinned. "Why? You know what I mean."

"I don't think I do," Betty said, then paused, color rising in her cheeks. "Or do I? Jim, you're a damned liar!"

"Buck don't think so, do you? He's been thinking about driving a few himself, ain't you, Bu—"

Harry Buck's knotted fist closed Jim Manly's mouth and flung him back into another table, bringing it down with a snapping of legs. The crash brought Temple Manly and Kohler in from the porch; they were blocking the door when Jim pushed himself erect.

His holster had slid around behind him and when he reached for this, whether to readjust it or bring out the gun, Harry Buck said, "Touch that and I'll blow a hole through you."

The warning took effect and Jim Manly forgot about his gun. "Step outside and I'll wrap you around the porch post," he said.

"Sit down and eat your supper," Harry said flatly. He looked at Betty Cardigan. "You want to stay here with him?"

"No," she said. "I've had enough of his mouth."

She wrapped her meat and pie in a napkin, stuffed four biscuits in her coat pocket, then waited for Harry Buck to come around the table. Jim stood rooted, bleeding slightly from the corner of his mouth. Harry Buck said, "You've got enough sense not to shoot me in the back, haven't you?"

Without waiting for an answer, he walked out. Temple Manly stepped aside for him and they passed onto the porch without a word. Returning to the hotel, Betty Cardigan walked ahead of him up the stairs to her room; Harry Buck held to a thoughtful silence. At her door she paused.

"You didn't believe him, did you, Harry?"

"No," Buck said. "He lies easy enough about everything else. I suspect he'd lie about that too."

"But it opened up an ugly possibility, didn't it?" She took his arm and shook it slightly. "Harry, it's important to me that there never be any doubt in your mind." Kohler came up the stairs then and went into his own room. Betty put the key into the lock and turned it. "Come in. We can't talk in the hall."

Buck closed the door gently and leaned his shoulders against it. She unwrapped the meat and made a sandwich of it. When she sat on the edge of the bed, Buck took the lone chair, extending his long legs, folding and unfolding his hands in uncomfortable silence.

Finally Betty said, "I'm not going to bite you, Harry."

He flashed her a look, then laughed, and the tension ran out of him. The manufacture of a cigarette gave him something to do with his hands and when it was finished he leaned back to enjoy it. "You're not in love with Jim Manly," he said. "A girl like you could never love a man like that." He hesitated, searching for words. "I mean, you're just too much woman for him."

"I never claimed to love him," she said. "Jim assumes a lot, Harry. I guess he's spread it around Gunlock—you know, what he implied in the restaurant." She put the sandwich aside and folded her hands. "Maybe it makes him feel more of a man to lie about a thing like that. Funny how I've walked down the street of that town and never thought that—well, now I'll be looking for sly glances, and wondering who he's told that to, and who's measuring me and wondering how their luck . . ."

"Shut up!" Harry Buck snapped.

His anger was quick and genuine; she stared at him for a moment, then dropped her glance to the rug. "Harry, what is it?"

He blew out an asthmatic breath and thrust his hands deep in his pockets. "I'm a poor man, Betty. Unless a man's got something to offer a woman, he's better off keeping his mouth shut." His boots stirred as he shifted his weight to stand up. "I guess I'd better go."

"Because you think you spoke out of turn?"

She got up and crossed to stand before him. He was tall and she had to tip her head back to look into his eyes. "Harry, put your arms around me. Put them around me because I've dreamed for so long how they would feel. Why wouldn't you ever look at me? I've asked myself that question a thousand times." He stood motionless, trying to read the brightness in her eyes. "At dances, I've wanted to go to you when you wouldn't come to me. Can you imagine what it was like, looking at myself in a mirror and wishing I was so beautiful you couldn't bear to stay away from me? Put your arms around me now. Please, even if you don't mean it."

"Mean it!" He smothered her with his embrace, yet he was gentle because his thoughts were gentle. She nestled close against him, drawing a moment's happiness from him. The expression of their love was wordless; she supposed that he would not often speak of it for he was silent about the things he felt most strongly.

He kissed her and it was as she had always hoped. Beneath the warmth of his lips were the biting hungers that are in all men, but loving her he offered only his restrained tenderness now. When they drew apart she wept, for the richness of this moment had been more overwhelming than she had hoped.

"I want to marry you," Buck said. "But I can offer you nothing, Betty."

"Nothing!" She wiped the back of her hand across her eyes. "Harry, you offer me yourself and I can be very proud of you. Do you think I want the things the Manlys have? Do you think I really need them to be happy?" She shook her head. "When we get back to Gunlock, I want to marry you, Harry."

He nodded; there was no need to voice his agreement. Crossing to the door, he paused there. "I'll help Wes first," he said.

He stepped into the hall and closed the door. When he looked up, he found Temple Manly standing in his open doorway. Manly said, "Will you step in, Buck? I want to talk to you."

"Sure," Buck said and went in. Manly closed the door. He limped when he walked across the room. Buck looked at the bandages but offered no sympathy.

"It's about my son," Temple Manly said. He did not look at Buck when he spoke. "The trouble you had tonight isn't over, but I'd like it to be." He swung around, leaning against the end of his bedstead. "Buck, I don't want you to kill my boy."

"Kill him?" For a moment Harry Buck suspected a grisly joke, then he saw the seriousness in Manly's eyes. "Mr. Manly, I never asked for trouble with Jim. But the lad has a knack for finding it."

"One man's dead," Manly said. "Not much of

a man, considering that he was half Injun, but he's dead nevertheless. I was as surprised as you when Jim killed Reilly. But I don't want it to happen again. The ease with which he did that can put strange notions in a man's head. He's young and impressionable. Buck, I don't want you to draw on my boy."

"You know I can beat him," Harry said evenly. "Mr. Manly, get the idea out of your head that I want to draw on any man." He stood up. "I guess you want to help Jim, but you won't do it this way. If he ever found out you talked like this, he'd hate your guts for it."

"I think he hates me now," Manly said dully.

"You act like the whole country's against you," Buck said. "Your conscience botherin' you a little?"

"A man always does some things he's not overly proud of," Manly said. "Goddamn it, Buck, I've been thinking of all the people I've stepped on, and wishing I hadn't!" He flung his arms out. "And I'm remembering all the times I pushed Jim aside because I was too busy, then bought him some gimcrack to make up for it." He pawed his mouth out of shape and was momentarily silent. "He's all I've got and I don't want him dead, simply because he ain't got sense enough to keep his big mouth shut."

"It's *his* mouth," Buck said harshly. "Mr. Manly, what are you going to do when the day

163

comes that Jim ups and leaves? How are you going to smooth out all the knocks for him then?" Manly opened his mouth to speak, then closed it before any sound came out. Buck smiled and added, "Mr. Manly, I guess you've done your damndest to keep the boy dependent on you so he couldn't leave. But you ain't satisfied with just one thing, you got to have him a man too. Can't have both, you know."

"All right, all right," Manly said, not wanting to talk any more about this unpleasantness. "We're leaving at daybreak. See that you're at the depot."

"I'll be there," Buck said, moving to the door. "Wouldn't want to miss your arrival in Gunlock."

He stepped out and closed the door, leaving Temple Manly alone with his thoughts. Looking out of the window, Manly could see clearly along the dark street. While he watched, Jim came to the lighted saloon porch for a moment, and from the way he swayed, Manly knew he had had too much to drink. His first impulse was to call down to the young man, but he stifled that. Then Jim went back into the saloon and Manly sat down on the edge of the bed, his head pillowed in his palms.

EIGHT

In order to survive in a land violently unsympathetic to any display of weakness, Harms had disciplined himself to live within the confines of a few simple rules, the primary one being never to do anything in a hurry; unpleasant bits of business had a way of dissipating themselves if left alone long enough. To people of shallow insight, this manner of living established Harms as a boondock sage; one given to deep preoccupation, a man of careful, even cautious decision. And Harms could never quite bring himself to admit, even to his few close friends, that this was the mere manifestation of an uncertain man performing in a fantastic drama that had no logical end.

When Harms first heard that Wes Cardigan had returned to Gunlock, he felt a vast sense of personal relief; he could hardly be expected to show surprise over another man's actions when his own were generally unpredictable. His first thought was that he should consult Temple Manly; the man must have a plan. But then he decided to wait. If Manly wished to consult him about anything, he would do so in his own good time.

A bath and shave refreshed Harms and in the

early evening hours he wandered downstairs to the street, standing on the hotel veranda to observe the mild traffic. Railroad men, he decided, were a quiet lot. The boom of road building had passed, leaving in its wake men with families and steady jobs, which all added up to steady habits.

While he lingered on the porch, he saw Jim Manly across the street. The young man came to the edge of the walk in front of the saloon, teetering uncertainly before going back inside. Harms frowned, for it was obvious that young Manly had been hitting the bottle, always a risky thing to do in a strange town. In a cattle town it might be all right, for a man was among his own kind there. But this town was too tame to tolerate a drunk. Likely there wasn't even a gambler or prostitute in Red Rock, which made a town pretty mild in Harms's estimation.

For a time Harms debated the wisdom of crossing the street to keep an eye on young Jim; it was always difficult for him to evaluate the amount of deference he should pay the Manlys; Temple Manly did not like interference, and the young man probably resented it as much as his father. Yet there was an anxious core of concern in Harms; he fancied himself a man of certain responsibilities; after all, he was a peace officer sworn to keep the peace. If he managed to keep young Manly from making a fool of himself, the father would be grateful. And Harms knew that one could never earn too much gratitude from the Manlys.

Easing his bulk across the street, Harms paused for a quick look through the front door of the saloon. He saw Jim Manly standing at the far end of the bar, his elbows hooked onto the wood, his face shadowed by his hat brim. Hank Wilson stood at the other end, his hands curled around a half-empty glass of beer. A few men were clustered about tables, talking quietly and playing cards. Harms stepped inside, drawing the usual, casual glances accorded strangers, then took a station halfway between Wilson and Jim Manly.

When the bartender approached, Harms said, "Beer, please." He laid a coin on the bar. He glanced at Wilson while the bartender drew from a keg, but Wilson had his head tipped forward, his hat brim boxing his face in shadows.

"Hear you've been on a manhunt," the bartender said.

"Yes," Harms admitted. "Seems that it's drawing to an end though."

"Must be some life," the bartender remarked. "I mean, being the law and all."

"It has its moments," Harms admitted. He took his beer and walked over to Hank Wilson.

The deputy spoke without looking up. "Back in Gunlock I'm forced to put up with having you around. I had to put up with your company coming here, but now I'd just like to stand here alone and enjoy my beer."

Harms showed no real offense; a slight frown marred the flesh of his forehead. "Don't be that way with me, Hank. I never intended any meanness to you."

This brought Wilson's head up and he stared at Harms. "You fat bastard, you never meant anything to anybody." He drank some of his beer.

There were dregs of anger in Harms; this was evident in his eyes. "You hate me, Hank? You want my job, is that it?"

"Ah, I guess it ain't really you," Wilson said. "Harms, I'm forty. You understand? Forty! I've got a hundred and thirty-seven dollars in the bank, a six-shooter, and a fifteen-dollar watch. That's what I got to show for forty years of living."

"This is my fault?" Harms asked, slightly bewildered. He had never understood this man and long ago had given up trying.

Hank shook his head as though there were no explicit answers. "Harms, I've been a deputy sheriff for eighteen years. I've worked for men who were lazy, or afraid, or tired, or just no damned good. Always worked *for* them and never had men working for me." He thumped his chest. "You want to know why? Because I've never rooted around a man's butt to get myself elected, that's why." He paused to finish his beer and signal the bartender for another. "Only this time it's going to be different. That express robbery was a windfall for me, don't think it wasn't. This ain't some steer that's been rustled, something you can shove aside and talk your way out of." He leaned forward, his face only a few inches from Harms's. "Cardigan beat it back to Gunlock—well, that's all right with me. Let him go back. To hell with Cardigan now. You can have him; he's no good to me any more. Make the arrest yourself and be a fat-bellied hero; that ought to make you happy. Only I want to end up with that money, Harms. You understand, *I want that money!* As far's anyone's concerned, it's never going to be found."

"What—what do you mean? Are you suggesting that I . . . ?"

"Uh-uh," Wilson said, smiling. "I'm not suggesting, I'm telling you. Arrest Cardigan; he's about ready to give up anyway. Arrest him and throw him in jail, then strut around the streets and take all the credit. Convict Cardigan and you'll get reelected for life. Think of that, Harms. A soft job where you can sit around on your butt and smoke ten-cent cigars, and slap people on the back so they'll forget how useless you really are." He stuck his forefinger against the sheriff's chest. "Go ahead and be the politician, but just remember that the express money ain't going to be found! You're going to turn it over to me, understand?"

"My God, Hank, I couldn't . . ."

"You can," Wilson contradicted. "Harms, you better listen to me. If you don't, I'll arrest Wes myself and make a damned fool of you. What difference does it make to you anyway? I want that money and when I get it, I'll get out."

Harms stared at him, his beer forgotten. "Hank, I always wondered what you liked best. I guess I know now."

"So what do you know? Repeat it and I'll call you a liar. And you don't have enough guts to call me on it." He chuckled softly. "Harms, I'm not a bad guy. I'm just tired of having nothing. Look, Cardigan's going to jail anyway for shooting Sims. So let him." He spread his hands. "Do you think anyone really cares? Hell, Manly will want to hang him for leading him on a wild-goose chase. You don't care about anything except how you look in public." He tipped his head down and studied the varnished bar top. "Better make up your mind, Harms. I'm not going to wait very long. You'll turn the money up, but you'll make everyone believe it was never found."

The sheriff stood silent for a time. Then he said, "Hank, I can see now why you wanted to hang Wes. Dead, he couldn't talk and convince anyone he was innocent. With him gone, folks would figure the money lost while you hunted it down and put it in your pocket."

"Wouldn't be the first robbery where the money never turned up," Hank Wilson said. "Harms, be smart now. I'm setting this up for you; you'll be a damned hero."

"And for yourself."

"Why sure. It all depends what a man wants. You want an easy job. I'll take the money." He took Harms by the sleeve and gave him a slight tug. "I'm waitin' for the answer."

"All right, Hank," Harms said slowly. "All right. I guess the express company was insured. It won't be like they lost it, would it?"

"Sure now, that's the way it is." Wilson was smiling. "You're being smart, Harms. Hell, a man forty ought to have a little something, hadn't he?"

From the other end of the bar, Jim Manly banged his empty glass, drawing the bartender's attention. Harms looked around, then left Wilson and walked up to side young Manly.

"If you're not used to that stuff, you ought to go easy," Harms said.

Jim Manly gave him an affronted stare. "If that's advice, I don't want it. I can hold my booze." He placed his hands on the bar and waited while the bartender stood there with bottle poised. This angered Jim Manly. "Goddamn it, pour! This fat sonofabitch don't give me orders! I give orders to him. You want to see?"

"Now, Jim," Harms said gently. His fat hands patted the bar and he looked at the bartender, his expression flaccid with apology. The men at the tables stopped playing cards to watch this.

"Call me Mr. Manly," Jim said.

"Jim," Harms pleaded. "Don't call attention to yourself this way."

"Ha," Jim Manly said. "Goddamn you, Fatty, I gave you an order. Now address me properly or I'll punch your fat mouth."

Harms took Jim Manly's arm and tried to coax him out of this, but the effort only angered the young man further. "Now, we don't want trouble," Harms was saying. "Jim, your father wouldn't like to see you acting this way." He knew a profound worry; a sensible man did not rough up Temple Manly's son just because he got a little loud-mouthed. And young Manly realized that he had the edge on Harms, playing heavily on the sheriff's sense of insecurity.

Angrily, Jim flung off Harms's offending hand. He drew his gun and held it cocked in his hand. "You butt-nosin' old fool, are you goin' to call me Mr. Manly, or do I have to blow a hole in your fat belly?"

If there was anything that Harms disliked, it was firearms; he carried his own gun with a certain element of loathing, a concession to the

172

job, nothing more. Staring down the bore of Jim Manly's gun shot him with numbing fear; his flabby cheeks turned ashen and he clutched the edge of the bar for support. It suddenly occurred to him that if Jim Manly did shoot him, very few people would consider it a tangible loss.

The bartender said, "Better put up the gun, sonny. We don't flash weapons around here in Red Rock."

Jim Manly glared at him. "You don't, huh? No wonder the town's so dead." He raised his gun, sighted along the barrel and shattered a bottle of whiskey that had been sitting on the bar. Harms stood motionless while Hank Wilson continued to stare at Jim Manly. A few men seated at the tables scraped back their chairs, remembering important affairs elsewhere, but Jim turned to them and said, "Now don't be in a hurry, gents. Why not stick around and see this fat toad croak." He pointed the gun at Harms's bulging stomach, the hammer going back in a series of dry clicks. "Sing somethin'."

"Sing?" the bartender asked.

"You want to join him?" Manly asked.

"No-no, sir."

"Then keep your mouth shut." He locked eyes with Harms. "Give us a rebel yell, jelly-belly."

"Now, Jim . . ." Harms tried a weak smile. Sweat made his cheeks oily. This was too serious to ignore as a joke. Jim Manly was just drunk enough to shoot and not sober enough to be sorry about it later.

"The rebel yell," Jim said harshly. "I won't tell you again."

Fear bubbled up strong in Harms, overriding shame and pride. One thought was uppermost in his mind; obedience would relieve this danger. He licked his lips and threw back his head. "YYYeeeehhooooo!"

Jim Manly pounded the bar gleefully with his free hand and stomped his feet in a lively jig. "Well now, that's right jolly, Harms. Now, give us a song." He prodded Harms with the gun. "I said sing!"

The shame Harms felt was a stain that would discolor the rest of his life. In a detached way, he realized too late that he never should have shown Jim Manly anything but firmness; he was old enough to know how difficult it was to reason with an intoxicated man. But the damage was done; even as Harms thought this he knew that he would submit rather than run the risk of being shot.

In a high, trembling tenor, he launched into "Yellow Rose," much to Jim Manly's amusement. The men at the tables were too embarrassed to look at Harms; they stared at folded hands, and card pips, although the game was now dead. Even Hank Wilson tipped his head forward and tried to find some meaning in the yeasty pattern of his beer foam. Jim Manly stomped his feet and flogged his hand against the bar, keeping time to Harms's erratic voice.

As Harms began the second chorus, the saloon door banged open and Marshal McKitrich stepped inside, his expression hardened. Jim Manly's glance whipped past Harms and the gun shifted slightly. This wavering was a release to Harms. A sudden flash of black rage swept over him and he smashed down with his hand, driving Manly's gun across the sawdust-covered floor. There was an animal noise in his throat as he flung himself at the young man. He struck Manly in the throat with his fist, then bore him to the floor beneath his ponderous weight. Jim Manly's neck was soft and delightfully yielding beneath Harms's fingers; he was all at once possessed with a Herculean strength; an unholy flame of vengeful anger gave him a killer's instinct.

Jim Manly thrashed about, trying to free himself, trying to suck air into his starving lungs. He raked Harms's face with his fingernails and struck the sheriff repeatedly, but Harms would not let go. He whooped as Jim Manly's eyes began to bulge and his complexion turned bluish.

Hands tugged at Harms but he rolled his shoulders, trying to throw them off. Marshal McKitrich had his arm around Harms's throat and a knee in his back. Then suddenly Temple

Manly was there, striking at Harms's forearms until he finally released the boy.

Jim Manly was unconscious, and his father was shouting, "Get a doctor! For Christ's sake, get a doctor!"

The marshal of Red Rock was sitting on Harms and the fat man was staring glassy-eyed at the ceiling lamps. Harms breathed heavily, but after a moment his eyes took on focus. "Think you can behave yourself?" McKitrich asked.

"I—I must have lost my head," Harms said dazedly. McKitrich let him up, then stood close by as though he didn't trust him. Harms looked at Jim Manly, and at Temple Manly, trying desperately to revive his son. Slowly Harms shifted his feet and brushed the sawdust from his clothes.

"What the hell happened here?" McKitrich asked. "Who fired the shot?"

The bartender nodded toward Jim Manly. "He had too much to drink. Started picking on this fella here. Pulled his gun and made him act like a fool." He blew out a long breath. "Trouble with you, McKitrich, is that you always get here too quick. This time you ought to have stayed away a few minutes more. Sonofabitches like him is better off dead."

This brought Temple Manly to his feet, his face dark with anger. "That's my son there! You dare talk like that about my boy?"

"If he's yours then you ought to put a chain on him," the bartender said. "Goddamn, do you think I want my place shot up? Customers threatened? He's going to jail for this."

Caution returned to Temple Manly as he realized that he was not in his own bailiwick. To McKitrich he said, "Can't I settle for the damages? We're leaving in the morning and I . . ." He kept his voice gentle, hinting that he was the most reasonable of men.

"Have to talk to the judge," McKitrich said. "That all right with you, Larry?"

The bartender thought about it for a moment, then shrugged. "As long as he don't stay around here, I don't give a damn what happens to him." He picked up his bar rag and found a spot that needed polishing farther down the bar.

Seconds later, the doctor arrived. He was a fussy little man, all business. Jim Manly was starting to come around. He couldn't speak and the doctor went quickly about his examination, making certain that the damage was superficial. When young Manly was able to stand, the doctor asked, "Any of you his friend?"

"I'm his father," Temple Manly said.

"He's had a close one," the doctor opined. "Throat's badly bruised. Be a week or so before he can swallow solid food without pain." He scribbled on a pad of paper. "Take this to the railroad chemist near the station house. He'll give you a salve to apply. Keep the throat bandaged. The soreness will go away."

He left them, his coattails flapping. McKitrich took Jim Manly by the arm. "I'll have to lock you up until I talk to the judge."

"Is that really necessary?" Temple Manly wanted to know.

"It is in Red Rock," McKitrich said and propelled Jim toward the front door. The whiskey was now taking full effect, leaving the young man very ill.

As soon as McKitrich left, Temple Manly whirled on Harms. "Goddamn you, what was the . . ." Then he waved his hands. "Never mind, Harms. Never mind." He walked out, banging the front doors behind him. For a moment the saloon was silent, then the cards began to fall again and talk picked up to a hushed murmur.

Harms sagged against the bar, sweating, and yet not wanting to draw attention to that fact by wiping his face. The bartender slid a whiskey glass in front of him and said, "On the house."

"Thank you," Harms said with feeling.

While he drank his whiskey, the bartender walked over to the wall and picked up Jim Manly's gun. He laid it on the bar by Harms's elbow and said, "Never liked to have these things lying around. Some damn fool's liable to point one at you."

This was, Harms supposed, the man's way

of detracting some of the shame from Harms's conduct, but it didn't seem to help much. The bartender went on about his business and Hank Wilson eased up. "Didn't know you could sing," Wilson said. He gave Harms a sidling glance that contained a deep-rooted amusement, as though his private opinion had just been substantiated.

"Leave me alone," Harms said dully. "Go away, Hank."

"Now that's no way to treat your deputy," Wilson said. "Harms, you and me are going to be friends. Oh, yes we are. Real friends." He wiggled his finger for the bartender. "Give my friend another whiskey here." Then he let his voice drop to a softly confidential tone. "Harms, I'm going to let you in on a secret. Now I'll do that because I know you'll keep it." He stopped talking while the bartender slid the drink in front of Harms. As soon as the man moved away, Wilson went on. "Cardigan didn't rob the express company."

For a moment, Harms remained still, then he looked narrow-eyed at Hank Wilson. "What's this? You said . . ."

"I said I saw Cardigan leaving town in a hurry, and that's a fact; I did. But Wes didn't steal any money. Likely it happened just like he told his sister. Sims got excited and flung a shot at him and Wes got excited and shot back."

"But, my God, you wanted to hang the man!"

"Keep your fool voice down," Wilson snapped. He sipped his beer and smiled. "Sure, why not hang him? The world's overrun now with nobodies. Who the hell would miss one?" He paused to wipe his mouth. "Wes didn't take the money, but he shot Sims. Now who the hell cares whether he meant it or not? Since he did shoot the old man, it won't be hard to convince people that he took the money too." Wilson smiled. "Hanging Wes is as good a way as any to keep him from denying that he took it. No sir, Wes is sure enough innocent; another man's guilty, but I don't give a damn about him either. Just the money."

"You begin to make sense to me," Harms said. "I see through you now, Hank. You always meant to steal this money back and keep it for yourself."

"Why not?" Wilson said. "Harms, this fella can't say a word without tipping his hand." His smile was deep and satisfied. "Perfect, ain't it? Wes goes to jail for everything and I end up with the money while the real thief just grits his teeth and takes it."

"Who robbed the express . . ."

"Uh-uh," Wilson said. "Now I share some of my secrets, but not all of 'em. Don't pay to trust a man too far, Harms, especially some gutless wonder like you." He let his smile fade. "All I got to do is find where he hid it, and I guess there'll be plenty of time after we get back to Gunlock."

"Yes," Harms said. "There'll be plenty of time." He tossed off his drink and left the saloon, crossing the street to the hotel. He sat on the porch, his feet on the railing, contemplating the dismal turn of events. Somehow he had never quite believed that Wes Cardigan was guilty; the man had run from panic, but that had cooled and now he had gone back home, seeking justice. It made sense.

Within Harms's jellied core, there still lurked some shreds of honesty, and the knowledge that Hank Wilson was trying to end up eight thousand dollars richer at another man's expense left Harms with a sick feeling. He supposed he could tell Temple Manly the whole story, but the outcome was uncomfortably predictable; Manly would kick him out of office without delay. He thought of recrossing the street and telling Hank to go to the devil, but that took a measure of courage and Harms realized that he could never carry it through.

Long ago he had learned how high was the price for being weak; unscrupulous men used him and threw him aside, but never before like this. His constantly overhauled set of principles had never forced him into a criminal act until now. Harms lighted a cigar but found little pleasure in the smoke. Perhaps if he studied the situation, he could come up with the robber's identity before Hank could go through with his plan. Knowing who had taken the money would be an advantage.

Perhaps he could even recover it before Hank got his hands on it. The thought carried a little hope, but that soon faded. Hank had no doubt considered that possibility already, and Harms didn't underestimate his deputy. Wilson would never stand by and watch the money slip through his fingers.

From down the street Marshal McKitrich walked Jim Manly back to the hotel. The young man's throat was thickly bandaged. When young Manly came onto the porch and saw Harms sitting there, he stopped. Manly's voice, when he spoke, was barely above a whisper.

"I'll settle with you," he promised.

"I think nearly everything's been settled," Harms said with unusual conviction. "Why don't you grow up?"

"Better get on up to your room," McKitrich said, and when Jim Manly hesitated, he gave him a shove. "Go on now. Do as I tell you."

As soon as Jim Manly entered the lobby, McKitrich perched on the porch rail, facing Harms. "You were rough on him." He shrugged. "Can't blame you though. Most of the trouble starts with the young ones. If they're lucky and live long enough, they wise up and turn out fairly decent." He nodded toward the upstairs. "The kid's old man's a bull who likes his own way, don't he?"

"He's an important man," Harms said.

"Not in Red Rock," McKitrich said. "You know the fella you're after?"

"Yes," Harms said. "I believe he's innocent."

"Like to see it turn out that way," McKitrich remarked. "That may sound strange from a man whose business it is to arrest people, but I'd rather see 'em innocent than guilty." He paused, as a man will when he has something on his mind and is unsure how to say it. "I've been on a posse or two in my time, but I've never seen anything like this one. Instead of sticking to business, they all act like they got reasons of their own for being here." He rubbed his hands together. "I guess I didn't say that very good."

"I believe you made your point," Harms said. He got up and cast his cigar into the street. "Well, it's late and there's the early morning train to catch." As he turned toward the door, Hank Wilson came out of the saloon and across the street. He passed Harms, nodding briefly to McKitrich, then went on up the stairs.

McKitrich left the porch, walking on down the street. Harms watched as he tried a door or two to see if they were locked, then lost interest in the man and went to his own room. He fumbled for the lamp, got it going, then lay back on his bed, the springs protesting at his weight. A step made a loose board squeak in the hall, and he felt an irresistible impulse to pick up his gun. With the weapon in his hand, he waited, then knuckles tapped lightly, startling him, even though he had somehow anticipated the knock.

"Who is it?"

"Temple Manly. Can I come in?"

Harms got up and opened the door; it had not been locked, but a man always opened doors for Temple Manly. Manly's expression was stern, but without anger, which was some relief to Harms.

After closing the door, Harms moved a chair closer. "Sit down, Mr. Manly. I'm real sorry about tonight, sir. Lost my head. I suppose the boy was just letting off steam."

"Yes," Manly said, "I suppose he was." He massaged his hands together and crossed his legs, only to promptly uncross them again. "Harms, I think we ought to reach an understanding."

"About what, Mr. Manly?"

"Wes Cardigan," Manly said. He gnawed at his lower lip for a moment, then added, "Naturally, I hold no personal animosity for the man. I myself would have fought with everything I had if faced with those odds. But I want that stolen money recovered. Do that, and I can guarantee that you'll be reelected until Doomsday."

"Well, Mr. Manly, I don't think Wes did . . ."

184

"I didn't come here to quibble about what he did or didn't do," Manly said flatly. "I've given this matter a lot of thought and I know what I'm doing. Harms, I just want you to present the facts to the jury: Cardigan shot Sims; likely he'll admit that on grounds that it was self-defense. And he *was* at the express office; by his own admission to his sister. The verdict I'm content to leave up to the jury. Do you understand?"

"Yes, sir. But the money . . ."

"I figure that he hasn't had time to spend it yet," Manly said. "The money has to be produced or we'll all look like fools." He got up and walked to the window, and stood there looking down at the dark street. "I'd like to help the boy, Harms. You know I would. But he's put me in a position where I can do little for him. Now, you find that money, Harms. You've got a good job and I'd like to see you keep it. We've always got along, you and me."

"I don't know about . . ."

Manly swung around, his expression inflexible. "Harms, I don't care what you know. You do as I say or, by God, we'll get a new sheriff!" He walked to the door and paused with his hand on the knob. "Use your head, man. More than likely he'll be ready to give himself up by the time we get back. Act right and the arrest will look good come election time. And I'll see that they remember how good it looked."

"All right, Mr. Manly. All right."

After Temple Manly stepped out and closed the door, Harms sat down wearily on the edge of the bed and stared hopelessly at the floor. This was, he decided, the most terrible moment of his life. He had always studiously evaded decisions and now he was being forced to make an impossible one.

Temple Manly's way, or Hank Wilson's? Either way he would have to lose; either way, he would have to face one of them afterward, and he was equipped to face neither.

NINE

Temple Manly breakfasted before daylight and with still twenty minutes to go until train time he walked to the station platform to stand, rifle in hand, saddle at his feet, an infinite patience masking his thoughts. Through the freight agent he had made arrangements to ship the horses as far as Willows; Harry Buck and Kohler had earlier supervised the loading into an empty cattle car. Manly was a little impatient for the train to arrive and take him home. He wondered if this was the same impatience a fighter must feel just before entering the ring; even as he dreaded facing Gunlock, he felt an eagerness to have it over with. That was his way, head-on, and this had pulled him through some bad moments in the past.

While Manly waited, Harry Buck came around the corner of the telegrapher's shack, his boots crunching the cinders. He dropped his saddle and settled his shoulders against the wall. The day was clear and cloudless; there was a promise of early heat in the sky. Buck shook out his sack of tobacco and rolled a cigarette. Afterward he offered the tobacco to Manly, who accepted it.

"Thanks. I ran out." His fingers creased the

paper with customary care, then he sifted in the tobacco and leveled it.

Harry Buck glanced briefly at Temple Manly. "That all you're out of, tobacco?" He chuckled. "You want to know the truth, I'm about run out of steam. That Wes has run me to a nub. Gunlock's going to seem different," he added. "Course, that's 'cause *we're* different."

"I'm the same," Temple Manly stated bluntly. Even as he spoke he recognized the native untruth in the statement; he had changed, but a man had to keep such admissions to himself.

"Maybe you're the same," Buck said, "but I sure as hell ain't." He drew deeply on his smoke. "Kohler ain't either. He's tired and disgusted and don't give a damn any more."

"He should have stayed home in the first place," Manly said. "He's soft in the head."

"Wilson ain't," Buck pointed out. "You been watchin' Wilson, Mr. Manly? He ain't got drunk since we started, and he could have got liquored up easy enough last night." Buck shied his smoke onto the cinders and thrust his hands deep into his pants pockets. "You know how Hank likes the stuff, yet he took the trouble to stay sober. I'd say he's changed some."

"Not for the good," Manly said. "Wilson's trash. Always has been and always will be."

"How about Jim?" Harry asked. "A week ago he was just a lazy kid who played a bad game of cards and laughed at everything. Now he's killed a man and . . ."

"My son is not a subject for discussion," Temple Manly warned.

Harry Buck's shoulders rose and fell. "I guess you'd stick up for him no matter what happened. Which is all right; kin should stick together." He fell into a thoughtful silence.

Manly glanced at him, hoping this would be the end of the talk. Yet he suspected that Buck was not through; the man's stubbornness nearly equaled his own, which made disliking him quite easy.

The arrival of the others kept Buck from renewing his pointed observations. Harms came first, puffing along, sweat ashine on his florid face. Kohler followed a moment or two later; he nodded to Manly but did not speak. Finally Hank Wilson arrived, his thin face expressionless.

Harms took out a dirty handkerchief and mopped his face. "Hot," he said, to no one in particular.

"Be hot in Gunlock too," Wilson murmured. "But I ain't going to mind it."

Manly shot him a quick, irritated glance, but the deputy was staring down the track as though watching for the train. Betty Cardigan walked onto the platform, saw Harry Buck, then went over to stand beside him. Manly observed this and wondered what lay between these two that he didn't know about.

"Be glad to get back though," Harms said, speaking to them all. "I sure hope Wes don't give us any trouble."

"What the hell do you think he's given us already?" Kohler snapped. He took off his hat, adjusted the crease, then put it back on his head. "I got better use for my time than to chase after a man you should have been able to catch by yourself, Harms."

To forestall further discussion, Temple Manly turned to Buck. "You're sure they'll pick up the car with the horses?"

"On the siding and waiting," Buck said.

Marshal McKitrich came down the street, Jim Manly parading sullenly before him. Temple Manly frowned when he saw this, for like most heavy-handed men, he resented this manner in others. There was no reason, to his way of thinking, for treating the boy this way, like a common criminal.

Jim Manly didn't speak to anyone; his throat was too sore to torture with words. Marshal McKitrich nodded to Temple Manly, who responded with restrained civility.

The marshal brought out his watch and said, "Ten minutes. I'll see you on the train."

"Is that really necessary?" Temple Manly demanded.

"The judge made it pretty clear," McKitrich said.

Out on the flats the westbound hooted for a grade crossing, then came on, belching smoke. As the train rumbled into the station, Temple Manly hefted his rifle and saddle, and when a vestibule step presented itself, Manly swung aboard. He went forward; there were plenty of vacant seats. Settling into one, he slid his saddle beneath his feet and propped his rifle against the window frame. A dozen passengers held scattered positions throughout the car. There were three men farther forward, and a woman with two small children. Her face wore a harried expression that spoke of tedious miles traveled.

Manly endured the aggravating lurch and shift of the coach while the cattle car was picked up. Then the engineer shrieked his whistle and the train pulled out of Red Rock with a snapping of couplings. Manly tipped his hat forward over his eyes and leaned back in the seat, letting the clack of the tracks lull him.

He slept, but not well; he began to wonder if he would ever be able to get a good night's sleep again. The children ran whooping up and down the aisle, climbing onto laps, and the woman was forever chasing and scolding them, but this wasn't what disturbed him most. A pall of anxiety weighed upon him and the ride seemed interminable; at times he wished that Kohler or

Buck would come forward and talk, but they left him alone. The recognition of his desire for companionship annoyed Manly, for he had always preferred solitude. Only lately had he found it almost unendurable.

Darkness had fallen by the time the train pulled into Willows, a small, two-street town, thirty-four miles north of Gunlock. Manly got off first and stood on the platform, looking at the town he had killed with his own personal ambition. Fifteen years before, this had been the cattle center for a hundred-mile radius, but he had put an end to that by growing big. Towns grew and flourished where the money was most plentiful, and Manly's payroll came to fifteen thousand a year. So he had nourished Gunlock at Willows's expense; a man couldn't run two towns and Gunlock had been closest to him. All that remained to keep the town alive now were a few hard-scrabble ranchers, men who did not fit into Temple Manly's plans.

Buck and Wilson went to the cattle car for their horses, and then the train pulled out of the small station, leaving behind the dampness of steam and the odors of hot oil.

John Kohler came up behind Manly and said, "Not much left of the place, is there?" He had known Willows in its heyday for he had once lived here. Yet there was no particular resentment in Kohler; he seemed to understand the price others had to pay for the success the Manlys of the world enjoyed.

"A town is like a man; it has to fight for life."

"That's a hard way to put it," Kohler said. "But then, you never were a man for doin' anything the easy way."

"It's suited me," Manly said. Silently, he cursed Kohler's attitude; he always felt a compulsion to apologize to his kind, much the same as he would reach down and pet a dog after accidentally stepping on its foot.

He was relieved when the horses were led up. Near the saloon sat the stage office, open and brightly lighted, for the southbound coach was due to arrive. A mild sprinkle of traffic cluttered the street and the saloon looked bright and inviting.

Hank Wilson said, "By God, I got time to get me a drink." He wiped a hand across his mouth and grinned.

"Just a minute," Manly said. "I'll ride your horse, Wilson. You and Jim take the stage into Gunlock." He spoke quickly, like he didn't want to argue about it. Then he waited to see how Wilson would take it.

"Like hell," Wilson said. "I bought that horse and no one rides him but me." He jerked his thumb toward Jim Manly. "Boss him all you want, but I do what I damned please!"

"I'll go on the stage," Betty Cardigan said.

"You can ride my horse, Mr. Manly." She was tired. Tired of trouble and tired of arguing. Vaguely she understood that Manly was trying to rid himself of two unsettling influences, and she pitied him because she knew it would not work.

"Thank you." He looked at his son. "Go with her."

John Kohler slid his mild voice into the conversation. "Mr. Manly, I'd as soon take the stage."

"All right," Manly said. "There's no sense standing here arguing about it." His glance touched Betty Cardigan. "If you need any money . . ."

"I'll buy her ticket," Kohler said flatly. He turned away, then looked back. "This has been one hell of a waste of time, if you ask me."

Harry Buck looked around, then threw his saddle and blanket on his horse and pulled tight the cinch. He watched Kohler and Betty Cardigan enter the stage office, then gave his attention to Hank Wilson. "That's one less man you have to worry about," he said. "Make you happy, Hank?"

"Don't make me sad," Wilson admitted. "We'll beat 'em to Gunlock by two hours if we get a move on."

"And what does two hours buy you?" Buck asked.

"Don't know for sure yet," Wilson admitted. "See when I get there." He swung up and a moment later Manly and the others were mounted.

Manly wasted no time in Willows; he rode down the main street and out on the south road, the posse strung out behind him. A few of the townspeople watched and wondered what this was all about, but he did not give them the opportunity to find out. He was more than a little disturbed for he had counted on ridding himself of his son and Hank Wilson; he had planned to make Cardigan's arrest his first aggressive act on returning to Gunlock, and he knew that it would be easier without Wilson and Jim. The fact that he now mistrusted his own son filled him with a momentary shame, but he pushed it aside. A fact was a fact to Temple Manly and Jim had proved how unreliable he really was.

He tried to understand the young man and failed utterly. How different he seemed now; he supposed the change had come about when Indian Reilly was killed. So sudden and positive, almost as though Jim had been eager to destroy something, anything, as a token of the anger that seethed within him.

Manly broke off this mental speculation and settled down to the ride. He made a few stops, but generally maintained a brisk pace. At eleven, he topped the last rise and stopped, the others bunched behind him. The sprinkled lights of Gunlock lay below and a mile beyond.

Harry Buck said, "Nothing looks as good as home, does it?"

"I got a bed down there," Harms said. "A damned soft bed."

"Then why don't you just go down there and sleep your head off," Hank Wilson said sarcastically.

Temple Manly still led them as they crossed the wooden bridge at the west end of Peace Street. The clatter alerted the fringe of traffic along the boardwalks, then the posse passed on between the avenue of buildings.

Gunlock was a town whose growth had long ago been established and had since been arrested; more than likely, a dozen years would not see it grow larger or shrink appreciably. Peace Street was comfortably wide, flanked by frame buildings, tree-shaded walks and hitch racks that extended three blocks east to Charity Street, the last cross street in town.

As Manly rode toward the hotel, someone on the boardwalk yelled, "Hey, it's Mr. Manly!" The call set up a commotion; doors banged as card games were suddenly abandoned. Apparently, the town had been waiting for Manly to arrive.

He had suspected that this might happen and silently he cursed the unidentified man for he would have preferred a quiet entrance. Now that hope was blasted. As he passed Lovering's saloon, men boiled out the door and forged into the street; he had no alternative but to swing in and dismount.

A crowd gathered on the run; he was surprised that so many people were still about at this late hour. Giles Stutchel, who was Gunlock's mayor, exited from the newspaper office at a run, coattails flapping. With Stutchel's arrival, some semblance of official dignity settled over the excited crowd. Manly was tying his horse; he stepped onto the boardwalk to meet Stutchel.

"Now move along, fellas," Stutchel was saying to the crowd. "Go on, there, give Mr. Manly some room." He was a moon-faced man, who tried his best to affect a dignified manner. The throng paid him no mind; their attention was on Temple Manly.

"To hell with you," one man said. "It's a free country. By God, we think as much of Mr. Manly as you do and we got a right to worry."

For an instant, Manly had difficulty resisting an impulse to place a finger in his ear to clear it; he was positive that he had heard incorrectly. He looked searchingly at the faces around him, fully expecting to see mocking laughter, but he read only relief, and the respect they had always accorded him. Manly felt shaken as his fears vanished, and was oddly humbled by the experience.

"Thank Heaven you got back safely," Stutchel was saying. "When Wes rode into town, big as you please, we all thought he'd maybe bushwhacked you someplace."

"That's hardly likely," Manly said slowly. That he could be so calm, pleased and surprised him; he knew that his manner impressed those looking on, yet he was not trying to impress them. Their genuine concern had left him slightly light-headed. They liked him as a man! Liked him in spite of the fact that he controlled their town.

"Where is Cardigan?" Harms asked.

"In jail," Stutchel said. "But don't concern yourself about it, Mr. Manly. He'll stay there and we'll see that he does. Didn't quite know what to do with him. Wait, that's what I said. Wait until Mr. Manly gets back."

"Who put Cardigan in jail?" Harry Buck asked. He looked at the sour-faced Wilson; the man was gnawing his lip and wondering what had gone wrong. These men should have been sneering and making a joke of this, yet they stood in respectful silence, waiting for Manly to speak.

"Wes locked himself in jail and threw the keys into the alley," Stutchel said. He looked questioningly at Temple Manly, wanting to be told what to do.

Manly let the silence run on for a moment; he needed time to overhaul his thinking. Since Cardigan's calculated move had been without effect, he decided that charity toward the man would be more understood than bitterness.

"Harms would have arrested him anyway," Manly said. "Leave him where he is."

One of the men standing on the walk reached out playfully and slapped Wilson's hat brim. "Cheer up, Hank. Don't look so damned disappointed."

A titter of amusement rippled through the crowd. "What's the matter, Hank?" another asked. "You want to hang someone so damned bad, then go throw your rope over a rafter in the stable and stretch your own neck."

Stutchel raised his hands for silence but he could not stop the laughter. Someone set up a cheer for Temple Manly and he had to smile and wave his hands before they would stop. Hank Wilson made an obscure remark in a disgusted voice and wheeled down the street, leading his horse. Jeers and ribald comments followed him while Harms smiled and turned politician, mingling jovially with the crowd.

"Everyone into Lovering's," Manly called. "The drinks are on me."

The crowd cheered again and started a small stampede toward the saloon. While the laughter died in his ears, Temple Manly stood with his head tipped forward, his expression composed.

"Different from what you expected, wasn't it?" Buck asked softly. He shrugged. "Maybe they

like you, Mr. Manly. Better than you thought."
He turned to his horse but stopped when Manly
spoke.

"Buck. Buck, I'd like to think that we parted
friends."

"Why sure," Buck said, a smile lifting his
lips. "There's no bone to pick between us, Mr.
Manly."

"I suppose you're going home now."

"No. I thought I'd wait in town for Betty."
He stepped into the saddle and rode toward the
stable.

Temple Manly turned to his son, who had stood
tightlipped and grim through all of this. "Go on
home, Jim. Tell your mother I'll not be late."

"Hell, I thought I'd stay and . . ."

Temple Manly unexpectedly flapped the back
of his hand across his son's face, then was
instantly sorry. "Jim! Jim, boy, I didn't mean
that!" He took Jim by the shoulder, gently. "I'm
all worked up, boy. Bone-tired and irritable." He
shook his son gently. "Jim, I'm sorry. Will you
just mind me, for once?"

"Sure," the young man said sullenly. "What
the hell does it matter now?"

Temple Manly watched him mount and ride
out. Then he walked down the street, his boots
thumping the boardwalk as he tried to ease
the torment of his blisters. In the darkness he
could let his relief soften his rigid expression;

he could hold close the knowledge that he was a man liked by his neighbor, a man trusted and respected. He wondered what had caused him to doubt himself. Tired probably. A man filled up with foolish notions when he was so tired.

On Charity Street he turned north toward the jail. The building sat on the corner of the courthouse plot, gray sandstone with the cell block shaped in an ell. The lamps were lit in the outer office and Manly found the door unlocked.

He went in and walked directly to the cell block. Wes Cardigan was asleep and Manly paused for a moment to study this man who had had such an effect on his life. Stranger still that the effect should all have been reflected, without personal contact. Cardigan was a man in his mid-twenties, an ordinary man, difficult to distinguish from the million others like him in the world. He was fair-haired, with a face so average that a man would forget it five minutes after he saw it. Cardigan was poor; his Levi's and brush jacket were many-windowed. His battered hat lay in forlorn proximity to his worn boots.

Temple Manly rattled the cell door and Cardigan sat up, shaking his head to clear the sleep from his eyes. He looked at Manly, then said, "You made good time getting here." He patted his pockets for tobacco and found none. "Got anything to smoke?"

"No, I'm out too. I'll have someone bring you a sack."

"I'd appreciate that," Cardigan said. "You mad about the horses?" He shook his head regretfully. "You kept on coming, Mr. Manly, and I was scared. I didn't know of any other way."

"A man can always buy another horse," Manly said. "But you had no reason to fear me, Cardigan."

"I guess not," the young man said. "Funny you can't see that at the time." He pawed his mouth out of shape and rested his elbows on his knees. "Mr. Manly, I've had a real scare." He searched Manly's face with serious eyes. "I don't want to hang for shootin' Sims."

"That's hardly likely," Manly said. "If the shooting was an accident like you say, then . . ."

"What I say and what it'll be after a lawyer gets through twisting it around is another thing." He stood up and came to the bars. "Mr. Manly, you're a big man and you don't owe me a damn thing, but I've got to have help. I know I got no right to ask but . . ."

"You'll have to stand trial," Manly said. "But there won't be any hanging. That's why I went along with Harms, to see that there wasn't any hanging."

"Funny thing," Cardigan said. "After Sims fell, all I wanted to do was run for home, but once I got there, I knew it wasn't safe for me. I trusted Harms, but not Wilson. He'd kill a man just to make himself look good. So I figured that the country was big enough to swallow me up. Only I didn't count on you, Mr. Manly. Kohler, I figured, would get tired and turn back. Buck would go with him. Then I discovered that you were along and all that country seemed to shrink up. Gunlock was the only place for me. Here in jail, where I belonged."

"I'll get you a lawyer in the morning," Manly said. "If you're innocent . . ."

"Hell, yes, I'm innocent!" Then Cardigan seemed to withdraw into himself. He stepped back, his eyes veiled by the shadows cast from the wall lamp. "No, Mr. Manly, don't get me a lawyer just yet. Give me time to think."

"All right," Manly said. "You know where to reach me if you want anything."

"Sure. My sister all right?"

"She's coming in on the stage," Manly said. He took out his watch and glanced at it. "Late. I have to go."

He left the cell block and found Harms just entering the outer office. Harms took off his coat and hat and hung them up. He nodded toward the back. "I ought to be mad at him, but somehow I ain't." He lowered his bulk into the chair behind the desk. "Turned out kind of surprising for Hank, didn't it? I mean, folks didn't . . ."

"Yes," Manly said briefly, hinting to Harms

that he was again talking too much. Then he recalled his final conversation with Harms in Red Rock; this had to be set right. "Ah, I don't think it's necessary to go ahead as we planned, Harms. Treat the boy with courtesy and I'll try to get him a good lawyer."

"But, Mr. Manly, you said you wanted him convicted."

"Damn it, I know what I said."

"All right, sir. You can rely on me."

This was debatable, but Manly decided not to challenge it. "There's no need to bring Buck or Kohler into the picture," he said. "I'll see Allendale in the morning. Perhaps we can get him to drop the charges against Cardigan." Manly stretched and walked tenderly to the door; his feet felt like two pods of fire. "I'm going home now."

The sheriff watched the door close, then he let the worry he felt stain his expression. By some miracle, Temple Manly had eased him off the hook, as far as he was concerned. But there was still the problem of Hank Wilson.

Harms walked to the cell block and found Wes Cardigan sitting on the bunk.

Cardigan asked, "Did you find the keys, Harms?"

"One of the boys picked them up and gave them to me," Harms said. "Mr. Manly's on your side, Wes. Takes a big man to feel that way after you did your damndest to make him look foolish." He took out his sack of tobacco and rolled a smoke, then passed the makings and matches through the bars. "What did you do with the money, Wes?"

"Money?" Cardigan looked up quickly. "Harms, I didn't rob that office. Christ, I thought you figured that out already."

"What I figured out ain't important," Harms said. "Mr. Manly wants to clear you, Wes, and it'll go a lot easier if you cooperate with us."

"But I don't have it! How the hell can I give you something I don't have?"

Harms shook his head. "Wes, there ain't no need to argue back and forth about whether you're innocent or guilty. We know you shot Sims and I guess it wouldn't be too hard for a jury to be convinced that you robbed the place too. You want to confess, I'll see that you get off as easy as the law allows."

"Ah, you go to hell," Cardigan said. "You don't give a damn about me, just how you're going to look at the trial."

"Important things first," Harms said. He drew on his smoke, his eyes squeezed nearly shut. "Wes, you think about it. And while you're thinking, remember that this is Manly's town. He's on your side now, but I wouldn't do anything to change that. Folks like us has just got to admit what's good for us and take it."

TEN

Temple Manly's ride to the home place was one of ease, for he felt at ease in his mind. He became almost maudlin as he recalled the reception that had awaited him in Gunlock, and in retrospect his previous fears seemed stupid and childish. For the first time in many years he reveled in the pleasure of being liked for himself; they surely must have felt that way for they had every reason to laugh. How ironic that he should underestimate his importance to the town. Had he actually felt so insecure as to think that a desperate man's gamble would unseat him?

I've thought too much about money, he decided, and made a mental vow to unbend a little in relations with his fellow man. When he rode into his own ranch yard, he found George waiting to take his horse. He was suddenly conscious of the fact that ever since he had hired the man eight years before, he could ride in, day or night, and find George there. He wondered if the man ever left his post to sleep.

George took the reins as Manly stepped down. He was a dry-expressioned man with a doglike loyalty. "Mr. James got home about twenty minutes ago, sir."

"Thank you, George. This is Betty Cardigan's

pony. See that it's taken care of and returned first thing in the morning."

"Yes, sir. Everything's all right here. I took Mrs. Manly to town like you said. Some things came in from Dallas."

"What things?"

"Stuff she wanted for the house," George said. "I believe Mrs. Manly is waiting in the parlor, sir. She's been worried about you."

Manly almost let his surprise show; Lila had not been much concerned with his coming and going for many years. "Ah, thank you, George. Better go to bed now."

"Yes, sir. It's good to have you back, Mr. Manly."

Manly turned, then looked back. "Why do you say that, George?"

The question was odd and unexpected; George seemed confused. "Why—we like it here, sir, working for you. We wouldn't want anything to change, that's all."

"Yes," Manly said briefly. "Good night, George."

"Good night, sir."

Manly walked slowly toward the house, walking carefully on his heels to favor the blisters. The front windows shed light onto the porch. When he stepped into the hall, Lila came to meet him.

He hung up his hat and coat and leaned his

rifle against the wall. Lila said, "You must be very tired, Temple."

"Yes. Yes, I am." He walked into the parlor and sank into his soft leather chair, stretching his feet out before him. He wanted to take off his boots to ease his blisters, but decided to wait for the privacy of his room. She would fuss over him in that gentle, detached way she had, as though he were a child who needed comfort, and Temple Manly did not want that kind of comfort.

"Jim is in his room," Lila said quietly. She sat down and picked up her sewing, her fingers beginning to move with maddening regularity. He watched her for a moment, then reached for the tobacco that lay on the table.

"I wish to God I'd never taken him along," Temple Manly said.

She spoke without looking at him. "Did he disgrace you, Temple?"

"No," he said. "No, it's not that. I just don't understand him any more."

"Temple, did you ever really try?"

He waved his hand in exasperation. "That's not what I'm talking about, Lila. Jim killed a man. He and Indian Reilly had some sort of argument; I don't think anyone really knew what it was about. Reilly made a flourish with his rifle and Jim just shot him. . . . Lila," he said, "didn't you hear me?"

"Yes, I heard you. Jim told me everything as soon as he got home." She put her sewing aside then and when she looked at him, her expression was aloof and quite strange to him. "He told me everything. How you rode him constantly and how you let the others ride him."

He half rose from his chair. "That's a damned lie!"

"Is it?" She shook her head. "Temple, the simple truth is, you've never been his friend. Why should I believe you and doubt Jim? Don't you think that I know my own son?"

His mind whirled, trying to grasp the meaning of this. Why would the boy say a thing like that? What had he done to deserve it? He said, "Lila, there are some men no one knows. Jim is like that."

"He's not. To you, who never cared, he may seem so. But not to me, his mother." She clasped her hands and found comfort in her unassailable position.

"*Lila, he killed a man!* I saw it." Manly moved his hands in a futile effort to find a medium of expression. "I've seen killings before—but this just came out of nowhere. It happened too fast, and he didn't care afterward. Of course it was self-defense but . . ."

"He explained that too, Temple." She gave him a slightly superior smile. "That horse has always been his favorite. Why, he'd hardly let George saddle him; you know that. He never let anyone touch him."

"That's not reason enough to kill a man!" Temple Manly said and stood up. He felt a sudden premonition, an undefined danger. The boy held the answer; Manly started for the hallway.

"Where are you going?" she asked quickly.

"To talk to him."

"I want you to leave him alone," she said firmly. "Temple, please sit down. There's something I want to talk to you about. Something very important."

"You think this isn't?"

"Please," she said, then waited until he resumed his seat. "While you were gone, I did some thinking. It's difficult to think around you, Temple. You overpower people. But you weren't here to do that to me, so I could make up my mind this time."

"Make it up about what?"

"Us," she said. "Temple, I know that I displease you. We seem to have lost something somewhere; I don't think we can ever get it back." Her fingers toyed nervously with a pleat in her blouse. "What I'm trying to say is that I was alone and I liked it. I may have liked it too much." She paused to take a deep breath. "Temple, I want to leave. Go back east and live."

He sat still in his chair, stunned beyond belief.

211

Finally he roused himself and said, "Did I hear you right?" He felt as though he was being buried alive; one unpleasantness was being heaped on another.

"It's a shock to you, I know," she said. "Yes, I meant what I said. I want to leave. I mean to leave. But of course I waited until you came back so I could tell you; it seemed quite heartless to leave only a letter."

He closed his eyes for a moment. "Lila, I don't know what to say."

"There's nothing to say," she said calmly. "I've asked George to drive me into Gunlock tomorrow morning; my things are all packed. I'll take the Willows stage and then a train to Philadelphia. Of course, you'll have to send me money regularly, but then . . ."

"Stop it!" He slammed his fists against the padded arms of his chair. "Lila, this is unthinkable!"

"Yes, I'm afraid it is, but I've made up my mind. Temple, do we really love each other any more? Once we did, but these last ten years have been busy ones for you and I'm no longer important to you." She looked at him squarely. "Would you really try to stop me, Temple? I'm afraid the gossip then would be worse than if you just let me go quietly."

"You have it all figured out, haven't you?"

"Yes. You could say that I'm visiting; everyone

212

knows that I have a brother in Philadelphia. In a few months, the visit can quietly be extended. The gossip will die out easy enough."

He tipped his head forward and closed his eyes. He had difficulty believing that she could mean what she said, yet he knew that she meant every word. He got up again and left the room, walking down the hall toward his son's room. Because of his deep preoccupation he opened the door without knocking, something he had never done before.

Jim Manly was sitting on his bed, staring at the floor. Temple Manly said, "Jim, it's time we had a talk. Did you have to lie to your mother?"

"Lie?" Jim Manly's voice was still a hoarse whisper in his injured throat. "Damn it, I didn't lie. Don't you recognize the truth when you see it?"

Conclusions came with smothering rapidity to Temple Manly and he leaned against the wall near the door, afraid that his legs would no longer sustain him. "You wanted to kill someone and Reilly was handy," he said. "Jim, what has gotten into you that you could do a thing like that?"

"Do I have to have a reason?" Jim said. His pistol belt lay on the bed and he took the holster and gun and held them in his lap, his fingers curled almost lovingly around the polished butt. "What's all the fuss anyway? Reilly was nothing but a dumb Injun."

"Jim, I just don't understand. Did you do it to hurt me?" Temple Manly could hear Lila's step coming down the hall and realized that his voice had carried. When he turned to close the door, Lila put her hand against it.

"Don't close me out, Temple. You've done that for the last time."

This angered him, this array of lies and deceit against him. "All right!" he said. He took her by the arm and pulled her into the room. "Look at him. Look at your son! He's not a damn bit sorry. Given a chance, he'll kill someone else."

She looked at the young man. "Would you, Jim?" She really needed no answer; Jim Manly was brazenly unashamed. She frowned slightly. "You'll have to understand that what you did was wrong, Jim." Somehow her voice seemed too calm, too gentle.

"I told you I was sorry," he said belligerently. He looked at his father. "Telling you that doesn't mean anything, does it?"

"You've told me that too many times," Temple Manly said wearily. "Jim, you can't keep buying yourself off with apologies."

"What do you want me to do?" Jim asked. "Hell, the man's dead. I can't bring him back to life." This was the extent of the sorrow; the I-didn't-mean-to stage. Temple Manly felt slightly ill.

"Reilly was a human being. Doesn't that mean anything to you?" Manly was suddenly aware

214

that he was capable of suspecting his son of anything.

"It's done and can't be undone," Lila said. "Jim, you're still our son. Do you think we're trying to punish you?"

"I think he needs punishment," Temple Manly said, but she put her hand on his arm and silenced him.

"We can talk about that later," Lila said. "Temple, give him a chance to think about it."

"Give him a chance? Jesus Christ, I've given him a thousand chances."

"Please! Let him alone, Temple."

"Jim, we're not through discussing this," Temple Manly warned.

"Perhaps in the morning," Lila said, taking her husband's arm. "Will a few hours matter?"

"I don't suppose anything matters any more," Manly said heavily. "Lila, the boy's completely without honor."

"That's a terrible thing to say!" She opened the door and urged Manly into the hall. "Temple, we must talk about this like sensible people. How can you believe he's really bad?"

"What more does he have to do to prove it? Good God, didn't you see him sitting there with his hand on his gun?"

"But he was frightened," Lila said. She forced him into his easy chair. "Temple, do try to understand him."

"Understand him?" He laughed hollowly. "Lila, that's the trouble; I'm afraid that I do now and I don't like what I know. That was no bluff with his gun. He would have shot me as quick as the next man."

"Please," she said. "We're not going to solve anything by getting hysterical. He's our son and we have to stand by him."

He stared at her. "Lila, I've lived my life by pretty strict rules of honor. Do you think I can lie to myself?"

"I think you'll have to compromise," she said. "Temple, this will be the last thing I'll ever ask you to do: stand by him now and see that no harm comes to him."

"You mean smooth this over?" He was really arguing against himself; in the back of his mind lay the certainty that he must protect the boy. Even now he was looking for a way.

She bit her lip slightly. "I didn't want to put it that way, but since you've said it, yes. You have money and power. What good are these things if you can't use them to help Jim?"

"How can I?" he asked. "Could I convince people that killing Reilly was accidental? Is that what you're asking?"

"Yes, if you have to. Just buy him another chance, Temple."

He rubbed his hands together. "Lila, I . . ."

"I've been a disappointment to you as a wife.

You don't have to tell me; I've known for a long time." She took a deep breath before plunging on. "Well, I'll stay with you and be the kind of wife you want, if you'll do what you can for Jim. And that means saving him from another mistake."

"A deal, Lila? I didn't know you made deals." He was shocked that she understood him so little as to think a bargain was necessary.

"I'm making one now," she said. "Am I so unattractive that you have to consider it, Temple?"

"Lila, don't you know that I love you, that I've always needed you?"

"This is the first real trouble you've ever let me share with you, Temple. Before, you've always fought your battles alone, leaving me on the outside of everything. You can starve a woman that way, Temple."

"Yes," he said. "I can see that now." He tipped his head forward for a time. "Let me be now. Many things that I've always believed in have turned out to be monstrous lies."

"You're closing me out again," she said. "But it's an old habit and we can't break it in a day."

A horse and buggy rattled into the yard and Temple Manly went to the front door in time to see Willis Havlock, Gunlock's newest and youngest lawyer, dismount and cross to the porch. Manly stepped aside and Havlock took off his hat. He was a neat man in his early thirties and he wore a plain suit, which was about all he could afford, having spent nearly all his money for law books and office rent a few months before.

"Mr. Manly?" He offered his hand. "I haven't had the pleasure of meeting you personally. I'm Willis Havlock. You may remember that I rented the office over the feed store a while back."

"Come in and sit down," Manly said. "Lila, will you see if there's coffee?"

"None for me, thanks," Havlock said. "It's late, Mr. Manly, and I'll come right to the point. Wes Cardigan is my client."

Manly frowned. "No money there, Havlock."

"There are some things we do that have no connection with money," Havlock said. He had serious brown eyes and a habit of scratching his right eyebrow. "Mr. Manly, I've had a long talk with Wes Cardigan and I believe the man's innocent, or at worst, a victim of unfortunate circumstances."

"We all are at times," Manly said, glancing at his wife. She pulled her eyes away quickly and took refuge in her needlework. "Just how do I fit into this, Mr. Havlock? I agreed earlier to help Cardigan all I could."

"I'm rather glad to hear that," Havlock said. "Frankly, Mr. Manly, you can do a lot for him; you're an important man in Gunlock and whichever way you blow, so blows the populace."

"Well, thank you, but do you think a man in my position ought to . . ."

"Yes, I do," Havlock said. "It's been my observation that ambitious men find philanthropy quite profitable. Anyway, that's neither here nor there right now. Mr. Manly, I think you should know that Wes Cardigan has come up with a most startling statement. He claims that as he rode up the street and approached the express office that evening, he saw your son run out with a sack in his hand. Sims fired then, and there was an exchange of shots. Your son allegedly dropped a pistol, which happened to be one Wes Cardigan traded to him a short time before."

"That's a confounded lie!" Manly bellowed this.

Willis Havlock seemed undisturbed. He held up his hands. "This is not the time to argue that, Mr. Manly. But I intend to get at the truth of the matter. Cardigan claims that the only reason he ran was to spare his sister; he believed that she and your son were in love."

"There's nothing to that at all," Manly said. "They don't even get along."

"Perhaps," Havlock said, rising. "Well, I've taken up too much of your time already, Mr. Manly. Perhaps you'd like to think over what I've said and drop into town in a day or so to talk it over."

"What's there to talk over?"

Havlock shrugged. "That's for you to decide, sir. Whatever the truth is here, it's bound to come out. Not even you could stop it."

"Now see here . . ."

"I'm not accusing you of anything, Mr. Manly. Nor your son. I'm merely exploring all the possibilities, which I've been retained to do. Good night, sir." He turned toward the hall, stopping when Manly spoke.

"Havlock, you're new to Gunlock. It's a nice town, but don't forget who runs it."

"I'm sure I won't forget," Havlock said, smiling briefly. "And, quite frankly, the fact that you do doesn't bother me. You see, Mr. Manly, I'll do what I have to do, what I believe is right. And if a few of the big trees get chopped down, well, they'll just have to fall like any others." He bowed slightly to Lila, then went out to his buggy and drove from the yard.

Manly returned to the parlor. Lila's sewing was on the floor, forgotten. She had tears in her eyes and desperation in her voice. "Temple, Temple. What are we going to do?"

"What do you think I'll do?" he snapped. "I'll make Cardigan and Havlock out for the liars they are! Hell, I can afford it even if it takes my last cent." He laughed without humor. "That's one thing for sure, Lila. I can stay in the game longer than they can simply because I've got the size."

"But I'm thinking of afterward," she said. "Temple, you didn't believe him? Oh, you couldn't think that Jim would . . ."

"I think nothing," he said, and to show her he held her blameless, he placed his hands on her shoulders. "You've made me do nothing that I wasn't willing to do. Only, like a coward, I used you to pry me into action. Someday I'll probably try to save my conscience by blaming you instead of myself."

"I love the boy," she said softly. "In spite of his weakness, I love him."

"Yes," he said. "He's our son, for good or bad. We have to stand by him; there's no other way." He left her to pace about the room. "One thing I learned tonight about Havlock; he's smart, and there isn't much that scares him. He'll fight for Wes, even if it ruins him." He stopped to fashion a smoke, bending over a lamp for his light. "I'll have to raise some cash; Allendale will want cash. I have nothing against Cardigan, but if he's acquitted, there'll be questions asked about Jim; I don't want the boy to have to defend himself against public gossip. So I've got to convict Cardigan, yet save him from hanging at the same time."

"Can you do that, Temple? Can you betray him after promising?"

He laughed. "Can I? God, I have to do it. What other way is there if I expect to keep my son's name clean?" He did not for a moment consider Havlock's half-accusations, not that he considered them beyond the realm of belief, but because he was afraid of the conclusions he might draw. Like most parents, Temple Manly was at that stage where he had to love his son the most, and at a time where the boy deserved this the least.

While he pondered a most dismal future, Jim came down the hall and entered the parlor. He helped himself to the whiskey on the sideboard. "You still cussing me out?" he asked.

Temple Manly looked at him. "What good would that do, Jim?"

"None," he said. "But sometimes it's a relief. Every time you made me do something, I'd get off by myself and call you every name in the book."

"Right now you should be worrying about what Cardigan's saying about you."

"Wes is just trying to save his own skin," Jim said. "I don't hold it against him; he's got a tough fight ahead."

"Did you ever have a tough fight? No, it's been too easy for you," Manly said. "You don't know what it's like to get out and earn an honest dollar. All your life you've been a privileged character around here. Cardigan's worked for what he has, just as I did. You seem to have difficulty understanding that. When you want people to like you, you first have to be likeable."

"Or have plenty of money," he said.

"You fool! Do you think I've ever deluded myself about people liking me?" He slapped his hands together in disgust. "Jim, you've never faced the truth about yourself. Not once in your life."

"What about yourself?" Jim Manly asked, grinning. "Don't kid me. Take a look at you, ready to lie, cheat, buy, and pull every dirty trick in the book to keep the Manly shirttail clean. You don't think you're doing it for me, do you? That's a laugh. You're doing it for yourself. Oh, yes, I heard what Havlock said about me."

Temple Manly's face was white. "I wouldn't lift a hand to save you if it wasn't for your mother," he said. "Now get out of my sight."

The calmness with which he spoke revealed the extent of the anger and outrage he felt. Jim Manly set his whiskey glass aside and left the room, leaving Temple Manly trembling in a deep pit of self-loathing.

ELEVEN

After a comfortless night, Temple Manly rose early, took a bath and shaved carefully before going into the kitchen. He put on a pot of coffee, then went outside to stand on the porch. George came out of the bunkhouse and Manly beckoned him over.

"Saddle a horse and go into town for Doctor Reichstad."

"Is Mrs. Manly sick, sir?"

Temple Manly smiled at this. The man never entertained the thought that Temple Manly himself might require medical attention. "No," he said. "Get on with it, George."

He returned to the kitchen and found Lila there. She was heating a skillet and slicing bacon on a board. "I heard what you said. What is it, Temple?"

She hadn't even noticed, he thought, then tried to decide whether he was hurt about it or proud that he had covered his limp so well. "I have a few broken blisters," he said. "Nothing serious." When she said nothing, he added, "Good God, I can afford a house call, can't I?"

He sat down at the table and watched her move about. She was silent, more so than usual.

She fried eggs to go along with the bacon, and

some potatoes. While she set the table, a rider came into the yard and dropped off at the porch. Then Harry Buck came to the back door and knocked, his face against the screen.

"Anybody home?"

"Come on in," Manly said, pulling a chair away from the table so Buck could sit down. Buck was dressed neatly in a clean shirt and a corduroy coat.

"Just took Betty Cardigan home," he said. "That coffee sure smells good."

"Had anything to eat?" Manly realized instantly that he had phrased the question improperly; Buck would not sponge a meal if he were starving. "Put on another plate, Lila."

"Well, I could take a bite," Harry said. He accepted a cup of coffee and sat with his palms cupped around it. "Saw George leave. That man's always in a rush."

Impulsively Manly said, "My feet are giving me hell. I sent George for the doctor."

"No wonder," Buck said. "You walked a damn far spell." He squirmed in his chair. "To tell the truth, the ride's galled me to where I can scarcely sit. Wet saddle did it, probably." He let a chuckle build into a laugh.

"What's so funny?" Manly asked.

"Just thinkin'," Buck said. "You got sore feet, I got a sore bu—" He glanced quickly at Lila, embarrassed. "Kohler's home in bed. Says he intends to sleep a week. And Wilson's drunk. The only man who came through without a scratch was old Harms. That's poetic."

"Or pathetic," Manly said. Lila placed his breakfast on the table and the two men filled their plates. She sat across from them with her cup of coffee, saying nothing, letting them blunt their appetites. Finally Manly said, "You're out early this morning, Buck."

"Said I'd been to town." He mopped up what was left of his eggs. "Seen Wes, Mr. Manly. I mean to thank you for offerin' to do what you can. Ain't many big men that's willin' to go out of their way to help a down-and-outer in trouble."

"Ah—yes," Manly said uncomfortably, his head tipped forward.

Buck finished his coffee and slid his chair back. "Many thanks, Mrs. Manly. I have to be goin'." When Temple Manly put aside his napkin and started to rise, Buck touched him on the shoulder. "Don't bother to get up. And again, thanks."

Temple Manly stayed at the table and listened to Buck ride out. Then he slammed down his fist and said, "Damn it, Lila, I want the respect of that man!"

"It seems that you have it," she said.

"No—no, I want to keep it. Somehow, he's come to like me, and it's important to me that he does." He shook his head sadly.

"Please, don't say it," she asked.

"Say it?"

"That you wish Jim was like him." She bit her lip. "That's what you were thinking, wasn't it?"

"Yes," he admitted, "but it won't do any good to talk about it."

He got up and went outside, limping noticeably. His blisters were much worse, sending shooting pains into the calves of his legs. Even his ankles were swollen. Being a rancher, he found plenty to occupy his time, although he had men who took care of the details. From the head foreman he got the estimated shipping figures; that time would arrive only too quickly, and there was winter feed to buy, about a hundred and thirty tons of it.

Manly returned to the house after several hours and as he gained the porch, he saw Doctor Manfried Reichstad's buggy raising a plume of dust on the road. He waited while Reichstad dismounted, an old man in a linen duster. Reichstad was blunt and irascible, and indescribably gentle. "Got the bellyache?" he asked as he clumped onto the porch.

"No," Manly said. "Come on in."

"Didn't expect to stand on the porch," Reichstad said. He seemed to take exception to everything said to him and people expected him to. He saw Manly's limp. "Step on a nail?"

"Blisters," Manly said and sat down to tug off his boots.

This proved unsuccessful for his morning's activity had further increased the swelling. Taking a pair of heavy shears from his bag, Doctor Reichstad began to cut the boots.

"What the hell, I paid thirty dollars for those in Dallas!"

"They're cheaper than feet," Reichstad remarked. He removed the boots and peeled away the crude bandages Manly had wrapped around his feet. Then he went into the kitchen, returning a moment later with a box of Epsom salts and a pan of hot water. "Put your feet in there," he ordered.

Manly tried, but the water was too hot; he jerked his feet away. Reichstad grabbed them and thrust them into the water. Manly snapped half erect and bit his lip. "Now keep them there," Reichstad said flatly. "And stay off of them for a few days. For a man as smart as you, you've acted stupidly. You want blood poisoning? Well, you almost have it."

"I have things to do," Manly said. "I can't sit . . ."

"You'll sit now or for the rest of your life," Reichstad said. He brought out salve and bandages, placing these on a small side table. "Keep it up and I'm afraid I'll have to amputate—that is, unless you give them a chance to heal properly."

Had this come from anyone else, Temple

Manly would have scoffed and treated it as a joke, but he had known Manfried Reichstad for nearly fifteen years and never once had he heard him joke about anything; he was as near humorless as a man could get.

"I'll be back in two days," Reichstad said, closing his bag. "Now, don't spend your time walking around. Soak those feet in salts at least three times a day. Hot water, you understand. As hot as you can stand."

The doctor went into the kitchen to talk to Lila; he had a habit of always leaving nursing orders with the wife, as if he assumed that in every household they ruled supreme.

He left by the back door and Manly heard him drive away. A moment later Lila came in, her expression anxious. "I had no idea how serious . . ."

"To hell with that," Manly said. "Lila, I have to get to town."

She put her hand on his shoulder, holding him in the chair. "You do as the doctor says. George can run your errands."

George did. Unable to go to Harms, Manly sent George for him. While he waited, Fred Allendale, the county attorney, drove into the yard. Manly was on the porch, both feet bandaged. Allendale noticed this, but made no comment; he had always felt it unwise to question Temple Manly about his personal business.

"I would have come earlier," Allendale said, lowering himself into a chair, "only Harms wanted to go over the evidence." He removed his hat and placed it on the porch. He was a man of forty some years, not too successful, but reliable; this was written in the uninspired angles of his face.

"I've sent for Harms," Temple Manly said slowly. "I think we have a case against young Cardigan."

Allendale let his surprise show. "Case? But, Mr. Manly, the way I understood it, you were going to help Cardigan." He spread his hands in bewilderment. "Why, Harms and I talked about releasing the boy, providing we could substantiate that the shooting was unintentional."

"I've changed my mind," Temple Manly said, studying the tips of his fingers. "We'll proceed on the premise that he's guilty."

"But, Mr. Manly . . ."

Manly speared him with a glance. "Did you come here to argue or to listen?"

"To—listen, sir," Allendale said. "We'll run this whichever way you say."

"That's fine," Manly said without conviction. He stared off onto the sun-brightened flats. "Wes admitted exchanging shots with Sims; that will establish the fact that he was capable of taking the money." He hesitated, then went on. "When Harms gets here, I'm going to have him search

231

Cardigan's property. No doubt the money's hidden there someplace."

"If the money's recovered," Allendale said, "we'll really have a case." He rubbed his hands together. "With robbery as the proved motive, I can ask for a mandatory death sentence and . . ."

"No hanging," Manly said flatly.

"But, sir, I thought you said . . ."

"I said we'd convict him, not hang him." He braced his hands on his knees and looked off into the distance again. "Mr. Allendale, you were an out-of-the-pants lawyer when I had you appointed county attorney. Since then you've made enough to buy a house in town, own two buggies, marry a local girl and send both of your kids to a good school. Under the circumstances, I don't think it's unreasonable to assume that my judgment should suffice concerning whether or not Wesley Cardigan should hang."

"Of course, sir, but it'll look better if he hangs."

"Convict him, but no hanging, Mr. Allendale. I think you understand that, so good day, sir."

"Yes, sir." Allendale retrieved his hat. "Good day, sir." He left the porch hastily and mounted his buggy. A moment later he wheeled out of the yard at a spry clip.

The door behind Temple Manly opened and Jim stepped out. He looked at Allendale's retreating rig, then said, "You're really covering for me. I guess I shot off my mouth again when I didn't know what I was talking about."

"That's not important now," Manly said. He busied his fingers with a smoke. "Jim, do you know what love is?"

"No," he said. "I never had any."

"Never?" Manly smiled bitterly. "Jim, even before you were born, your mother and I used to sit by the hour and talk about you. We talked about the color of your hair and eyes, and whether you'd be tall when you grew up. Love you? Boy, you were loved from the time we knew you were on the way." He paused to puff his cigarette. "The night you were born it rained hard. I rode for the doctor. Dragged him cussing out of a warm bed." He shook his head sadly. "I always figured that you'd know someday, because you'd have a son of your own. Then you'd sit by the hour and watch him crawl around the floor, or count the days until he spoke his first word."

"All that was for a baby," Jim Manly said. "I don't remember any of it. All I remember is the lickings I got, and the times you didn't talk to me."

Temple Manly tipped his head forward and studied the crooked ash on his smoke. "I know of those times, Jim. But the love was still there. I guess every man is impatient for his son to grow and put aside the foolish things. Maybe I've been too hard on you, or too easy. One way is as bad as the other."

"Whatever I am, you've made me."

"Yes, I'll have to accept the responsibility for that."

"You get me out of this and there'll never be another time," Jim Manly promised.

Turning his head, Temple Manly looked at his son. "Have you any idea how many times you've told me that?"

"I mean it this time!"

"And that too," Manly said. "I'm sorry, Jim, but I can't believe you now."

"Did you ever believe me?"

"Oh yes," Temple Manly said. "Yes, until you proved to me that I couldn't. Jim, we all have to learn the same lessons, but somehow, you never did. You could never understand why it was wrong to beat your horse because you were mad at George. Jim, we just can't go through life striking out all the time. We have to live for something else besides getting even."

"You through with the lecture?"

"Yes," Temple Manly said. "You didn't understand a word of it, did you?"

"Understand?" Jim Manly laughed brittlely. "Hell, I didn't even listen."

Harms put in an appearance around noon; he had a habit of timing his visits to coincide

234

with mealtime. The day had turned off hot and Manly had Lila bring sandwiches and coffee to the porch. Harms settled himself in a chair and placed his hat on his lap.

"Came as soon as I could, Mr. Manly. Allendale was mighty disturbed. Met him on the way out."

"Allendale will do as he's told," Manly said. He took a handkerchief from an inner pocket and wiped his face. "Cardigan's been spreading lies about Jim; I want them stopped, Harms." He did not look at the sheriff when he talked. "If Cardigan's convicted for the robbery and shooting, then he can hardly accuse Jim and have anyone believe him, can he?"

"No, but I thought that you . . ."

"Damn it, Harms, don't play stupid with me!" He waved his hand impatiently. "I want you to go to Cardigan's place and turn up that money." He took a roll of bills from his pocket and tossed them into Harms's lap. "That's all the cash I have. If the money isn't there, then 'discover' this."

Across Harms's moon face there spread a look of bafflement, but he had always done what he had been told to do and the habit was strong. Sighing, he stood up and put on his hat, tugging it in place. The money was tucked into his coat pocket before he stepped off the porch. At the base of the steps he paused and turned back. "Mr. Manly, I guess I got a lot to thank you for;

235

the whole county has. I've done your biddin' a number of years now, and I can say that up to this moment I ain't been ashamed of what I done." He met Manly's eyes squarely and gathered shards of courage he never knew he had. "I'll do this thing for you, Mr. Manly. But I want you to know that when it's over, you'll have to find someone else, because I'm through."

"You'll never quit me, Harms. You're old and fat, and being sheriff is the only thing you can do."

"Then I'll take to sweepin' out Lovering's saloon," Harms said. "There's no disgrace to cleanin' out a spittoon; that ain't as low as what I'm doin' now."

The man was right, and Manly knew a profound shame. There, he told himself, stands a man with more real courage than I'll ever have. And he regretted the times past when he had accused Harms of weakness and stupidity. The man possessed honor, for in this moment he could face himself and take action against what he saw.

Harms went to his horse and pulled himself into the saddle, riding out immediately. He cut toward the Cardigan ranch in the breaks, holding his horse to a walk, for he dreaded every step that closed the distance. Alone and away from Temple Manly's influence, Harms wondered why he had taken his stand. His debt of gratitude was great and Harms recognized this act as the final payment for all the years of uselessness that Manly had tolerated.

He did not pretend to understand Temple Manly, nor the factors that drove him to this radical change of position concerning Wes Cardigan. He knew only that he must break with Temple Manly, and yet, such an act was alien to Harms's nature for he was a born leaner. For many years now, he had garnered a reflected importance from Manly, but suddenly, he no longer needed that reflection. Since pocketing the money, Harms had felt indescribably soiled, as most men do when their last remnant of honor is threatened with annihilation.

When he reached the last hill overlooking the Cardigan place, he stopped. The cabin was small and the barn untidily built, but many men were in a hurry when they first got started on their own. Harms saw Betty Cardigan carry a basket of washing from the cabin, as he rode off the slope, she strung it on the line stretching from the cabin corner to the well house. As he entered the yard, Betty turned, raising a hand to her forehead to shield her eyes from the sun's glare.

Harms took off his hat and swung down, grunting a little as his legs took up his ponderous weight. "Lonesome out here," he said, looking around at the bowl of hills that contained this property.

"You can't get lonesome with two weeks' back washing to do," she said. "Care for some coffee?"

"I'd thank you for it," Harms said and followed her inside. The cabin was rough, the furniture homemade. It reminded him of the fact that most people started small and stayed that way; only a few ever grew big.

He settled at the table while she poured. "What brings you out here?" she asked. "A little out of your way, isn't it?"

"Just wanted to see how you're getting along," Harms said uncomfortably. When he moved, he felt the money crinkle in his pocket and he darted a look at her as though wondering if she had heard it and divined the purpose of his visit. But she was looking out the open doorway so he said, "Talked to Wes last night. He ain't despondent or nothing like that."

"Thank you," she said. "I worry about him, Harms. He loses his temper. Oh, not now. He believes that everything will work out all right because he's innocent. But if anything goes wrong, well . . ."

"What can go wrong?" Harms asked carefully. "Willis Havlock will get him off." He drank some of his coffee and wondered how he was going to lead up to the point of searching the place. Finally he said, "Havlock's a careful man, Betty. He wanted me to come out and have a look around."

She glanced at him sharply, questioningly. "What for?"

"Oh, nothin' in particular," Harms said. He drained what remained of his coffee and stood up. "Best get at it if you have no objections."

"I guess not," Betty said, frowning. "Seems like a waste of time to me though."

"Got to keep the lawyers happy," Harms said and waddled out. He walked to the barn and spent more than a half-hour puttering around, digging into the bins. There were many good hiding places and he considered each one in turn, then passed it up for another. Twice he took the money out of his pocket, only to return it, and was taking it out for the third time when he heard Harry Buck ride into the yard.

Harms could hear Betty Cardigan talking to Buck, then the tall man came on to the barn, dismounting just outside the door. As Buck stepped toward him, Harms came out, pretending surprise.

"You got a quiet horse," he said. "Didn't hear you, Harry."

"What you looking for?" Harry Buck asked, his tone severe.

"Just routine," Harms said evasively. "Nothing in particular, Harry." He walked back to the cabin and stood near the door. "Hot day," he said. "I'm getting too old and fat for all this riding." Buck was rolling a cigarette when Harms glanced at

239

him. Betty Cardigan had her shoulder braced against the door frame, her bare arms crossed casually. Harms sighed and removed his hat to mop away the sweat trapped there. "I've been thinkin' of givin' up this job," he said.

They looked at him quickly, disbelief in their eyes. "Why?" Buck asked. "You've nosed Manly for years to keep it."

"It needs a younger man," Harms said. "A man like you, Buck."

This struck Harry Buck as funny and he laughed. Then the humor vanished, leaving him serious-eyed. "This a joke, Harms?"

"Nope," Harms said with a trace of regret. "A man should know when he's reached the end of his rope. I'd like to recommend you to the mayor, Harry. You'd be my choice."

"I'd do a better job than you ever did," Harry said, without meaning to be rude. "You know what I mean, Harms: I'd never lick Manly's boots."

"I know," Harms murmured. "My feelings ain't hurt." He clapped his hat back on his head and turned to his horse. "Come in town late this afternoon, Harry. I'll have the badge polished for you."

Harry Buck's eyes narrowed. "What's Temple Manly say about this?"

"Don't know," Harms admitted. "I haven't told him."

"Ah, now I know it's a joke," Harry said. "Harms, you haven't taken a decent breath in years without Manly's approval."

"This is my first," Harms admitted. "You don't believe me, then come into town this afternoon." He rode out then, quickly, before he could change his mind.

Betty Cardigan and Harry Buck watched him until he started up the hill toward the town road. Buck said incredulously, "This has to be a joke, Betty."

"I don't think so," she said. "He acted so strange; I noticed that as soon as he stepped off his horse. I don't know *this* Harms, Harry."

"Well, if he means it, I don't know him either," Buck said. "Unless Manly's put him up to this."

"Are you going to town?" she asked.

"I might," he said. "I just might."

He had things on his mind which made him restless; she did not try to hold him, and ten minutes later he was mounted and cutting toward Temple Manly's ranch. He rode the ridges, dropping across several valleys to come upon the trail that led from the high country into the broad valley.

As he made one crest, he stopped, for his eye had caught a shaded movement below. After a moment's study, Buck made out Jim Manly moving slowly through the brush. He sat there for a time, watching the young man, and when he lifted the reins to move on, he saw someone else, farther south, but obviously trailing young Manly. This wove a frown on Harry Buck's forehead and he studied the second man until he recognized Hank Wilson. The native dislike Buck felt for this man prodded him into action, and into doing something he rarely did, take sides.

Because Wilson was concentrating on following Jim Manly, he made the task relatively easy for Harry Buck, who could move like an Indian when the fancy seized him. Twenty minutes of rapid, but cautious movement brought Buck into a dense thicket that lay along the path Wilson was following. Dismounting, Buck picketed his horse, then moved a hundred yards up the faint trail, far enough so his horse wouldn't catch the scent of Wilson's animal and give him away prematurely.

The wait was a short one, no more than ten minutes. Wilson rode bent over the horse's neck, his eyes on the ground. He was noticeably surprised when Harry Buck said, "You ought to watch where you're going before you run into a tree."

Wilson's hand made a practiced stab for his holstered revolver, then he reconsidered and crossed his hands on the saddle. "I'm on official business," he said. "You're interferin' with it, Buck."

"Official business, hell!" Buck said. "What you Injunin' up on Manly for?"

"I said it was business," Wilson repeated. He kept looking past Buck, as though eager to get on with his purpose, yet he made no move to pass Buck.

"Been my observation that Manly business is their own, and they don't welcome interference," Buck said.

"So?"

"So I'll ride into town with you," Buck said. "You don't mind the company, do you?"

"Damned right I mind," Wilson snapped, his expression going flat. "Buck, you goin' to let me pass, or do I have to make my own way?"

"Every man has to make his own way," Buck said softly. "And you said once that you had something to settle. So let's settle it right here."

Wilson understood and hastily considered the possibilities: Buck was on the ground and would have to bring his gun up a little high to reach him, a mounted man. Yet shooting down was an odd angle for a man, and from a horse it was especially risky. Should he miss, the horse would pitch, and Buck would stand there and pick him off between jumps. The risks were a little more than Wilson cared to assume, so he said, "I like witnesses when I cut a man down to size."

"Witnesses, or an edge?" Buck asked. He waved his hand. "Get out of here, Hank."

"Sure," Wilson said, wheeling his horse. He flogged him into a run and when he disappeared, Harry Buck went back to his own horse. Swinging up, he rode in the other direction, toward the spot where he had last seen Jim Manly.

For better than an hour, Buck picked his way along the faint trail and finally emerged in a small clearing where a line shack stood. Manly's horse was there and as Buck rode up, Jim came from behind the cabin, an old shovel in his hand.

He showed surprise, then this was replaced by an innate caution. "What are you doing on the old man's place, Buck?"

"Following you. Bury something?"

"No," Manly said flatly. "I ought to tell the old man."

"Tell him," Buck said. "While you're at it, tell him that Hank Wilson was following you too."

"Wilson? Where?"

"A mile or so back," Buck said. He cuffed his hat to the back of his head. "You in some kind of trouble, Jim? I'd help a man."

"The hell you would," Jim Manly said. He threw the rusty shovel into the line shack and stepped into the saddle. "Since you got no business here in the first place, I won't keep you any longer."

"Fair enough," Buck agreed. They rode out, taking different routes. Buck retraced his track along the trail for a time, then cut off toward the town road. A glance now and then at the sky told him that the day was wearing out; he judged it was after four when he came to the road.

Increasing his pace, he raised Gunlock at supper time and put up his horse at the stable before going to the small restaurant on Hope Street for his evening meal. While he sat there, waiting for his order to arrive, Willis Havlock came in, placed his hat on a vacant chair, and sat down near Buck's right elbow.

"I was wondering if you'd come," Havlock said. "Not many people pay attention to Harms's talk."

"Then he resigned?"

Havlock nodded. "Damndest uproar you ever heard. The judge has called a meeting. Someone's sent for Temple Manly." Havlock took out his watch and glanced at it. "Probably be here by eight-thirty. The meeting's scheduled for nine."

The talk stopped when Buck's meal arrived, then as soon as Buck began to eat, Havlock continued. "I heard it from Reichstad, but I couldn't believe it. Buck, if we get you into office, do you realize that this will be the first law in years that wasn't owned by Temple Manly?"

"Maybe I'm a Manly man myself," Buck said easily.

"No," Havlock said, shaking his head. "You're

too small to be a Manly man. No offense, Buck, but you could never do anything for E. Temple Manly, so he wouldn't fool with you."

"I've just been recommended," Buck said. "If the council don't accept it, you'll still end up with a Manly-picked sheriff."

"We're going to fight!" Havlock said. "This was a windfall for us, and we can thank the unpredictable Harms for that. All along we figured we'd have to wait for election year, then slug it out and be defeated by Manly-paid votes." He enumerated the score on his fingers. "The judge is for Manly, right down the line. So is Allendale. But Doctor Reichstad's got a mind of his own and so have I."

"Two against two? What kind of a deal is that?"

"Don't forget Lovering," Havlock said. "He's the deciding vote. Harry, I want you to go with me and talk to him."

"What'll I say?" Buck asked. "Hell, Willis, he knows me."

"No—no—no," Willis Havlock said, trying to make his point. "Yes, he knows you, but Manly's coming in. He'll sit there, and stab everyone with his eyes, and Lovering can't take that by himself. He has to have our backing, yours and mine." He took Harry Buck's sleeve and tugged at it. "Listen to me, Harry. You know Manly, and how he gets his way. God, he can look at a man and make him feel he's two inches high. You stand up to Manly, and if Lovering knows that you'll be there, he'll come to our side."

Harry Buck ate awhile and thought about this. When he turned to his coffee, he said, "Willis, what do you hope to gain by making me sheriff?"

"Political freedom," Havlock said. "Oh, I know what Manly's done for the town, but one man can't go on telling everyone what to do. We all have to decide, as individuals, what's good for us." He gnawed his lip. "Then there's the matter of Wes Cardigan. I know that I'm defending him, but he needs a defense, Harry. The whole thing has been a bit of Manly's business from the very beginning, and it'll go on being Manly's business unless we do something about it. Do you think Wes is going to get much of a trial, Harry? Hell, there won't be a man in that jury box who won't look at Manly before he makes up his mind."

"I know," Buck said softly. "That's been in the back of my mind all along, Willis, ever since I moved to this country. But Manly's been pretty square; you got to admit that."

"But there's no guarantee that he'll stay square," Havlock said. "Harry, will you go with me to see Lovering?"

"Yeah," Buck said, and finished his coffee. He picked up his hat and put it on, pausing then.

"Willis, what the hell do you suppose come over Harms?"

"I don't know," Havlock said, "but I bless him."

TWELVE

Temple Manly was eating his supper when a horseman rode into the yard and exchanged a few hurried words with George. Manly raised his head and looked out the window in time to see George come across the porch.

Hat in hand, George paused in the doorway. Manly said, "What is it, man? Who was that?" There was suspicion in his voice although he tried to keep it out.

"One of the fellas from town, sir. Sheriff Harms has resigned." He spoke calmly for this had no special significance for him; his world was bounded by the Manly ranch.

Lila was lifting her coffee cup; she set it back with a click. Manly frowned. "If this is a joke, I don't like it." He felt sure it was not and a genuine alarm shook him.

"It's no joke, sir," George insisted. "Harms resigned and recommended Harry Buck to the judge. They want you to come in, sir. There's a meeting tonight."

"You can't go, Temple," Lila said quickly. "Doctor Reichstad . . ."

"Hang Reichstad! Hitch up a team to the buggy and bring it around to the porch, George."

"Yes, sir." He went out immediately and hurried across the yard.

Manly pushed his plate aside and hobbled painfully toward the hall closet. While he got his hat and coat, Lila found an old pair of comfortable slippers and a pair of heavy socks. "If it's late," he said, "I may stay over at the hotel and come back first thing in the morning."

"All right," she said. "Temple, what reason did Harms have for resigning?"

"He's an old fool," Manly said. "That's reason enough for a lot of things."

With the socks and slippers on, he stood up, testing them for comfort. She held his coat for him while he got into it. "Where's Jim?" he asked.

"I don't know," Lila admitted. "He saddled a horse around noon and rode out."

"You'd think he'd have sense enough to stay home once in a while," Manly said irritably. George brought the buggy to the porch and stopped. Manly put his arms around Lila and kissed her gently. "Try not to worry," he said.

"That's an odd thing," she said. "You've always told me not to worry, and I never have. I mean that. There's never been any doubt in my mind but what you'd always do what you set out to do."

He was not certain whether he should be flattered by this confidence, or warned by it. He went out, walking carefully, and George handed him into the buggy. "Get in," Manly said. "You can drive."

He settled on the high seat while George wheeled out of the yard. Manly was glad that George was not a garrulous type; he had selected him as a general aide-de-camp because of this quiet habit. While the miles rattled away beneath the iron-bound wheels, Temple Manly planned the moves he would have to make in Gunlock. That fool, Harms, with his tardy display of morals could throw everything out of kilter, but Manly was confident that there was still a chance to save the game. No bull rush this time, but a steady, polite pressure.

In spite of the fact that he knew Harry Buck as a man who would never take orders, he recognized that he would make an excellent sheriff. And at any other time, Manly would have welcomed the change; Harms would eventually have to be replaced and it was always smart to look for a replacement while there was time to make a careful selection.

They arrived in Gunlock a little after eight, and Manly checked in at the hotel while George took the team to the stable. Ever mindful of Doctor Reichstad's warning, he kept his walking to a minimum and took a chair in the lobby.

The town was wide awake, he noticed; the word had spread quickly, and any threatened change in local politics was of wide interest. Within minutes, the judge arrived, a rail-thin man with white sideburns and a habit of clearing his throat with annoying regularity.

He shook hands with Manly, then pulled a chair close. "Ah, sir," the judge said, clearing his throat, "so glad you could come. This whole affair has been rather a surprise. Harms gave us no notice, sir. None at all." The judge adjusted the lapels of his coat and eased back in the chair. His name, before Manly's helpful push onto the bench, had been Leander Pomeroy Friedkin, but once the judicial robes had been donned, he announced that either His Honor or The Judge would be a proper address.

"Judge," Manly said, "what the devil's the rush here? Couldn't this meeting have waited a few days or a week?"

"Hhhhmmm, impossible, sir," the judge said. "With a prisoner in the jail, a properly con-stituted law officer has to be in charge." He bent forward and spoke more confidentially. "Knowing your views on Hank Wilson, I hardly thought it likely that . . ."

"Yes, yes," Manly said, waving his hand. "Well, we'll appoint a new sheriff tonight then, and be done with it."

"Ah, the opposition has seized upon this opportunity, as it were, and they mean to make the most of it. Of course, sir, myself and

Mr. Allendale stand staunchly behind you, as always."

The Manly clan was gathered with the arrival of Allendale, the county attorney. He took a chair near the judge and they all waited for Reichstad, Havlock and Jake Lovering. The hotel lobby joined the bar and from that room came the babble of men's voices, with shards of laughter sprinkled over the deeper tones.

Havlock and Doctor Reichstad came in together. They nodded to Manly, and the two men sitting with him. Then Havlock went over to the clerk's desk and spoke softly. He came back a moment later and said, "I think a room would be better than the lobby, gentlemen."

"Where's Lovering?" Allendale asked.

"He'll be along," Havlock said and led the way. While Manly was getting up, Harry Buck entered from the barroom. Letting the others go on ahead, Manly hung back to speak to Buck.

The young man had bought a new pair of jeans and shirt. A shave and haircut spruced up his appearance and Manly noticed that Buck was not wearing his gun. Manly said, "I won't insult you by offering congratulations, Harry. If I can, I'm going to keep you out of the job." He dared not exhibit any show of concern; he knew that Buck could be merciless when there was a job to do.

"Sure," Buck said, a slight smile lifting his lips. "No hard feelings, Mr. Manly." This was a clear-cut statement from a man whose life ran along clear-cut channels; there was no deceit in Harry Buck.

"There's nothing personal here," Manly went on to say. "Frankly, I have a lot of respect for you."

"I would never be your man," Harry Buck said. "I wouldn't take your orders. Maybe you can find some clerk to pin a badge on, someone who'd do what you want, but not me."

Manly nodded. "Did it ever occur to you that I might be tired of giving orders? Harry, I have everything a man could ask for. As far as I'm concerned, someone else can run things."

"You expect me to believe that?" Buck asked. "This is still your town, Mr. Manly, and people jump when you nod." He indicated the door through which the others had disappeared. "And to prove it, you came to town tonight to make a few of them jump."

"I asked you once before," Manly said, "and now I'll ask you again: are you after me, Harry?"

"Personally, no. Politically, yes."

A frown marred Manly's forehead. "Why? God, man, I've made this town what it is."

"And I guess folks are properly grateful," Harry Buck said. "But now that it's fat and prosperous, we'd sort of like to keep it that way ourselves, without anyone with the power to wreck it if he wanted to."

Havlock chose that time to put his head out the door. "Mr. Manly, Harry, would you step in here, please?"

At the door, Manly stopped and touched Harry Buck on the arm. "Once we're in there, I'm against you, boy."

"Same here," Buck said and stepped inside.

The others were gathered around a table. Reichstad's foul cigars were already at work turning the air close and blue. Manly and Buck sat down as the judge cleared his throat for order.

"Where is Lovering?" he asked.

"He'll be along," Havlock repeated and dropped his head to examine his fingernails.

"Gentlemen, hhhmmmmm. We're here to select a new sheriff, and upon Harms's recommendation of Harry Buck, we are now prepared to vote."

"Not until Lovering gets here," Havlock said easily. Then he looked up at each of them. "Let's not talk about a quorum; this isn't the Moose Lodge. Until Lovering gets here, there'll be no voting."

Allendale slapped the table in annoyance. "Why the devil isn't he here then?" He glanced at Temple Manly, as though expecting him to intercede. But Manly remained thoughtfully silent; outside of being the most influential man in the county, he had no official voice here.

"I think Mr. Lovering wishes to avoid the small talk," Reichstad said dryly. He looked at his huge stem-winder. "I'd just as soon pass it up myself. I have a delivery to make in about an hour and a half, if this particular woman's labor pains prove reliable, and they have on the last eight."

"I see no reason why we can't take a preliminary ballot," Allendale said. "Purely for the sake of discussion." He had the persistence of a woodsman walking around a chosen tree, looking for a crack in which to insert the splitting wedge.

"An oral vote," Havlock said smoothly. "We wouldn't want anything hasty placed in the record."

This angered Allendale. "Damn it, you're set on splitting hairs tonight, aren't you?"

"Just keeping it legal," Havlock said. He was the newest member, appointed when Olson, the grocer, died suddenly. None of these men knew Havlock too well, but they were getting acquainted rapidly.

Manly said nothing. Normally, he would have spoken to quiet this disagreement, but with Havlock apparently reading from the law book, he thought it best to let his presence alone exert the necessary pressure.

After twenty sullenly silent minutes had passed, the judge said, "Well, we can't wait for Lovering much longer. I move that we vote."

"Second that," Havlock said unexpectedly.

They all stared at him and Allendale said, "What did you say?"

"I said, second the motion." He looked at each of them, his expression innocent. "I believe that was in order."

"What the hell's going on here?" Allendale wanted to know. "A little while ago, you were strong for waiting. Now you've changed your mind."

"There you are quite mistaken," Havlock said. "I thought that a little delay would cement your decisions firmly and make the first ballot the final one." This man, Manly decided, was extremely clever. He had, without raising his voice, controlled this meeting completely.

"Hhhhmmmmm, we'll take the vote," the judge said. He glanced at Harry Buck, who sat stiff and silent and very uneasy. "Mr. Buck has been recommended to succeed Harms as sheriff." He tore off pieces of paper from a pad and passed them around. "The question is: is this recommendation to be supported by the council? Signify by a written yes or no and pass them to the head of the table."

Each man voted, folded his paper and passed it forward. Manly observed this with a casual interest; he could guess at the decision: two for and two against. And with Reichstad the weaker yes, it was only a matter of time before it became three no, and one yes.

The judge was opening the folded slips of paper. "A vote no," he said, making a note of this for the record. "Another vote no. A vote yes. Two votes yes." Then he looked at an envelope that had been with the slips of paper, a frown furrowing his shaggy brows. "What's this?"

"That is Mr. Lovering's vote," Havlock said evenly. He met their surprise, which soon changed to anger.

Allendale slapped his palm against the table. "I won't have it!"

Havlock spread his hands in open appeal. "I'm afraid you must, Councilor. The law clearly states that a member may cast an absentee ballot, when it is properly sealed and witnessed." He smiled faintly. "And I can assure you that this was witnessed by at least thirty men in Jake Lovering's saloon. Open it, Your Honor."

The judge glanced at Temple Manly, who was sitting very straight in his chair. He tore open the envelope and said, "A vote yes. Harry Buck is the new sheriff." He looked briefly at Buck. "If you'll remain, I'll swear you in as soon as the meeting adjourns."

And adjourn it did, very rapidly, and without official approval. Temple Manly was the first to leave, and he did so half angrily, slamming the door behind him. Allendale and Doctor Reichstad left together and Allendale was in an obviously bitter frame of mind.

Touching Harry Buck lightly on the shoulder, Havlock said, "If you hadn't talked to Lovering, we'd never have made it." He went out then and found Temple Manly in the lobby.

Manly turned and said, "That was a damned sly way of doing business, Havlock."

"Sly? Mr. Manly, that depends on the point of view. Suppose Lovering had come. You'd have stared at him all the while he sat there and when it came time to vote, he would have followed Allendale's lead."

"Buck may be sheriff," Manly said, "but this is still my town. I'm not going to let you forget that either."

"We have no intention of forgetting it," Havlock said.

Harry Buck came out of the room then, Harms's badge pinned to his shirt front. True to his word, Harms had polished it until it reflected the lamplight brightly. He walked over to where Manly and Havlock stood. "How much trouble can I expect from you, Mr. Manly?"

"How much are you prepared to give me?" He could harbor no real anger against this man, for he could not blame Buck because Havlock had outsmarted Allendale.

"Didn't figure on giving you any," Buck said. "I'll uphold the law and there won't be any short cuts."

"That sounds fair enough," Manly said. "Step

over to Lovering's and I'll buy you a drink."

"Well, thanks," Buck said. "Join us, Willis?"

"Ah—no," Havlock said. "I've got a few things to take care of."

Manly and Buck stepped to the hotel porch and Manly paused to study the street. Men were gathered into quiet cells of conversation along the walk. A few of the business houses were open, shedding lamplight through their windows. Laughter floated from Lovering's place and a man whooped in a high, ringing voice.

"What are they laughing about?" Manly asked suddenly. "I lost, didn't I?" He glanced quickly at Harry Buck, ashamed that for an instant he had allowed his emotion to show. "What are you going to do with your ranch? Let it go?"

"Hire someone to keep it up," Buck said. "The sheriff's salary is a hundred a month. I can get a good man for fifty and still show a profit."

"A man can't run two businesses at a time," Manly warned.

Buck laughed. "From you, that's funny. For years now, you've been running your own and everyone else's." He stepped off the walk. "Let's get that drink."

The saloon was crowded and two bartenders sweated up and down the polished mahogany, dispensing drinks. As soon as Temple Manly approached the bar, a lane opened and he raised his hand to get immediate service.

"To luck," he said and lifted his glass.

"We may both need it," Buck said and tossed off his drink.

Through the back bar mirror he saw Harms at a table, drinking alone. Buck turned and hooked his elbows on the edge of the bar and said, "Harms, come over here."

Conversation dribbled away like water from a well spout when the handle stops working. Harms scraped back his chair; the sound was loud and harsh, and Manly's face was stiff as Harms approached the bar. He cast Manly a brief, apologetic glance. "Evenin', Mr. Manly."

"Hello, Judas," Manly said. He closed his mouth with a snap and motioned for the bartender to fill Harms's beer stein.

"I told you, Mr. Manly," Harms said. "Told you, but you wouldn't believe me." He thrust a hand inside his shirt and brought out a wrinkled envelope. "Guess I'd better give you this."

The moment Manly touched it, he recognized the money, and a small fury seized him. Confound the fat fool! Until this moment there had been no doubt in his mind that Harms had carried out his order before quitting.

"What's that?" Harry Buck asked easily.

"Huh?" Manly glanced down at the envelope. "Some papers. All right, Harms, that'll be all."

The tone, the words, turned Harms, but Harry Buck reached out and took the ex-sheriff by the arm, pulling him back. "Manly may not like your company, but I do." He looked past the fat man to Manly. "You got to get rid of that habit of just waving your hand to make a man disappear, Mr. Manly."

"See here, Buck . . ."

"Now, I don't mean to argue about it," Buck said, holding up his hands. "I just don't like it, that's all." He motioned toward the empty glasses. "Care for another? I'll buy."

The refusal was on the tip of Temple Manly's tongue, but he held it back. Nodding, he faced the bar again while the bartender upended the bottle. Someone shuffled near the other end of the room and Manly looked into the mirror in time to see Hank Wilson detaching himself and easing toward them. Buck saw this too for he turned as Wilson edged in.

"Well, now," Wilson said. "Quarrelin' already?" He laughed shortly. "Buck, you should know better than that." He ignored Temple Manly's scowl of dislike, and Harms's uneasiness. Tapping the badge on Buck's shirt with his finger, he said, "Now, ain't that pretty? Jesus, Buck, it seems that you're into everything lately. Just this afternoon you were sticking your bill in where it didn't belong. Now you've gone and got yourself a badge to hide behind."

"When did I ever hide from you, Hank?"

Hank Wilson's easy voice irritated Temple

Manly; he felt like telling Buck to throw the man out, yet he realized that he dared not do that. Buck would make up his own mind and resent any interference.

"Well, I can't really say's you have," Wilson was saying. "Of course, you and me haven't really tangled over anything yet."

"Then maybe I ought to give you a reason," Buck said softly. "Hank, take off that badge and lay it on the bar. As sheriff, I won't be needing you."

"Huh?" Wilson reared his head back slightly, then laughed. "Harry, if I didn't know you was joking, I'd take real offense at that." His glance swept Harms. "You fat bastard, see what you've done?"

Reaching out, Buck fastened his fingers around the badge and jerked it free, tearing Wilson's shirt to the waist before the pin parted company with the cloth. Hank tipped his head forward and looked down at his ruined shirt.

"You shouldn't have done that, Harry. No man fires me unless I'm ready to quit."

"You've been fired," Buck said. "Harms might have been scared of you, but I'm not."

"You're not carrying a gun," Wilson pointed out. "That's too bad, because I'm going to have to do something now." He pawed a hand across his mouth and his eyes pinched together until they were nearly closed.

There was little hesitation in Harry Buck; he knew how to deal with this and sledged Wilson in the mouth as the man shifted his weight to step back.

Wilson was flung sideways into Manly, who shoved him away toward the center of the room. Harry Buck placed the badge carefully on the bar and turned as Wilson bore in. The men who watched in silence had seen their share of fights, and they made their judgments early as to the probable winner.

Whipping aside, Harry Buck clubbed down with his forearm, catching Wilson across the back of the neck as the man's head rebounded from the bar, where his charge had flung him. There was a detached coolness in Buck that the onlookers did not miss; he went after Wilson, hitting him again, short, efficient blows that hurt. Wilson was trying to flail his fists about, but Buck shocked him with a clipped punch underneath the heart. With mouth agape, Wilson staggered to the center of the room and sat down abruptly, sawing painfully for wind.

From behind the bar, Lovering said, "You going to throw him out or will I have to?"

Hank Wilson raised his head and glared at Jake Lovering. Then he looked at Buck and Manly. "Sonofabitches," he said. "Dirty sonofabitches, all of you."

Lovering snapped, "He's shot off his mouth for

the last time in my place. Without the star, he's just another bum."

"You heard Lovering," Buck said. "He don't want you in his place."

Rubbing a hand across his eyes, Wilson shifted to a sitting position. One side of his face was beet-red, and sawdust clung to his clothes. Looking at Manly, he said, "This is what you wanted, ain't it? Me thrown out. Well, I ain't finished with you yet, Manly. Not by a damned sight, I ain't finished."

"You'd better shut up," Manly said coldly.

"You going to shut me up?" Wilson pushed to his feet and stood there, weaving slightly. "Big man," he sneered. "Big, hell! I could tell plenty, and maybe I will. Maybe I will, and then you won't be so damned big any more." He turned to the door, his feet dragging. There, he turned and pointed his finger at Harry Buck. "And when I'm ready, I'll get you."

His boots thumped the walk and outside a man cursed as Wilson rammed him before driving off down the street. For a full minute, silence hung like a pall over the saloon. Then Lovering said, "On the house," and everything loosened up again.

Manly said, "Care for another?" Buck shook his head. "You went after him hard, Buck. Been thinking about it long?"

"Considerable," Buck admitted. He picked up

the badge and dropped it into his pocket. "Looks like I'll have to roust me a new deputy, don't it?"

"Might be hard to find," Manly said. "You're not on the right side of the fence."

"I ain't on any side," Buck said, "and I got him all picked out. Harms."

Manly felt like laughing, then he realized how devoid of humor this was. Harms had crossed him once, thrown him over; the thought that he would again be wearing a badge and siding Harry Buck disturbed Manly. He turned to Harms and said, "You ought to take another job, Harms. I mean that."

"He can make up his own mind," Harry Buck said evenly. "How about it, Harms?"

Everyone watched Harms curiously, for the habit of bowing when Manly spoke was deeply ingrained in the man; they all wondered if he could break it now. Harms did not look at Manly. Finally he said, "If Buck wants me, I'd be mighty grateful."

Manly stood still, thinking of all the times he had considered the moment when his authority might be disputed, and he was surprised to find it completely unlike his imaginings. How had he expected it? An uproar of sound and fury? An open fight with his enemies, and what big man lacks them?

Instead, only a pot-bellied man stood in a

saloon and spoke quietly, and his words shattered the pillars supporting the Manly power.

Manly said, "You're an ungrateful dog, Harms."

"Am I?" Harms looked at him then; he dared now. "Mr. Manly, I got to do this. You know why." He thrust his pudgy hands into his pockets, then took them out immediately. "Mr. Manly, everything was going all right until this morning. Now you know that's the truth, and I don't have to say no more about it." He began to sweat; talking back to Manly was a nerve-stretching experience for better men than he. "The thing is done, Mr. Manly, and I don't intend to speak of it; that is, as long as I can live my life as I see fit." This was as near a threat as his courage permitted him to make, yet Manly understood.

"You go right ahead, Harms," Manly said. "I'd be the last to try and stop you." His glance touched Harry Buck briefly. "Good luck with the job."

He laid a coin on the bar and walked out. On the porch, the evening breeze cooled the sweat on his forehead and upper lip. Behind him, in the saloon, voices commenced to pick up the threads of conversation and weave them into the multicolored cloth that constituted public opinion.

A small boy ran by. Manly hailed him and had George summoned from the stable. While he waited for the buggy, he considered the night's events and tried to evaluate their importance. He had to concede complete defeat as far as the law was concerned, not that he had made a habit of abusing it in the past; he would merely have to learn to live without its being at his easy beck and call.

Unpleasant as it was to think about, he tried to divine Havlock's intention regarding the story that was bound to be circulated about Jim. Of course Cardigan had to be lying, trying to throw some of the suspicion in another direction. Manly could scarcely blame him for that; desperate situations called for desperate measures. With Harms in office, Manly could have counted on a most inefficient investigation into any charges Havlock might bring, but Harry Buck was a different kind of man; one who would delve into all the attending circumstances, even Indian Reilly's death. All this could lead to plenty of unpleasantness.

George arrived with the buggy and Manly eased himself onto the seat. As the rig made a U-turn to leave town, Fred Allendale came out of his office on the corner and signaled. At Manly's motion, George wheeled the rig to the curb and stopped.

"I've got to talk to you," Allendale said. He glanced at George, then promptly forgot him; he was a man who considered any menial deaf and dumb to anything but the commands of their betters.

"Can't it wait until tomorrow?" Manly asked impatiently. "It'll be one o'clock by the time I get home, as it is."

"What happened tonight was no accident," Allendale said severely.

"I never thought it was," Manly murmured. "Fred, the trouble with you is that you think the entire world is populated with fools. Therefore, you were surprised when Willis Havlock outsmarted you."

"I don't need it rubbed in," Allendale said. "Damn it, Cardigan's spreading rumors about your son."

"That was to be expected," Manly said calmly. "Fred, don't you think I've been talked about before?"

"As an attorney," Allendale said, "I'd advise you to talk with the boy and see if you can't establish his whereabouts at the time of the robbery." He held up his hand to ward off any verbal blast Temple Manly might fling at him. "I'm serious, Mr. Manly. A witness would be all he would need to make Cardigan a liar."

"I'll find a witness," Temple Manly said. "Drive on, George."

THIRTEEN

The ranch house was dark and seemingly deserted when Manly returned home. He expected Lila to be in bed, and dismounted quietly at the porch, then stood there while George took the rig to the barn. While he waited, he heard a door open and close, then a light came down the hall. Lila said, "Temple? Is that you?" She was at the front door, shining the light onto the porch. "Why are you standing out there?"

He said nothing, just brushed past her and went into the parlor where he lighted another lamp. He seemed older and very tired as he lowered himself into his favorite chair.

She studied him for a moment, then said, "Harry Buck is the sheriff?"

"Yes. Willis Havlock did it. Damned clever of him."

Lila placed her lamp on a small table, then sat down near the arm of his chair. "Temple, does it really matter so much as all that? I mean, you own your land; nothing can really hurt you." She laid her head in his lap. "You've always worried so about everything. Is it such a tragedy if Buck's the sheriff?"

"Yes, it's a tragedy," Manly said tonelessly. "It's a tragedy to have everything I've worked so hard to build threatened." He waved his hands aimlessly. "I'm not talking about the land. I'm talking about the Temple Manly name, the Manly reputation."

"And the Temple Manly control? Temple, is that so important?"

"To me it is," he said. "Did Jim get home?"

"Several hours ago. He's sleeping."

"Would you ask him to come to the parlor?" He patted her hand when she hesitated. "Lila, it's important."

"All right, Temple."

After she went down the hall, Manly took out his tobacco and rolled a cigarette.

The cigarette was finished by the time Jim came from his room. He had slipped into a pair of trousers and a shirt, but the tail hung outside. His hair was tousled and he rubbed his face vigorously. "What's the matter? The house afire?"

"Sit down," Temple Manly said. He looked at his wife. "Would it be too much trouble to fix us some coffee?"

"There's some on the back of the stove that just needs warming."

Manly waited until she left, then said, "Jim, you overheard what Havlock said. I mean, what Cardigan told him. I didn't worry too much about it at the time, because I thought that Harms would take care of things."

"You think I did it?"

"Now, I didn't say that at all," Manly assured him. "Jim, don't get on your high horse about this." He paused a moment. "Harms stood up to me. Quit. Tonight the council appointed another man for sheriff. Harry Buck."

"What?" Jim Manly stared, then anger came into his face. "How the hell could you let that happen? I thought you had some control over people around here!"

Lila returned with the coffee and while she poured, neither spoke, giving them both time to reorganize their thoughts. Finally Temple Manly said, "I've never liked to be in a position where I had to prove anything about myself; my word should be sufficient, but somehow, somewhere, that's slipped away from me. Perhaps it started with Cardigan, and the night the posse came here. I shouldn't have gone with them, nor allowed you to go either, Jim. That was none of my business, actually. And yet it was." He brushed a hand across his eyes. "Sometimes it's difficult for me to determine where my business leaves off and others' begins." Absently, he added canned milk and sugar to his coffee, and then stirred it slowly. "Harry Buck won't take orders from me or any other man, Jim. And because of that, I'm afraid that we're going to have to prove where you were when the express company was robbed."

"Temple!" Lila said, but he silenced her with a wave of the hand.

Jim Manly hesitated, then said, "I told you that I was at Betty Cardigan's. Ain't my word enough?"

"It's not a question of your word being enough, Jim. Things have got to the point where my word can be doubted. We'll have to get Betty Cardigan to admit that you were there."

"She won't admit that," Jim said flatly. "Hell, that's her brother in jail! You think she'd say anything to make him look bad?" He licked his lips and slapped the arms of his chair. "What a mess. How am I going to prove I was there?"

"There must be a way," Temple Manly said. "I'll find a way."

"Sure," Jim said, grinning slightly. "We got to stick together now, huh, sir?"

"Yes," Manly said, warmed by the thought that he and his son were finally pulling in the same direction. "We can quarrel amongst ourselves but we stand united against the world. A good feeling, isn't it?" He drank some of his coffee, then put the cup aside, for he had allowed it to grow cold. "I don't pretend to understand what's happened these past few days. Perhaps, while we were trailing Cardigan, I allowed weakness to show, and my enemies seized upon it. Or perhaps I violated my basic rule and allowed

274

them to know me too well. Never let a man do that, son, for the worst enemy you will ever have is the man who was once a close friend; no other man can know you so well."

"I never had any friends," Jim Manly said.

"I'll have to talk to Betty Cardigan," Manly said. "I like her and I think she'll tell me the truth."

"She'll lie to save her brother," Jim said. "Wouldn't you lie to save me, your son?"

The boy had used the wrong tense; Temple Manly had already lied to himself for a number of years, yet he did not admit this. Instead he said, "I'll have to try anyway, Jim. Allendale feels that a witness would blow Cardigan's preposterous statements sky-high." Manly laughed briefly. "The whole thing is ridiculous, Jim. Why would you want to rob the express office anyway? If you wanted money, all you'd have to do is ask for it."

"Sure," Jim said. "Cardigan's guilty as hell and trying to make me out a goat to throw blame away from himself." He stood up and yawned. "Can I go back to bed now, sir?"

"Yes," Manly said. "Good night, son."

They sat in silence until Jim's footfalls receded down the hall. "More coffee?" Lila asked.

Temple Manly shook his head. "It'll keep me awake."

Lila gathered the cups, placing them on a tray.

Then she turned to him and said, "Temple, are you so afraid of being hurt?"

"Hurt?" He looked at her blankly. What nonsense was this?

"I never understood this before," she said, "but you're very unsure inside."

"That's utter nonsense," he said.

"You want to run everything because you trust no one," she said. "That's true, isn't it?"

"No," he said, without conviction. "I'm a builder, Lila, and I'm angered by anything that threatens my plans."

"What are you going to do if Jim is right, if Betty Cardigan refuses to help you?"

"I don't know," he said. "But there's always something a man can do."

"Something honest, Temple?"

That she could suspect him of dishonesty was at first a shock, then he realized that her suspicion was well grounded; he was now capable of anything.

"You fight fire with fire," he said and got to his feet, hobbling painfully to the bedroom.

There are some men whose personalities are so definitely established that no amount of fortune or misfortune can alter them, even slightly. Harry Buck was such a man. He accepted his appointment as sheriff with bland unconcern. After Temple Manly left town, Harry Buck walked to the jail. The office lamp was turned low and he brightened the flame before going into the cell block.

Wes Cardigan was on the bunk, a hand flung over his face. He looked up as Buck paused by the barred door.

"Get your supper all right?" Buck asked.

"Harms brought it in," Cardigan said. He sat up then, noticing for the first time the badge pinned to Buck's shirt. "What is this, Harry? You made a deputy or something?"

"Sheriff," Buck said dryly. "Harms resigned sudden-like."

"Resigned! Why he was Manly's . . ." He slumped back, his shoulders against the wall. "What's happening out there, Harry? What's going on?"

"A little early to tell yet," Buck admitted. He took a ring of keys from his pocket and opened the cell door. Then he stepped inside and placed his shoulders against the bars. "You told Willis Havlock a story, Wes. How straight was that?"

"Mighty straight," Cardigan said. "Harry, I wouldn't lie to you."

"Tell me about it," Buck invited.

"Just like I told Havlock, I came into town. It got dark early because of the storm. Not much traffic. In fact, after thinking about it, there wasn't hardly any at all. I guess everyone was home waiting for the cyclone." He paused, as though to straighten out a few facts in his mind. "When I neared the express office, a fella ran out. Couldn't see too good; gloomy, like I said. But I recognized his horse, and when he swung up, I got a good look at his face. It was Jim Manly."

"Wes, you can't be mistaken now?"

"No. No mistake. Sims came out then, just as Jim wheeled to ride out. Sims shot; the damned bullet passed within inches of me. For a minute I thought he had mistaken me for Jim. I yelled. Sims shot again and I answered him back. I guess Jim did too; there were three shots fired, then Sims fell off the porch. About that time, Hank Wilson came boiling out of Lovering's place. Jim was running down the street; I guess Hank saw us both. Me, I got the hell out of there, fast."

"Why didn't you tell Betty this?" Buck asked.

Wes Cardigan shrugged. "I wasn't thinking straight, I guess. No. That ain't it either. I thought she loved him, Harry. Hell, he was always smelling around the place, and she fed him and talked nice to him."

"Is that the truth, or just a story you're giving me?"

"What? Why would I give you a story, Harry?"

Buck tipped his head forward and concentrated on the making of a cigarette. "You're lying to me, Wes. That ain't the reason."

"I guess not," Cardigan said with a sigh. He wiped his mouth and worry deepened the lines around his mouth and eyes. "Harry, that was a Manly I saw. You understand, Temple Manly's kid. You think I dared to say anything? Christ, I was scared, Harry; Manly scares me. Can you believe that?"

"That I can believe," Harry Buck said. "Now it makes sense, why you ran instead of holding your ground." He laughed. "You know, all the time I was in that posse, I was trying to figure out what the hell you were running from. I guess I knew all along."

"What you going to do about this?" Cardigan asked.

Buck's shoulder lifted and fell. "I guess I'll try to prove the truth, Wes. It's all a man can do."

"Against Jim Manly!"

"Jim Manly's no different from anyone else," Harry Buck said. "Neither is the old man."

"God," Wes said, sagging down on his bunk. "I believe you, Harry. You've given me some hope."

"Likely Manly's going to set the date for a quick trial," Buck said. "If I'm going to prove anything, I'll have to do it fast." He opened the door again, stepped into the hall and locked it. "Harms is the deputy now; I kicked Wilson out. If I ain't here, just ask him and he'll get what you want."

In the outer office Buck turned the desk lamp down again and went to the street. He considered sleep and found the thought enticing, yet he knew that this was not possible, not if he expected to get the jump on Temple Manly, a man who had been getting the jump on people all his life.

At the stable he saddled his horse and rode out a few minutes later, taking care that he didn't arouse a lot of attention by parading down the main street. With Gunlock behind him, Buck swung toward the breaks and the Cardigan ranch a few hours' ride away.

The night was like ink with only the faintest sliver of moon, and Buck held his pace down to a walk. In an hour he left the main road, taking a little-used trail, and once on this, he urged the horse to a trot.

By the time he broke out of the fringe timber above the Cardigan place, he estimated that it was well after one in the morning. No lights showed below, but then, he hadn't expected any. Easing down, Buck rode into the yard, exercising his customary care. He did not make a lot of noise, but neither did he try to be silent; he wanted to announce his arrival to Betty Cardigan and still not alarm her.

As he dismounted, Betty spoke from a doorway. "Sing out who's there! I've got a rifle here!"

"Harry." He heard her move and a moment later the yellow smear of lamplight brightened the room. He stepped inside and paused. She wore a long, cotton nightgown; her pale hair was a shining aureole around her face.

"Can I fix you something, Harry?" She looked at him, squinting her eyes against the lamp's unaccustomed glare.

"A cup of coffee maybe," he said.

She turned to the stove and a near dead fire, then stopped suddenly and turned back, noticing for the first time the badge he wore. "Harry!" She threw down the stick of wood and came up to him, the question in her eyes.

"A long story," he said. "Harms meant what he said, Betty." He took off his hat and sat down at the table. "Manly came to town but Willis Havlock outsmarted him. I got the appointment, at least until election time. Then Manly will pull the votes to the man he backs."

Feeding the fire gave her time to think about this and after putting on the coffeepot she came to the table. When she passed in front of the lamp, she was sharply outlined through the nightgown; Buck tipped his head down and looked at his hands until she sat down.

"I talked to Wes," Buck said softly. "He claims that he saw Jim Manly come out of the express office. Because of what he saw he was afraid of what Manly might do. That's understandable."

"Yes," she said. "Yes, he had something to be afraid of. And if you push this, Harry, Manly will give you something to fear."

"Maybe," Buck said. He fell silent for a moment and the only sounds were the roar of the fire and his horse stirring outside. "When I was a kid in south Kansas, a man was reckoned to be grown when he could lift a rifle and take a shot at his neighbor. We had our share of the Manlys, and we had our share of fear, but in the end we bucked them and to our surprise we found that they were just as afraid of us as we were of them. You ever wonder why Manly tries to run everything? Because he's scared. He's scared that someday all the little men he's walked on will get up and stomp his guts out."

She reached across the table and took his hand. "Harry, Wes is my brother and I love him, but I don't want him dead just because he had to prove something."

"He's going to be dead if I don't prove it," Harry Buck said grimly. "Wes said that Jim Manly robbed the express company and shot at Sims. I'm the sheriff now and I'm going to find out whether or not that's a fact."

"Do you think Temple Manly will stand by and allow you to do that?"

"No," he admitted. "But I won't let that stop me."

The coffeepot began to rock and she took it

off the stove. Filling two cups, she brought them to the table. "You're tired, Harry. You can have Wes's bed."

He pursed his lips and considered this a moment. "Thanks, no. I'd better get back to town."

She studied him thoughtfully, then smiled. "Now who's afraid, Harry?"

"I am," he admitted. "Not of you, Betty, but of myself. A man can want something a long time. Want so bad that he can't trust himself." He lifted his coffee. "Waitin' a week or so more won't kill me."

"Does everything have to be exactly right with you?"

"Nope. But there are some things that's either right or wrong. Sleepin' with a woman when I ain't married is one of 'em." After he said it, he realized that he had been too blunt; there was bright color in her face and anger in her eyes. He realized then that he had cheapened her by implying that she had extended an invitation. So he said, "I guess I could talk you into doing something that ain't right. And if I couldn't talk you into it, I'm ornery enough to take what I want. It's just as well that we're not alone in the same house until we're married."

"Whatever you say, Harry."

"Jim—he came around here some, didn't he?"

She paused. "Yes. Too often."

"I was wonderin'," Buck said, "whether he showed up the day the express office was robbed."

"No," she said solemnly. "I was alone all day. Wes took a string of saddle horses over to Kohler's, then went on to Gunlock from there. I remember that I did my baking that day."

"You might have to repeat that under oath," Buck said easily.

"I would," she assured him, "it's the truth."

He finished the rest of his coffee and stood up. She got up too and came around the table. "Harry, I love you. If Wes doesn't get hurt, then that's all I ask. I don't care whether the Manlys get their lumps or not."

"There's a matter of simple right to consider," Harry Buck said.

"Yes, you'd think like that," she said. She slipped her arms around his waist and lay against him, her head on his chest. "Men always consider that, don't they?"

"Wouldn't be much of a world if a man looked out only for himself." The warmth of her disturbed him and gently he put his arms around her. When she raised her lips, he kissed her with an open hunger, then released her abruptly.

"Late," he said and put on his hat, moving toward the door. She walked with him and stood there, outlined by the lamp, while he mounted. By exerting a definite will he managed to turn the horse instead of going back inside with her and closing the door.

Quickly he stormed from the yard, not looking back until he topped the rise a quarter of a mile from the cabin. The return to Gunlock was made in easy stages while Harry Buck turned over several possibilities in his mind. He had enough now, he felt, to arrest Jim Manly and put him in jail, but that hardly seemed smart. Temple Manly would only go bail and have him released, and, if that failed, he would hire a Dallas lawyer and get the boy off scot-free.

No, he would have to be as smart as Temple Manly, Buck decided. As smart and as careful. If he could accumulate enough evidence, then spring it on Manly, he would have a closed case. But he would need more evidence than he now had.

"Then I'll get it," Harry Buck said to the night and rode on toward Gunlock.

Temple Manly had an early breakfast after soaking his feet, and went to the porch to sit. He noticed with some satisfaction that the swelling had decreased and some of the soreness had left his calves and ankles.

The sun was bright and hot and he smoked a cigarette while the hands went about their work, detailed by three loud-voiced foremen. At one time, Manly had handled all the supervisory work on the ranch, but he had outgrown that, as he had almost everything else. Now he rarely offered more than a suggestion, and this only when a foreman happened to be in his office. Contact with his ranch had grown less and less until he often thought of himself as a visitor to the place he had created. That was the way things went when one outgrew a way of life. The conditions of pasture and water he now heard first-hand from his foremen; he no longer felt the urge to look for himself.

After the yard cleared, Manly waited until George came from the barn, then signaled for the man to come over.

George removed his hat as he always did in Manly's presence. "Yes, sir?"

"Sit down, George," Manly said, indicating a rocker.

For a heartbeat, George just stood there; he was like a barnyard dog suddenly invited to lie on the hearth rug. But an order was an order and George had spent a lifetime trying not to offend his betters. After he sat down, Manly said, "You've been with me a long time, haven't you, George?"

"Yes, sir."

"Happy here?" Then Manly laughed. "Of course you're happy here. And I'm mighty happy to have you working for me, George." He took out his sack tobacco and after rolling a smoke, offered the makings to George, who accepted after some hesitation. "How much am I paying you now?"

"Forty a month, Mr. Manly."

"That hardly seems enough," Manly said. "I'll have Schroeder raise you to fifty." From George's expression, Manly realized that he had offered too much; men like George were suspicious of gratuities; a hard life of servitude was their lot, almost a birthright.

Manly reached out and slapped George on the arm. "Yes, I said fifty and I meant it. I believe in rewarding a loyal man." He paused to draw on his cigarette and stare out onto the flats. "And I think you are a loyal man, George."

"Yes, sir. There ain't anything I wouldn't do for you and Mrs. Manly."

"That's fine," Manly said. "Really fine, George."

"I—I'd better get on, Mr. Manly. There's harness to fix and that roan's back sores need doctoring." He started to get up but Manly's hand pulled him back.

"No hurry about that," he said. "George, there's been some trouble; likely you've got wind of it. They have Wes Cardigan in jail."

"Well, I don't pay much attention to what goes on outside the ranch, Mr. Manly. To tell the truth, I keep pretty busy here, just mindin' my own business."

"That's commendable," Manly said. "But to get back to what I was saying, this fella has accused Jim of some pretty serious things. Now you know Jim. He's full of hell, but he's not bad. What I mean is, the sheriff has quit and Buck's wearing the badge. He don't mean to make trouble, but you know how a new man is, real conscientious."

"Sure," George said. "I remember when Tim first come here. He was trying to do everything and I . . ."

"That's it exactly," Manly said, smiling. "What I'm trying to say is that when Buck comes around, I want you to tell him that Jim was here all afternoon the day the express company was held up."

George looked at Temple Manly, then at the cigarette held between his fingers. "Mr. Manly, Jim wasn't here."

"I know that," Manly said, trying to keep his voice pleasant. "But we've got to avoid trouble, George."

"You want me to lie, Mr. Manly?"

Leave it to the fool to be so bluntly honest! "Ah, George, it's not exactly a lie."

"It ain't the truth, Mr. Manly."

With an effort, Manly tapped the well of his patience. "Now, George, I don't want to split hairs with you. Just think of it as another order; I've given you a thousand that you never questioned."

"But I ain't lied, Mr. Manly. Never!"

The man's insistence was beginning to anger Manly and he was sore put to control his temper. "I want to do what's right, but I need your help, George. I need a man I can trust implicitly."

"Well, I guess I can be trusted," George said, "but I sure don't want to lie about anything. Nosiree, I sure don't."

"Now, see here," Manly said. "I have important things to do and sitting here quibbling about this isn't one of them. Buck will come here and when he does, you'll tell him that Jim never left the place all that afternoon."

Slowly, carefully, George got out of the rocking chair, and threw away the cigarette Manly had given him. "Mr. Manly, I can't do that."

Why, Manly asked himself, did all the know-nothings, do-nothings, have so many damned principles? Probably because they were free and could so easily be afforded.

"I just offered you a raise, George. Can you turn that down?"

"Yes, sir. I didn't need any raise, Mr. Manly. Now, if it's all right with you, I got that harness to mend and the roan's back to . . ."

"Goddamn you!" Manly shouted, rearing to his feet. "You going to obey me or not?" He did not need an answer; by the way George backed off the porch, he could see that the man would remain stupidly stubborn. "All right, you ungrateful bastard! Get off my place! Right now! Start down the road a-running." He pawed through his pockets, finding a few bills. "Here! Here's your goddamned pay, now get the hell out of my sight!"

George was starting and swallowing hard, then he was running out of the yard, taking the town road. The cook came from the mess shack and stared, but went back inside a moment later. Lila's heels tapped the bare hall floor as she hurried through the house. She came out, saw George's retreating figure and her husband's furiously angry face.

"Temple, what in heaven's name happened?"

"The moral sonofabitch!" Manly said. "Flung it in my teeth, that's what he did." He waved his hand toward the disappearing man. "The bastard can sweep out saloons for all I care. Damn his moral soul anyway!"

"Temple, you tried to buy him!" She said it like an accusation.

He whirled on her, the threat of violence in his manner. "Buy him? Hell yes, I tried to buy him, just like I have everything I own. Only he wouldn't sell. The stupid fool. He wouldn't sell!"

FOURTEEN

Temple Manly's moment of fury passed and he was ashamed that she saw him now as a man whose courage and honor were only a studied pose. He quailed inwardly before the shock in her eyes. He read scorn in the planes of her cheeks and imagined that she loathed him even as he silently pleaded for her understanding.

"He was just a hired man," Lila said. "Temple, what did you expect him to do?"

"Show his loyalty to the hand that's fed him." He could not bear to admit the totality of his error so he groped to fling blame on George who would never dream of defending himself.

"What do you mean fed him?" she asked. "Temple, you've always taken credit for 'feeding' people after they work hard for their bread. George has earned his pay these many years; he owes you nothing!"

"And I suppose you feel the same way?" he snapped.

"You're my husband," she said softly. "No, of course, I feel differently." Gently she took his arm. "Temple, why don't we go away for a while?"

"Run?" He said the word as though it were indescribably filthy.

"I don't think of it as running," she said. "I would rather think of it as the only remaining solution; we have both gone too far to turn back. We could sell this place and settle in Dallas or Fort Worth. If you insist on staying here, you'll only destroy yourself, along with the people who have trusted you for many years."

He laughed at this. "Fool woman," he said. "Destroy myself?" He struck his own chest. "I'm a builder, not a destroyer! And I'm not through building!" He wheeled and started for the door. "I'm going to town. I'll be back when I get here."

She must have thought to stop him for she lifted her hand, then let it drop limply to her side. When she heard him banging around the hall closet she went inside. He was shrugging into his coat. His rifle leaned against the wall.

"What are you doing with the rifle?" she asked.

"Quite obviously I intend to take it to town with me."

"The rifle won't help you," she said evenly.

He picked up the gun and tucked it in the crook of his arm. "Have someone hitch the—never mind, I'll take care of it myself."

When he turned back toward the front door she caught his arm and held him. "Temple, I love Jim as much as you do but I don't want you to destroy yourself for him."

"A little late to think of me, isn't it?" He

pulled himself erect, the old pride making his eyes stabbing as they regarded her. "To accuse my son is to accuse me. Somewhere along the line, people have lost their respect for the Manly word. So I'll have to go out and get it back."

He left her standing there with her unspoken protests while he limped across the yard to the barn. Hitching his own buggy offered moments of frustration for it had been years since Temple Manly had waited on himself. One of the foremen came in to offer his help, but Manly sent him away with a curse.

Mounted at last, he spun out of the yard, taking the town road. The wind in his face seemed to fan away the heat of his temper until his thoughts became once again organized and clear.

Manly found that he could now think of George with somewhat less heat. The man had only reacted from simple instinct and training. *Damn it,* Manly thought. *I trained him too well.* Or had he trained him at all? Manly was forced to admit that a possibility existed that his judgment of people was not always accurate. How easy it was for a man to fool himself about others. He had supposed that his authority was absolute; it had never been strongly questioned before.

"But I'll straighten it all out," Manly said to the empty land, and with this thought settled himself to endure the remaining miles.

When he came to the cutoff leading to Wes

Cardigan's place, Manly halted, and on impulse turned off. "I'll talk to the girl," he said to himself. While he drove along he considered the things he would say. Polite things, to be sure. Polite but firm. A man always caught the most flies with honey. Too bad he hadn't thought of that while dealing with George and Harms.

The ride proved rough and tiring and by the time Temple Manly arrived at the Cardigan place, he was in anything but a pleasant frame of mind. His shirt was sweated through and dust had been ground into the collar. The jolting buggy had worked a new ache in his legs.

Betty Cardigan heard the rig rattle down the hill and came out to see who it was. When Manly wheeled into the yard, she stepped to windward in order to escape the settling dust. "I certainly never expected to see you," she said. "Would you care for some cold buttermilk?"

He almost admitted to having a great thirst. Then he decided it would be better if he declined, for when a man accepted a gift his position was always weakened slightly.

"Thank you, no," he said, trying to keep his voice pleasant. "I merely came for a talk and I'll be very brief."

"All right, Mr. Manly," Betty said. "You suit yourself."

"Your brother has been circulating talk about my son," Manly said. "I want it stopped."

"Wes is in jail; how could he spread talk?"

"I don't mean to quibble," he said sharply. "Miss Cardigan, Wes fed Havlock a cock-and-bull story and Havlock's passed it all over town."

"Then you ought to see Havlock," she said.

"I intend to," Manly said. "But I'm warning you, girl. I won't stand to have my boy slandered."

She looked at him squarely and shrugged. "I'm sure Wes wouldn't say anything about a man that wasn't true, Mr. Manly."

His face took on color and angry lights brightened his eyes. "Are you saying that my son is a thief?"

"I didn't say anything," Betty pointed out. "Wes said it, and you ought to know Jim well enough to decide who's telling the truth."

"I know the truth," Manly said, his voice rigidly controlled. "And I mean to throw the lie in Wes Cardigan's teeth." He bent forward slightly and looked down at her, menace heavy in his expression. "My son informs me that he was here with you the evening the express office was robbed. I know that he got home late and I have no reason to doubt him. When I spoke to him about this, he said that you would deny seeing him to save your brother. Now I want the truth from you and no nonsense about it."

"Do you think you can stand the truth?"

"Don't toy with me, young woman," Manly said. "I have no patience with that now."

"The truth is that Jim's a liar," Betty said evenly. "He was never here that afternoon."

There was no change in Temple Manly's expression. He nodded, as though her answer had been exactly as he had expected. "My son was right; you're a cheap slut who would lie her head off to save her kin."

"Just as you're denying the truth about your own son. Or is it yourself that you wish to save, Mr. Manly?"

He flung his hands wide. "Don't worry about me, girl; I'll be here when trash like you are gone!" He pulled his voice into tempered softness. "I'll ask again, and this time I expect the truth."

"You wouldn't know it if you were slapped across the face with it," she said. "If you expect me to say that Jim's lily-white, then you're wasting your time. Good day, Mr. Manly."

"Good day, is it?" He lifted the reins, ready to move out. "Don't think I'm finished! If you were a man I'd beat the truth out of you! I know your kind; I've fought them all my life. A lot of creeping things, ready to swallow a man like locusts stripping a field." He stabbed her with his eyes. "I'll clear this up, you wait and see, and when I do I'll see you gone from this land!"

With that said, he wheeled the buggy and

stormed up the hill, not once looking back. He chided himself for ever entertaining the thought that she would help him. And the way she quietly defied him left him oddly nervous. Had she flown into a rage, thrown something, sworn at him, he would have felt better because that was the way people were supposed to act when hard-pressed. But she had presented only a stony indifference.

A sense of acute failure began to dog him and he thought of returning home, but the thought of facing Lila pushed him on toward Gunlock.

Maybe a showdown with Harry Buck would be the thing; without a doubt it had been building for a long time, and incidents during the posse's tedious chase only added fuel to an already smoldering clash of personalities. The thought of hitting out at someone, anyone, pleased Temple Manly and made the ride endurable.

There was a mild scatter of traffic on Gunlock's main stem as Manly drove along. Halfway down he turned on Charity Street, toward the jail.

Manly was almost overjoyed to find Harry Buck's saddle horse tied at the hitch rack. Dismounting carefully, Manly hobbled across the walk. The office door was open, but Buck was not there. Manly hesitated for an instant, then walked through the short hallway to the cell block.

From his bunk, Wes Cardigan rolled over,

saw Manly standing there, then slowly sat up. "Huh," Cardigan said. "Surprised to see you here."

"I'll bet you are," Temple Manly said. "I've come to call you a goddamn liar, Cardigan!"

"Call me anything you want," Cardigan said. "A day or so ago I'd have mumbled something to myself and took it, but I sure as hell don't have to take it now. You can kiss my butt as far as I'm concerned."

"I see through you, Cardigan; you're telling lies about my boy to make things look better for yourself. Well, I won't stand for that." He suddenly grasped the barred door and jerked it as though trying to remove it from the hinges. "If this wasn't between us, I'd beat the truth out of you!"

"By God!" Cardigan flared, suddenly goaded to reveal all the vague angers he felt against an unsympathetic world. "I wish this door was open! I'd smash your sonofabitchin' face!"

The words, the tone, inflamed the underlying passion that was the only thing these two men had in common. By common consent they flattened themselves against the bars, arms hooked through, awkwardly pounding, flogging each other. Manly wrapped his arms around Wes Cardigan's neck, pressing the young man's face cruelly against the bars while his free hand flailed away. And Cardigan's hand sought Manly's throat, as though his one passion in life was to tear it from the man's body.

Their breathing was hoarse and heavy and now and then their fists found a mark, never solidly, but hard enough to draw blood. They strained against the separating bars, strained to expel the frustration and resentment bottled within them. They were like two men going down with a ship, and ignoring that danger to settle forever between themselves all those grievances accumulated against mankind after a lifetime of silent endurance; they fought there in the cell block as though they might never get another chance to settle these undefined differences.

This was the way Harry Buck found them, bleeding and still trying to hurt each other. Roughly he jerked Temple Manly away from the door. Manly's face was bleeding; his upper lip was split and there was a cut above his eye. Cardigan's nose was dribbling blood and his left eye was closing rapidly. Both men breathed like wrestlers in the last stages of exhaustion.

"You damn fools!" Buck said. He whirled to Manly. "What the hell are you doing here?"

"Searching for the truth."

"Get out of here!"

"When I'm ready I'll . . ."

Buck seized Manly with unexpected fervor and half spun him toward the hall door. There was a moment of insulted objection and Harry Buck lashed out with his fist, driving Manly toward the exit. The blow shocked Manly more than it injured him and then he stepped into the office while Buck closed the door in between.

"You come in here again like that," Buck said flatly, "and I'll put you into a cell of your own." He waved his hand toward the corner wash basin. "Go wash your face. You look like some overgrown kid who's been rollin' in the street."

Harry Buck's simile shook Manly badly, for he knew then of this man's magnificent contempt. While Manly washed, Buck sat on the corner of his desk, watching; this in itself aggravated Manly.

Finally he turned to Buck. "Do you think I'm going to take these filthy lies about Jim without striking back?"

"What filthy lies?" Buck asked gently.

"You know what I mean. That bald-faced lie about my son." Harry Buck shook out his sack of tobacco and rolled a smoke. Temple Manly waited, expecting him to speak, and when Buck didn't, Manly wiped his dripping face and hung up the towel. "I suppose you're like the others. You'd believe trash like Cardigan instead of . . ."

"Who says Cardigan is trash?" Buck asked. He looked intently at Manly as though any answer the man might give would be immeasurably important.

A sudden and complete caution filled Temple

Manly. "Why," he said, "I mean, what is Cardigan anyway?"

"A man."

"But not a very important man," Manly said. "Hell, Buck, don't twist my words!"

"I'm not. They're your definitions." He slid off the desk corner and picked up his cartridge belt, buckling it around his waist. "My horse is outside, Mr. Manly. I want you to come with me."

"What for? Where?"

"You just come along," Buck said, opening the front door. He stood there patiently as though he intended to stand there forever, or as long as necessary to get his way. Manly sighed and stepped out, pausing while Buck locked the door.

Harms came out of the corner bakery and approached the jail, a sack of cookies in his hand. He saw Manly standing there, the habitual scowl marring his forehead. When Harms reached them, he spoke to Buck. "I guess I'll hang around the jail until you get back, Harry." His glance touched Temple Manly. "Run afoul of the law, Mr. Manly?"

"You go to hell, Harms."

"Likely I'll meet you there," Harms said dryly and inserted his key in the lock.

Buck untied his horse as Manly swung up into the buggy. Instead of riding, Buck looped the reins on the back of the buggy and got in beside

Manly. "Take the road to your place," Buck said. Manly stifled his objections and swung the rig around in the street.

As they clattered out of town, Manly said, "Just because I've agreed to this doesn't mean that you've buffaloed me, Buck."

"Sure. I didn't think that," Buck said. He cocked a foot on the dashboard and reared back in the seat, one arm flung across the back to brace himself. "Mr. Manly, I could have arrested Jim on Cardigan's say-so. You wonder why I didn't?"

"I don't give a damn," Manly snapped. "I'd have had him free within forty-eight hours."

"That's why I didn't arrest him," Buck said. "I wanted to be able to hold him when I did put him in jail."

Manly's head came around with a jerk. "Why damn you! You're just like the others!"

"Nope," Buck said. "I'm different." He tapped the star on his shirt front. "This makes me different, Mr. Manly."

The point of this escaped Temple Manly, but he remained silent, not wishing to argue with Buck. For over an hour they drove in silence, then Buck indicated a turn-off. Temple Manly said, "That goes to my winter range."

"That's where we're going," Buck told him.

"Nothing up there," Manly said. "Just a line cabin and an old horse corral."

"We'll go anyway," Buck said flatly and Manly swung up the faintly marked trail. The horses strained in the harness and the ride turned rough for there was considerable brush and dead limbs choking the road. An hour passed, then Manly broke into a brief clearing and stopped to rest the team.

"What's up here that's so important?" Manly asked.

"We'll see," Harry Buck said easily. He took out his tobacco, offered it to Manly, then rolled a smoke for himself. After he got it drawing he said, "You shouldn't have jumped Cardigan like that. The news will get out and you'll look pretty bad."

"I do what I do," Manly snapped. "I ask no man to understand it."

"No," Buck admitted, "I guess that's the truth. You just *tell* him to understand it."

"That's wrong?" Manly snorted through his nose. "In the army a general doesn't have to tell why he gives an order."

"This ain't the army, and you ain't a general," Buck pointed out.

"I built this country and that gives me some rights."

"There's where you and me differ in opinion," Buck said. "Mr. Manly, you built this country because you wanted to; no one asked you. And because of that, you got no rights that are special. How long do folks have to keep paying? You ever establish a price or a time limit?"

"Well, that's a hell of a way to put it!"

"What other way is there?" He butted out his smoke. "Let's go."

Manly drove on, pushing higher until he came to the winding trail marking the last mile and a half to his line cabin. As they drew into the clearing, Harry Buck reached over and took the reins from Manly's hand.

He sawed the team to a halt and looked at the ground, his eyes moving ahead toward the cabin and the huge corral. "Had visitors," he said softly. "Well, no use getting down here. Might as well drive the rest of the way." He clucked to the team and approached the cabin, stopping there. He swung down and had his careful look around, examining meticulously the bare ground by the door.

Manly dismounted and hobbled painfully to the watering trough where he sat down. He watched Buck for a time, then said, "What the hell are we here for?"

"To recover the money taken from the express office," Buck said mildly. He kept swinging his head, scanning the circle of choking brush that ringed the yard. Temple Manly opened his mouth to speak, then thought better of it and closed it quickly. Without looking at Manly, Buck said, "Get your rifle out of the buggy, Mr. Manly."

He had spoken softly and Manly jerked his head up. "What?"

"Go on, go on, man," Buck urged. "A set of tracks came in, but they haven't gone out."

Manly stood up and took a few steps toward the rig; he stopped quickly when Hank Wilson said, "That's far enough, Manly!"

Immediately, Harry Buck pinpointed Wilson's position behind a clump of dense brush; Buck stood motionless, his hands idle at his sides. "Why don't you come out, Hank? I knew you were around someplace." There was no hint of tension in Buck's voice, although a heavy silence seemed to settle over the clearing.

"Sure you did," Wilson said. "Saw you playin' Injun." He stood erect then, his head and shoulders above an alder thicket. Manly shifted his feet and Wilson said, "Forget the rifle, Manly. I've got both of you on the hip, haven't I? You can't see my hands and I might have a gun pointed your way."

"Did you get what you came after?" Buck asked quietly.

"Sure," Wilson said. "Always knew I would." He laughed triumphantly. "I'd have got it the other day if you hadn't butted your nose in."

"Eight thousand won't take you far," Buck said. "Besides, you'll have to cross Texas to get to Mexico. You think the Rangers will let you do that?"

"They won't stop me," Hank Wilson said. "Harry, use your head now. A couple of shots and I'm a free man. Who's to say I did the killing? Not you two."

"Thought you liked witnesses," Buck said.

"Now, I don't have the time now," Wilson said. He laughed again. "Do I make you nervous, Harry, standing like this, where you can't see my hands? Got you guessing, ain't I? Where's my gun? In my hand or in my holster?" Wilson paused to let this soak in. "Why don't you take a chance, Harry? You was real willing the other day."

"My God," Manly said, "this is mur—"

"Shut up," Harry Buck said softly. He never once removed his attention from Hank Wilson, still in the same position.

Temple Manly felt the dry nettle stinging of sweat on his forehead and stifled the impulse to raise his hand and wipe it away. He studied Harry Buck; the man seemed completely calm and he wondered how this could be possible. In his own mind he tried to summon his knowledge of Hank Wilson in order to guess the man's next move, and found that his observations stood him in little use now. Whether the man had his gun in hand or holstered was only a guess at best, and Manly was sure that Wilson would fire the first shot before either of them could lift a weapon. Manly looked again at Buck; the decision here was his. Buck could not afford to await Wilson's first move, yet Manly wondered if Buck could put aside every instinct and cut the man down by surprise.

Harry Buck must have been debating this too, for quite unexpectedly he drew. The man was as fast as Manly had ever seen. Buck's gun rose hip high and he wiped his palm across the hammer, rolling his shots into the bushes. Hank Wilson fired once; Manly heard the shot whip through the trees, then the man wilted from sight. Manly would have gone forward then if Buck hadn't said, "Wait." He was kicking out the spent shells and reloading. With his gun ready, he went ahead, approaching the brush carefully. Hank Wilson lay on his back, his stomach a red damage; he seemed undeniably dead to Temple Manly. Wilson's horse was nearby and Harry Buck removed the saddlebags. Unbuckling a strap, he brought out the stolen express money.

"Do you want to know how I knew what he was after, Mr. Manly?"

"A lucky guess," Manly said.

"Not a guess at all," Harry Buck said. "Mr. Manly, I know that your son buried the money here. Hank Wilson was following him when I stopped him."

"That's a lie . . ." Manly stopped, his face chalky.

"Is it a lie?" Buck asked. "This is a moment of

truth, Mr. Manly. This money"—he waved it at Manly—"was found by Harms and me together, only we left it where it was buried. I wanted your son to come after it, but Hank Wilson beat him to it."

"Then you haven't a thing on him," Temple Manly said, the sunshine of hope reflected in his face. "You'd never get a conviction on what you have, Buck, and you know it."

"Maybe I wouldn't," Buck admitted. "Maybe a jury would turn him loose, but I know that now you're going to stop lying to yourself about your son, Mr. Manly. And maybe you'll stop lying to yourself about what kind of man you are." He paused. "Harms told me why he quit, and I know what was in the envelope he gave back."

"The fat fool!"

"And George told me why you fired him," Buck said. He shook his head sadly. "Mr. Manly, didn't you know they'd tell?" He asked this as though completely baffled how any man could overlook so elemental a fact of human nature.

The false pride and the false anger drained out of Temple Manly; his shoulders sagged appreciably and he looked older, more haggard. "I suppose I'm under arrest now?"

"No," Buck said softly. "I think you've got something to do first."

"Ah," Manly said, anguish in his voice, "is there no mercy in you, Buck? None at all? God, he's my son!"

"Mr. Manly, don't tell me how much you've done for him, how many times you've lied for him, because you never did any of those things for Jim."

"I did, I did!" Manly yelled, and the timber swallowed up the boom of his voice. "Do you think I really cared about myself?" He stopped then, aware of what he said. "No, it must have been more than that, Buck. It has to be more than that. I didn't build all of this on deceit, Buck!" He smashed his fist against his chest. "There is honor in me, man! You know that it wasn't all a lie!"

"No, not all," Buck said. "I'm going to arrest Jim, Mr. Manly. If you try to stop me, I guess I'll have to shoot you."

"Arrest my boy?" Temple Manly shook his head. "By God, no, Buck! I'll bring him in. You have my word on that."

"Your word isn't any good any more, Mr. Manly."

The truth of this was a crushing weight on Temple Manly, but he did not get angry. "All right, Buck. But give me a chance. Come with me. I'd want that because now I know I'm weak and I might fail."

"Could be this time you won't fail," Buck said.

"A man is never so strong as when he admits his weakness."

"I won't spare him this time," Manly promised while mounting the buggy. "Do you believe me, Buck?"

"Let's say that I'd like to believe you, Mr. Manly."

"But I want to make everything right," Manly was saying as he wheeled the team around. "Buck, I mean to make it right."

"Your intentions may be good," Buck said, clinging to the pitching rig, "but I don't think it can be set right now. You're too late on a lot of things."

With a complete disregard for safety, Temple Manly flung his team and buggy down the rutted trail, not slacking his pace until he came out on the flats and drove toward the succession of gates that led to his own ranch yard. Harry Buck did not speak during the ride; there were times when a man was best left alone to sort out his thoughts.

Buck dismounted several times to open and close gates. The ranch house and outbuildings were less than a mile away when Buck came to the last gate. As he moved to close it, Temple Manly suddenly lashed the team into a wild run, leaving Buck to yell and charge after him through a cloud of dust. With Buck's saddle horse tied to the back of the buggy, Manly had no fear of pursuit. This maneuver gained ten precious minutes for him.

He drove into the yard, halting by the porch. Lila ran out, her eyes filled with worry. "Temple, what is it?"

He got down, unmindful of the pain in his feet. "Where is Jim?"

"In the barn, I think. Temple, is there something wrong?"

"Go into the house and stay there."

"But what is it?" Then she saw Harry Buck running on the flats. "Isn't that Harry out there?" She stepped toward him but he pushed her roughly aside.

"Damn it, woman, I said get into the house!" He swung his head toward the barn in time to see Jim come to the doorway and look out. Without hesitation, Manly started to limp across the yard. Lila called to him but he did not seem to hear her.

When Temple Manly drew near enough to speak, Jim said, "You look like you're in one hell of a hurry."

"You insolent dog," Temple Manly said. "What have I whelped?"

The tone caused Jim Manly to take a backward step. He raised his hands in mock defense. "Hey! What the hell's the matt—"

Manly was now close enough to strike; his fist smashed into his son's mouth, sending him crashing back against the door. In a rush, Temple Manly closed with him. He took the young man's gun and flung it away, then he seized Jim by the hair and began to drag him across the yard. With a shriek, Lila left the porch, meeting her husband in the middle of the yard. She began to hammer at Manly with her fists. "Let him go! Let him go!"

"He robbed the express company," Manly said, not looking at her. "This pup did it, can't you understand that?"

She began to cry and tug at his arms vised so tightly around Jim Manly's neck. "Didn't you know? Were you so blind with yourself that you didn't know?" Tears streaked her face. "Oh, you're hurting him! He's bleeding!"

"I could kill him," Temple Manly said. "With my bare hands, I could kill him!"

She slapped Manly and pulled at his hair; her fingernails left raw tracks across his cheeks. "Blind! Blind, blind fool! You couldn't look at anyone but yourself long enough to see the truth!"

Out of breath, Harry Buck made the last dash across the yard. Roughly, he pulled Lila away; she fell to the ground and sat there, weeping. Buck broke Manly's grip on the young man and from his hip pocket he produced a set of handcuffs. He clamped them on Jim Manly's wrists, then stood back, sawing painfully for wind.

Temple Manly looked at the circlets of steel and the last shred of veneer vanished. Suddenly he flung his arms around his son and clutched him tightly. "Boy, boy, where have I been all these years? Where did I lose you?"

FIFTEEN

Temple Manly insisted on driving his son to town while Harry Buck rode along behind. There was no talk between them; they were years too late for that. Lila did not go with them and Harry Buck could understand why. He supposed that Temple Manly also understood, although that too might have come too late.

The sun was almost down by the time they reached Gunlock. Harry Buck was surprised to find John Kohler and Betty Cardigan waiting outside the jail. Harms was sitting behind the desk when Temple Manly came in with his son.

At Buck's nod, Harms took Jim Manly into the cell block and locked him up. When he returned, Wes Cardigan was with him.

"Figured this was all right now," Harms said. He avoided meeting Temple Manly's eyes.

"Yes, it's all right," Buck said. "I'll explain it to the judge and Fred Allendale." He made a motion with his hand. "Do you mind stepping outside for a minute?" This motion included them all and he waited until the door was closed.

Temple Manly stood in the center of the room, his head bent forward. "I suppose it will be all over town in an hour?"

"About Jim?" Buck nodded. "Yes, a man could

315

never hide that, Mr. Manly. You were a fool to even try."

"And they'll know about me too," Manly said. "Buck, I did the right thing, didn't I? I mean, at the last, I did."

"I guess you did, Mr. Manly, but it was pretty late to fix anything."

Temple Manly nodded. "It's not easy to see what I worked so hard to build go like this. Mighty hard, Buck."

For a moment, Buck said nothing, busying himself instead with the manufacture of a cigarette. He passed the tobacco to Manly and waited until the man had it ready for a match. "All the way in I've been thinking," Buck said. "Thinking about those years when you built something. I guess it wouldn't be right to let all those people know how you really were. It would make them doubt the things they always believed in." He paused to pull deeply on his cigarette. "Harms won't say anything, and I guess George wouldn't either. He's been with you a long time, Mr. Manly, and he'd think kindly of you." He raised his head and looked at Temple Manly. "That seems important to me, Mr. Manly, that people think kindly of you after you're gone. Not important for you, but for them."

"Gone?" Manly said. "What do you want me to do, Buck?"

"You're learning to face the truth," Buck said. "You tell me."

For a time Temple Manly was silent, then he said, "My wife has talked of selling out and moving to Dallas. Maybe that would be best for everybody."

"Dallas is a nice town," Harry Buck said. "Got drunk there once, when I was young and didn't have better sense."

This struck Temple Manly as odd, and he looked intently at Harry Buck. "Young? Yes, you do seem old, Buck. You've put your fun behind you." He shifted his feet uneasily. "Will you tell the Cardigan boy how sorry I am?"

"No," Buck said, without hesitation. "There are some angry men around here, Mr. Manly. The less said, the better it will be."

"I guess you're right." He turned toward the door. "Shall I go and see Jim?"

"I don't think he wants to see you right now," Harry Buck said. "If he does, I'll let you know. Likely it'll be a week or so before you and your wife move to Dallas."

"Yes," Manly said. He stepped outside quickly and crossed the walk to his buggy. Kohler and a few of the townsmen stood there, watching. Harry Buck joined them as Manly lifted the reins and turned down the street.

"Goddamn, but he's getting off easy," Kohler said.

The man's remark irritated Harry Buck and

he swung around. "John, you got to forget!"

"You think so?" Kohler made a face. "You telling me or asking me?"

"I'm telling you," Buck said. "John, if the mistakes we made were unforgiven, we'd be hated by everyone. It's what a man does in the final reckoning that matters." He turned his head in time to see the buggy disappear around the far corner. In a more subdued voice he said, "John, you wanted to know once about the rules Manly lived by, whether they were the same for himself as they were for you and me."

"I remember," Kohler said.

"Well, I found out today," Buck said. He looked at the men standing on the walk, and his glance lingered longest on Betty Cardigan and her brother. There was a question in Buck's mind as to whether or not they would understand the struggle that took place in a man when he had to make the ultimate decision with his conscience. The fact that it could never be clear-cut might leave them wondering, and he didn't want that. He said, "Manly brought his own son in. I guess I don't have to say any more."

Kohler was not a man who liked to admit that he was in debt, even to the extent of an apology, but he swallowed his pride because the others did and he didn't like standing alone. "I guess a man can't stay mad forever," he said. "And like you say, Manly did bring his kid in, didn't he?"

He clapped Wes Cardigan on the arm. "Let's go home. I've been taking care of your stock and it's high time you took 'em off my hands."

Betty Cardigan remained and neither her brother nor John Kohler questioned her about it; they both knew that she would be staying in town. When the two men walked toward the stable, and the townsmen drifted away, Harms said, "Gettin' near my supper time."

"Yes, it is," Buck said. "Send two trays back to the office here, will you, Harms? And in the morning, take two men and go out to Manly's line cabin and bring Hank Wilson back."

He omitted the details of the fight, which annoyed Harms. Turning, the fat man waddled down the street. After he drew out of earshot, Betty Cardigan said, "Harry, you can still smell the dust from Manly's buggy."

"Yeah," Buck said gently. "The man's gone, but there's a lot he's left behind. Good things and bad things, Betty." There was a tinge of regret in his voice. "But the dust will fade in a minute. Everything fades, Betty."

He took her arm then and eased her ahead of him into the office. She did not notice, for her thoughts were on tomorrow and the endless tomorrows to come, but Harry Buck paused an instant in the doorway to gaze down the road where Temple Manly had traveled.

Then he quickly closed the door.

Center Point Large Print
600 Brooks Road / PO Box 1
Thorndike, ME 04986-0001 USA

(207) 568-3717

US & Canada:
1 800 929-9108
www.centerpointlargeprint.com